From Dawn to Death

A Legion Archer
Book #7

J. Clifton Slater

Finding motivations for historic characters and inventing the whys of their behavior are research challenges. Then, intermixing fictional characters and their backgrounds in events and blending the real with the invented to create a comprehensive story is a labor of love, and at times, insanity. But watching the boundaries of logic, and armed with her red pen, Hollis Jones hovers over the process. Through her keen eyes, she controls the chaos and guides me through the history and the fiction to a satisfying end. For her, I am eternally grateful.

As always, my warmest 'thanks' goes to you. My readers are the reason I can spend my days doing research and writing stories. Rendering a hand salute to you for being there for me. Ready, two!

If you have comments, contact me:

www.GalacticCouncilRealm@gmail.com

To follow my progress on upcoming books, read blogs on ancient topics, or to sign up for my monthly Author Report, go to my website:

www.JCliftonSlater.com

Act 1

As if a leviathan resting to catch its breath, Hannibal Barca and his great army camped in the southeast of the Italian Peninsula. After twelve years of war, he required a rest. Although he won every battle, Hannibal achieved little. Many cities and tribes that declared for him, fled back to the arms of the Republic once the Carthaginian moved his army away. Blinded by his hatred of Rome, the forty-one-year-old general failed to understand the draw of cities to a steady currency, fair laws, and an abundance of trading partners.

Even if Capua and cities of that ilk returned to Rome, Hannibal had willing allies in foreign powers. Phillip V of Macedonia, the Aetolian League's city-states of central Greece, and both eastern and western Numidia supported him. They sent replacements, grain, and coins to further the Carthaginian cause against a mutual enemy. Their help was appreciated and needed. Supplies from his breadbasket and mercenary breeding ground of Iberia had dwindled from an ocean to a river. But things would be better soon, once Hannibal and his army rested and Iberia was returned to Carthaginian control.

Mago Barca, Hannibal's younger brother, was gathering a vast hoard to drive the Roman Republic from the city of New Carthage. Then, Mago would push the brash Latian General to the base of the mountains and trap him and his Legions against the foot of the Pyrenees. Soon, Cornelius Scipio and his allies would be crushed under a Barca's heel. Rome's hold on Iberia, at last, would end.

"Any day," Hannibal prayed, "let my brother and his Carthaginian army wipe the Legions from Iberia."

A thousand miles away, a twenty-eight-year-old Cornelius Scipio also prayed. The Roman General's prayer was simple and more fatalistic.

"Allow me to rise before my enemy and fight him from dawn to death, or to victory. Whichever the Gods will allow."

Welcome to 206 B.C.

Chapter 1 – Light of Knowledge

"The Roman is a fool," Mago announced.

"How so, General Barca?" General Hilles of the African Corps asked.

"He runs around Iberia negotiating trade deals with Iberian tribes," Mago replied. A Captain of the African Corps ushered in a courier. The two waited respectfully at the entrance. Mago continued. "While he expands his energy and coins trying to bring war chiefs under control, he leaves New Carthage lightly defended."

"Then we'll relieve the Roman of the responsibility for such a valuable property," Hilles assured Mago. Next, he turned to the entrance. "You wanted to see me, Captain?"

"No, sir. The courier is here to report to General Barca."

"Out with it, Numidian," Mago instructed.

"Sir, the Legions are three days march from here," the courier reported.

"Legions, you say?" Mago questioned. "How many are in the Republic force."

Mago Barca reclined on his sofa and took a sip of sweet wine. He didn't expect more than a casual scouting report. And that would be exaggerated. The real numbers could be ascertained later.

"According to my Captain," the cavalryman responded while unrolling a scroll. "General Scipio has twelve thousand heavy infantry, thirteen thousand light infantry, and twenty thousand Iberian spearmen. Plus, three thousand mounted, including fifteen hundred Celtiberi heavy cavalry."

With his mouth hanging open, Mago sat upright. Bewilderment showed on his face. Either from the thoroughness of the report or the raw numbers of enemy troops heading for his camp. Then General Hilles began laughing.

"Congratulations, General Barca," he exclaimed. "You won't have to chase Scipio down to beat him. The Roman is coming right to you. After this, you can take your time recapturing New Carthage."

"How many in the African Corps?" Mago inquired.

"Thirteen thousand of the best heavy infantry in the Carthaginian trading empire," Hilles told him. "And to cover our flanks, you have over sixty thousand spearmen."

"If I might, General Barca," the Numidian requested. Mago waved a hand in an out-with-it motion. "Sir, you have four thousand cavalry and thirty-two war elephants."

"We can sit here and let the Roman dash his army against our shields," Hilles ventured. "And as sure as if he was a ship-of-war in a storm on a rocky coast, his Legions will break."

Mago stood and an evil grin came to his face.

3

"I owe Scipio for Carmona. His light cavalry rode in and butchered my infantry and spearmen. And he captured Hanno the Elder," Mago shot out an arm and pointed a finger at the courier. "Get me your Senior Captain. I have a mission for him."

"Sir," the courier acknowledged before rushing out of the pavilion.

"What do you have in mind, General Barca?" Hilles asked.

"A little scuffle to pay Scipio back before the big battle," Mago responded. He sat, lifted his glass in salute, and repeated. "The Roman is a fool."

***

Dawn found the Carthaginian camp at Ilipa buzzing with activity. Sergeants rousted men from their blankets and readied them for inspection by their Captains and Lieutenants or by their War Leaders. While that activity was the norm throughout the fortified position, at the main gate different activities occurred.

"There must be a thousand of them," a heavy infantryman noted. "Where are they going?"

A Lieutenant of the African Corps came from between the tents.

"General Barca is sending the Roman's a welcome to the neighborhood present," the officer stated.

"Sir, what kind of present is delivered by a thousand cavalrymen?"

"The kind unprepared infantrymen don't ever want," the Lieutenant replied. "Show me your armor. And I better not find any rust on it this time."

"Not my armor, sir. It's scoured, scrubbed, and oiled."

The rest of their conversation was drowned out by cavalry Captain Vermina.

"Numidians, forward."

It wasn't Vermina's single voice but the officers and NCOs passing along his order to march that dampened conversation along the main route to the exit. Once outside the Carthaginian camp, Vermina waved four scouts to his side.

"This is a straightforward raid," he instructed. "Locate the Legion's vanguard and report back to me. I want their route of march, and the fastest way in to kill them and our quickest route away. I'll not lose men to a General's whim."

"We understand, sir," the scouts stated.

While the scouts galloped to the northeast, the columns allowed their mounts to prance away from the Carthaginian encampment.

***

The afternoon of the next day, three of the scouts trotted into view. In the distance, a profile of low mountains filled the horizon.

"This is good land for us," a Lieutenant offered to Vermina. "If we catch the Legions coming through a narrow pass, it'll be like cutting the head off a snake."

The scouts reined in and were all smiles.

"Their vanguard is on the far side of the range," a scout reported. "They'll come through bunched up and ready for us to chop off the head of the Legion."

"Seems I've heard that recently," Vermina remarked before asking. "Where are they coming through?"

"Near the village of Osuna, sir. That's only a mile from the mountain pass," the third scout reported. "If we're fast, we can kill a mile of them before they can get reinforcements through to help."

"The head of the snake," the Numidian Lieutenant restated.

***

One mile to the west of Osuna, where trees grew dense along the small river, Vermina stationed his horsemen. Facing the town, they waited for the Latian vanguard to appear and the signal from their Captain to attack.

"The elders at home will sing about this ambush for ages," a Numidian rider proposed. "But I'm bothered about one thing."

"What's that, Sinissa?" his friend asked.

"The Captain wants us to ride through and kill as many as possible," Cavalryman Sinissa whined. "Then wheel around and comeback to finish them off."

"What's wrong with that?"

"I wanted a chance to loot the bodies," Sinissa protested. "In a quick raid, we won't have a chance to collect trophies."

Through the trees, they noted the caravan town of Osuna. Beyond the structures of traders and homes of residents, a pair of hills rose from the plain. Between the heights a low sling saddle connected the hills. The elevations would force the Legions to march to the west of the town and right into the ambush.

"Ready yourself," the word filtered through the riders.

Moments later, columns of infantrymen marched through the pass and onto the plain. As hoped, they followed the trail to the west of Osuna.

"Something bothers me about them," Sinissa mentioned.

"Again?" his friend questioned. "What is it this time?"

"Infantrymen on a long march have bundles and carry their helmets and shields over their shoulders," the Numidian observed. "Those troops are armored. And they're carrying shields as well as spears and javelins."

"It's the vanguard, they have to be on alert," the other cavalryman pushed back. "Now stop worrying, you're making your horse nervous."

"My mount is fine," Sinissa boasted before suggesting. "Maybe it's you who's nervous."

"I wasn't until you started complaining."

Only about two hundred infantrymen came through the mountain pass. Behind them, twenty cavalrymen walked their mounts onto the flatland. By then, the leading edge of the infantrymen approached Osuna.

"Mount and hold," the word was passed from Captain Vermina.

"It's about time," Sinissa declared.

"On that, we can agree," his friend assured him.

They mounted, pulled throwing spears from sheathes, and waited.

***

Numidian light cavalry was feared throughout Iberia, and to be honest, around the Republic as well. Their ability to rapidly close with an enemy, throw spears with accuracy, and follow up with lances made them a nightmare for disorganized infantry. And a bane for Legion cavalry as the Numidians hit, retreated, and charged again in lightning quick attacks.

The order to execute the ambush rolled through the waiting line of riders.

"Numidian cavalry, assault."

Being spread in a long line caused a delay in response. As a result, the northern end broke from the trees first. And as if a whip before snapping, the emerging lines of riders coiled around the head of the Legion infantry.

The infantry shields snapped together in a fruitless shield wall as the rest of the Numidians galloped from the trees. At the rear, the last of the Numidian riders curled around the Legion cavalrymen, preventing them from retreating back to the mountain pass.

Captain Vermina reined in to watch the slaughter unfold.

"Had you waited, sir," the Lieutenant offered, "you could have caught more of them in the kill zone."

"I'll take two hundred and twenty easy kills in place of a prolonged battle, any day," Vermina informed the junior officer.

***

Sinissa and his friend put heels to flanks, jumping their horses through the branches.

"May Hawot ride the tip of my spears," Sinissa beseeched the God of the Dead.

The Legion riders were cut off from their line of retreat. Sinissa laughed as the enemy cavalrymen released their horses and ran for the protection of the infantry shields.

His riding companion shouted, "at least we won't have to chase them down to kill them."

Yet, in a puzzling maneuver, the panicked infantrymen, caught in the open and vulnerable, didn't run. Rather, they gathered back-to-back and formed a knot of infantry shields.

"It'll take more than two passes to eliminate them," Sinissa thought as his first spear sank harmlessly into the wood of a Legion infantry shield. Before Sinissa galloped by the Legion formation, a gladius blade appeared from the mound of shields and chopped away the shaft of his spear. While drawing a second spear, the Numidian confirmed. "Definitely, more than two passes."

A thousand riders trying to attack a single cluster of infantrymen allowed the unimpeded riders to race quickly by the enemy position. In the frustration of knowing only a few would have a chance for glory, many riders reached Osuna, turned their mounts, and sat to watch the show.

With over eight hundred pairs of eyes on the mound of shields, Captain Vermina considered calling those uninvolved in the assault back to the river.

"This isn't good," the Lieutenant sighed.

Mistaking the sound as one of pain or helplessness, Vermina looked away from the battle. He scanned the junior officer for injuries. Seeing no blood, he focused on the mountain pass. When no Legion reinforcement poured from the gap, the Captain turned back to the Lieutenant.

"What do you mean?" Vermina inquired.

"This should have been a quick raid, sir. But it'll take a while to break this hard nut."

Vanguards typically were light infantry or skirmishers. When the infantrymen came through the gap, they should have been strolling, not marching. And their cavalry escort could have raced for Osuna and escaped over the hills to the east. But the Legion riders dismounted and joined the infantry formation.

As if exposed to a bright light suddenly brought into a dark room, the Captain's eyes slammed shut. The light of knowledge flared as his brain slogged through the clues. Then, in terror, he opened his eyes and gazed at the hills on the other side of Osuna.

***

Single columns came around the outside of the twin hills and two other columns cantered between them. With lances leveled, the Celtiberi heavy cavalry broke into a charge on the downhill slope.

As if straw targets, the Numidians sat watching their companions hurl spears at the pile of hardwood shields. Although quick and agile once in motion, the riders from Africia were limited by the reaction of their horses.

"Retreat," Captain Vermina bellowed while waving his arms.

A few of his riders noted the arms waving and waved back. Then the arms fell into a recognizable pattern of fallback and the ones aware kicked their mounts into motion. The other Numidians became aware of the danger when the thunder of hoofs from fifteen hundred tough mountain horses overwhelmed them. Acting as if flood waters washing through a village in a valley, the Celtiberi punched into the light cavalry.

Chapter 2 - The Anticipation Trap

With knee pressure, Sinissa brought his mount around. As he flashed by the turtle shell of shields, he flung his spear. Jerking the reins, he circled, against orders, for another attack run.

"There must be an opening," his friend shouted as he mirrored the turn.

"No," Sinissa yelled. But it wasn't a response to his friend's comment.

A lance pierced his linen armor, lifted him off his horse, then deposited the Numidian on the ground. As he collided with the earth, his head bounced, and the world went black.

By hugging his mount's neck, Sinissa's friend avoided the other lance. Although the steel tip grazed his shoulder. Bleeding and hanging on, the cavalryman allowed his horse to chase after Captain Vermina and the Lieutenant. While he and a few other Numidians escaped the Celtiberi heavy cavalry, most were trapped.

***

At the cries of dying men and horses, the testudo broke, and the Legionaries lowered their shields. Thrown javelins cleared Numidian riders, creating a safe zone around the Legion heavy infantrymen.

"That was intense," Battle Commander Zeno announced as he rotated, observing the cavalry battle. "My thanks to First Century and Nineteenth Century."

"I still don't know why you came out here, Colonel," First Centurion Rosato remarked.

"I'm a Roman Battle Commander for an Iberian Legion. If I want the respect of my heavy infantry, I have to be more than a Latin politician," Zeno told him. He lowered his eyes and glanced around the ring of infantrymen. "I will never ask you to do something, I wouldn't do myself."

"Sir, you mean like walking into a trap to hold the Numidians in place for the Celtiberi?" a Legionary inquired.

"That's exactly what I mean," Zeno assured him.

"A Rah for Colonel Zeno, Battle Commander of Steed Legion," another infantryman shouted.

A chorus of Rahs rang out from the circular shield wall. But the voices carried only a short distance. Beyond the shields, the sounds of battle easily drowned out the cheering.

***

As if the hands of a killer embracing the neck of a victim, Captain Bekeres and his riders came from the right and Captain Darsosin and his units approached from the left. When the commanders of the Celtiberi cavalry met, they sealed off the last escape route.

"General Scipio wants ten alive and able to ride," they reminded the squadrons behind them. "Kill everyone else."

Slower this time, the heavy cavalry trotted inward, closing the noose around the necks of the trapped Numidian cavalrymen.

***

A short while later, two hundred Velites jogged onto the plain from the mountain pass. Behind them, twenty cavalrymen walked their horses. Without being given an order, the Legion's vanguard halted. Slowly, as if

12

disbelieving their eyes, they peered at almost six hundred dead Numidian cavalrymen.

"That could have been us," observed First Centurion Turibas.

"Thanks to General Scipio's vision, it wasn't us," Senior Tribune Ceradin reminded the senior combat officer. "Centurion Usico. Guide us farther to the west and away from the looting and the smell."

"Yes, sir," the Standard Bearer for Winds of Nortus confirmed.

***

Already confused at not being mounted, Sinissa was further baffled when a pair of strong arms pulled him from the ground and flung him into the air. Despite a splitting headache, he opened his eyes when his body was dumped over his saddle.

"Maybe we won the fight," he thought, "and my friends are taking me to shelter."

But even with the odd angle of his head and downward view, he noted the number of bloody, punctured, and torn bodies of Numidians and their agile horses. The evidence dashed any hope of a victory for the light cavalryman. To put a finer point on the idea, when he craned his neck to get a broader view, a hand slapped the back of his skull.

"Don't think about it," a man with a Republic accent warned.

Sinissa's head hurt, and his ribs ached. Other than pain and confusion, he wasn't thinking about anything.

"What have we here?" a decidedly Latian voice inquired.

"We found him unconscious, Colonel. Figured if he came around with some sense, you could use him."

The horse walked by a pair of infantry shields and stopped.

"My friend, you have a nasty lump on your head," the Latian observed. "Help him off the horse. Gently now. Rest him by the others."

While bent over his sore ribs, arms carried Sinissa to a group of nine wounded Numidian cavalrymen. The porters sat him between two bleeding men.

"What's going on?" Sinissa whispered.

"The lucky ones died on Celtiberi lances," one survivor replied.

On the other side of Sinissa, another Numidian growled, "and all we have to look forward to is torture and death on a Legion cross."

"That's where you're wrong," the Latian informed them. Sinissa raised his head and discovered the speaker was a Legion Battle Commander. Then, the officer instructed. "Get me a couple of Legionaries with medical experience. I want these men stitched up and ready to travel."

As vinegar flushed wounds and sutures closed gashes, fires were lit. Sinissa peered beyond the flames to the trail from the pass. Hundreds of marching feet passed by. And they continued to flow from the mountain in a never-ending parade of Legion infantry, spearmen, and cavalry.

"Impressive aren't they," the Battle Commander offered. He scanned the ten prisoners as if searching for something. A moment later, he declared. "You must be thirsty after your ordeal. Optio, get these warriors vino."

"Right away, Colonel Marcius."

At the end of the line, the Legion NCO handed a Numidian a wineskin. After taking a long stream, the cavalryman started to hand it back.

"No. That one's yours," the Optio told him. "I have more coming. One for each of you."

True to his word, the Optio began distributing nine additional wineskins.

"Now that your throats have been wet," Lucius Marcius proposed, "I expect you're hungry."

"You can torture us, but it'll do you no good," a Numidian uttered. "We're simple cavalrymen and not privileged to the plans of our officers."

Marcius tapped a finger against his chin in contemplation before asking, "First Optio, do you know General Scipio's plans?"

"Sir, how would I know what the Gods say to the General?" the NCO replied.

"That's right, he is a seer," Marcius admitted. "It's how he knew where you would wait in ambush for us. The Gods told Scipio."

"The Gods told him?" Sinissa inquired. "I had a bad feeling about this."

"Perhaps you should have paid attention to your feelings," Marcius proposed. Then in an explosion of embarrassment, he said. "Oh but, I am a terrible host."

The Numidians glanced at each other at the announcement.

"You there, what do you have in your satchel?" Marcius inquired of a Legion cavalryman.

"Sir, I have pork," the Legion rider answered.

Lucius Marcius scrunched his eyebrows as if in deep contemplation.

"Is pork alright?" he asked the prisoners. "If you'd rather we can get beef or fish."

"Pork is fine, sir," a Numidian replied.

"Good, good," Marcius stated. Then to the cavalryman, he asked. "Can you spare ten slices?"

"Sir, you can take the satchel. I'll just get another from the supply wagon."

The First Optio took the sack with the pork. At the fires, he sliced generous portions, skewed the pieces on sticks, and placed them over the fires.

"Do any of you Legionaries want pork?" Marcius asked the guards.

"No thank you, sir," the squad leader replied. "We're still stuffed from the big breakfast."

"I hate to waste it," Marcius complained. "I know. Optio. Cook all the pork. We'll sent it with the Numidians."

"You're letting us go?" Sinissa questioned.

"After you answer a few questions."

"But sir, we don't know anything," Sinissa protested.

Fat fell into the fires sending up an aromatic smoke. Adding to the delicious aromas, roasting pork crackled in the flames.

In the distance, a Century of heavy infantry and another of light stepped out of the march. In an arrangement where the Legionaries were flanked by half the light infantry on each side, the detachment marched towards the town of

Osuna. Before they reached the buildings, a Tribune left the march and raced up to them and reined in.

"You aren't a scouting party," he advised. "You're a combat patrol. Come back with blood on your spears."

"Yes, sir," the Centurions acknowledged.

Leaving the detachment, the Tribune trotted back to the marching Legions. As he passed the prisoners, he saluted Colonel Marcius.

***

"Let me explain a few things," Marcius proposed to the Numidians. "The Legions are here to break Mago Barca and Hasdrubal Gisco. We have provisions to last us all summer. And while your army will soon starve, we'll supplement our supplies with your grain. We'll capture the wagons and prevent the food from reaching you. I want to know which tribes are in league with Mago and Gisco. Then you can go."

"The Turdules, Counel, Vettones, Lusitanes, and Astures," one answered.

"Plus, they have thirty-two war elephants," another volunteered.

"That's good," Marcius stated. "They're big. When food runs out you can dine on elephants. Have you ever had elephant meat?"

The ten prisoners admitted they'd never eaten elephant.

"Optio, help me hand out this pork," Marcius instructed. "As good as the pork is, elephant is just plain nasty. I've had it but it soaked in brine for three weeks before it was tender enough to cut. It didn't help the taste, but at least we managed to cut it down to bite size pieces."

Between the wine and meat on the sticks, the nine prisoners relaxed. Although the unpleasant thought of eating elephant lingered in the back of their minds.

"Colonel, General Scipio's party is coming through the gap," the First Optio warned.

"Stop eating and lower your eyes," Marcius ordered. "Under penalty of death, everyone, lower your eyes."

Officers, NCOs, Legionaries, cavalrymen, and Numidians dipped their chins to avoid eye contact with General Scipio. Except for Sinissa, he twisted his head and caught sight of Cornelius Scipio.

Gold armor reflected the morning sun. And light beamed off the General's upturned face as if the Gods were shining illumination down on him. Behind Scipio, eight banners hung from tall standards. In that moment, if Sinissa could have thought of the word majestic, he would have ascribed it to the vision.

The General's entourage moved by, and Marcius released a long-held breath.

"Is everyone alright?" he questioned.

Legion groups reported that everyone was safe.

"How about you?" Marcius asked the Numidians.

"Why shouldn't we be?" Sinissa inquired.

"Sometimes when General Scipio is praying, people who look at him go blind."

"Sometimes?" Sinissa uttered while rubbing his eyes.

"Not always," Marcius assured him. "Only if the Gods notice the interloper."

"Colonel Marcius, we need to catch up with the Legion," the Optio suggested.

"You'll be followed until you're out of our area," Marcius informed the prisoners. "Grab the pork, mount up, and get out of here before I change my mind."

They all stumbled from injuries but managed to mount. And, as a people born to ride, the ten raced away.

The First Optio faced Marcius and asked, "Colonel, when did you eat elephant?"

"Never. I've only seen the beasts from a distance," Lucius Marcius admitted. "It's like going blind from looking at General Scipio. Or the formation of our patrols. All lies."

"Then why do it, sir?"

"Because those ten will tell everyone about the abundance of vino and food we have," Marcius revealed. "Like General Scipio said, there is no more powerful weapon than fear. And those ten will warn about the Carthaginian army starving long before they run out of food."

"Plus, the fear that the Gods are on General Scipio's side," the Optio ventured.

"That, First Optio, was not a lie."

***

As he had done since he commanded the first long march, Cornelius pushed the Legions until late in the day. Yet, on this day, he exceeded the normal extended hike.

"It'll be dark soon, sir," Gaius Laelius pointed out.

"I have eyes, Colonel."

"I understand, General. It's just we'll need light to set up the marching camps."

"Not here, and not in this location," Cornelius informed the Battle Commander of Eagle Legion. "We're less than thirty miles from Ilipa. If we stop here then move forward at dawn, Mago and Gisco will be on us like locusts. Before they can catch us stretched out on the march, we need to arrive at our destination and build our defensives."

"A night march, sir?"

"All night, Colonel," General Scipio confirmed.

***

Not unusual for Scipio Legions, the Legionaries, Velites, spearmen, draft animals, and animal handlers arrived exhausted and footsore. But they had marched within three miles of the Carthaginian camp under cover of darkness.

"Use all the torches and firewood you need to get the work done," Cornelius instructed his five Battle Commanders.

"Sir, the fires will let the Carthaginians know we're here and that we're close," Zeno remarked. "They can't help but respond."

"They have over seventy thousand men under arms," Cornelius pointed out. "Have you any idea how long it takes to mobilize that many warriors?"

"No, sir."

"I'd judge about the time we finish our stockades, they'll be lined up admiring our work," Cornelius told him. "And that's all they'll do, stand around and admire our walls."

"Yes, sir," Zeno replied.

The five began walking away when Cornelius called them back.

"Our formations, gentlemen, from Legion maneuvers, down to the smallest patrol, must have Legionaries in the center with Velites flanking on both sides."

"Sir, that's the Legion standard for the most," Marcius stated.

"And here, at Ilipa, it's the order of the day, every day. No deviations, none."

"Yes, General," the five replied.

They rode back to their Legions to order the construction of five marching camps. One big camp would have been easier to administer and to guard.

But as General Scipio said, "One marching camp wouldn't create the illusion of a barrier, barring the Carthaginians from the plain of Andalusia and their supply routes."

Sunrise found thousands of spearmen and heavy infantrymen, both Iberian and African Corps, on their battle works, gawking at the five stockade structures in the distance. And as predicted, other than a few mounted patrols, no infantry companies came out to challenge the Legions. It appeared as if Scipio really was consulting with the Gods on the Ilipa campaign.

Chapter 3 – The Formation

The midday sun beat down on the Legion patrol. And although hot, the going was easy on the dry wagon trail.

"I can feel eyes on us, Centurion," the Optio remarked.

"If you can see the Carthaginian camp through the trees and over the miles, Sergeant, you're certainly blessed with magnificent vision," Centurion Arathia offered. "Remind me later. I'll join you in your sacrifice to Theia."

"Sir, I hadn't planned on a sacrifice to the Goddess of Sight," the NCO told him.

From deeper in the Twenty-fifth Century, the Tesserarius called forward, "Centurion, we have visitors. Request permission to send out the Velites to investigate."

The combat officer shortened his strides and allowed the ranks of heavy infantrymen, and their light infantry escort, to move by him.

When the Corporal approached, the Centurion fell into step with him.

"Tell me where without pointing," Arathia urged.

"I caught a bright reflection from the trees ahead on the left side of the road," the Corporal reported. "It was brief. But, sir, I'm sure it's the sun reflecting off a blade."

"First squad. Keep your covers on your shields, your spears on your shoulders, and continue forward as if nothing is happening," Arathia advised. "Velites. Same instructions."

"Yes, sir," the Decanus responded. "First squad maintain your march."

"Yes, sir," the Decani from the four squads of light infantrymen acknowledged.

"Twenty-fifth Century, below your waists, remove your covers and unbundle your javelins," Arathia commanded. "And for Hades sake, don't look down while you do it. That'll tipoff the Carthaginian patrol."

"What patrol, sir?" a Legionary inquired.

"The one your Optio felt and your Tesserarius saw," Arathia answered. Then he declared. "Give me a Rah for the third best pair of NCOs in Steed of Aeneas Legion."

"Rah," the eighty Legionaries bellowed.

"Sir. If they're third best," a Legionary inquired, "who are the best NCOs in the Legion?"

"I don't know," Centurion Arathia admitted.

The combat officer fast walked by Legionaries as they removed covers from their shields and untied bundles of javelins. Near the forward ranks, the last squad marched along as if nothing was out of the ordinary.

When he reached the front rank, the Optio cocked his head and asked, "Third-best, sir?"

"Just wanted to give you something to strive for," Centurion Arathia told him.

***

In a well-coordinated ambush, slingers rose from concealment on the right side of the road. Pellets slashed into the ranks of Velites on that side, and several of the light infantrymen dropped to the ground, bleeding from head wounds. Next, a row of big shields and long spears broke from the trees on the left side. Each shield propelled by a battletested infantryman from the African Corps.

"Second Squad, move out and shield our Velites. Then show our appreciation for the skills of the slingers," Arathia commanded. "Third through Eight Squads, give me an assault line. Let's see if the Corps is as tough as their reputation."

After giving the orders, Arathia marched a few steps towards the Corps' line.

"Sir, you should get behind our lines," the Optio encouraged.

Centurion Arathia tossed his red cloak over his shoulder and drew his gladius. Standing in front of his attack line, he hoisted his weapon overhead and shouted, "Second and third ranks, two javelins on my command."

"Two javelins on your command, Centurion," the Legionaries repeated.

In the instant it took for the Legionaries to position two javelins for the throws, the African Corps closed to within eighteen feet of the Legion line.

"Sir, please get behind our ranks," the Optio begged.

Arathia stood rock solid in the face of the approaching enemy. At twelve feet, he ordered, "Century, standby."

"Standing by, Centurion," the Legionaries blurted out. By rushing the words, they hoped to get their combat officer to order the throw and move back.

Although well disciplined, the sight of a Legion officer standing alone proved too much. The center of the Corps' line bowed outward as African heavy infantrymen rushed to be the first to kill the foolhardy Centurion.

In a few steps, a pair of steel tips were aimed at Arathia's chest.

Two steps and a jab away from his death, the combat officer thundered the order that released his Legionaries.

"Throw javelins. Advance, advance, advance. Send them to Hades."

A flight of forty iron tips flashed by on either side of the Centurion. But he didn't notice the javelins or the damage they inflicted. The raised gladius swiped across his chest, striking the two spears still in front to him. A single gladius against two spears was a bad situation. Even as forty more javelins punched infantryman from the African Corps out of their attack line, Arathia fought a helpless duel. The spears attempted to get inside the Centurion's guard. Slashing with all his strength, Arathia fought against the odds.

When it seemed, he couldn't hold the spears back any longer, a roar came from behind the Legion officer. Third and Forth Squads of the Twenty-fifth Century appeared on either side of their Centurion. Following immediately behind them, the Fifth and Sixth stomped forward.

"Advance," they screamed as their shields flowed around Arathia, driving the spears away from their officer. Then their gladii cut deeply into the bowed section of the enemy's line.

And while the Legion lines were arrow straight across their front, the bowed section of the African Corps' ranks collapsed in the center. Divided, they began to fight as two separate combat lines.

"Seventh and Eight Squads left diagonal. Second and Third, right diagonal," Arathia ordered. "Show the Corps why it's a bad idea to get out of alignment."

At an angle, the squads attacked the raw ends of the Crops ranks. Now fighting head on while also having their end infantrymen pushed back and away from their companions, the ranks of Africans broke.

"Hold," Arathia shouted when his Legionaries began giving chase. "Save your strength. Let them go."

Spinning on his heels, the Centurion ran to the opposite side of the road. But once near his squads, he slowed and assumed a more dignified pace.

"What have you got there?" he inquired.

The Tesserarius held out a hand. Strings of leather with small leather patches dangled from his fingers.

"Gifts from the slingers," the Corporal answered. "Their bodies are out in the field. Orders, sir?"

"Don't you think this is an odd place to stage an ambush?" Arathia pointed out. "We're in the middle of nowhere, on a deserted road, miles from the Carthaginian and the Legion camps."

"Now that you mention it, sir," the Tesserarius observed, "there's not a creek or a spring nearby."

"That begs the question, what was an African Corps patrol doing out here?"

"I could ask the same thing, sir," the Corporal noted. "What are we doing on this road?"

"You are a bright Legionary," Arathia complimented. "Perhaps the fourth best Tesserarius in the Legion."

"Sir, I thought I was third best?"

"That was before," Arathia said. He turned and started back to the road.

"Before what, Centurion?"

"Before I realized how smart you are and your potential as a leader. Now you'll have to work harder to impress me."

"What did I say, sir?" the Corporal inquired.

"This nowhere acre of Iberia shouldn't rate two heavy infantry patrols," Arathia described. "And as you almost said, the only reason is a supply caravan. Send out two squads of Velites and see if they can locate the supply wagons."

***

Late in the day, the gate guards of Steed's stockade called the Sergeant of the Guard.

"We have a patrol coming, Optio. And they have four wagons."

"Where did a patrol get four wagons?"

"No idea but you might want to get the Senior Centurion or the Battle Commander," the gate guard suggested. "There's got to be a story in this."

When Arathia guided his Century, the light infantry squads, and the wagons through the gateway, he was met by Colonel Zeno, and Senior Centurion Thiphilia.

"Centurion Arathia. I sent the Twenty-fifth out to clear the land of Carthaginians and you came back with supply wagons," Thiphilia proclaimed. "Do you have an explanation for the extra equipment?"

"Well, Senior Centurion," Arathia started to say when the gate guard shouted.

"General Scipio is coming, sirs."

"Hold that thought, Centurion," Zeno urged.

Moments later, Cornelius reined in and dismounted. In his wake, the General's entourage halted, kicking dust up. After marching to Arathia, Scipio instructed, "Tell me about your patrol."

Dust washed over the General and the Centurion. They ignored the grit.

"My Optio and Tesserarius noticed signs of an ambush," Arathia reported. "I had the First Squad continue forward while the rest prepared for battle."

"Most Centurions would have sent the Velites out to check," Cornelius proposed.

"I didn't sir, because we were ordered to maintain the sausage formation."

"The sausage formation?" Cornelius questioned.

"Yes, General Scipio. It's what the Legionaries call it. With your permission?"

"Go ahead."

"Twenty-fifth, what is the sausage formation," Arathia called to his Century.

"Centurion, the sausage formation has a dense, meaty, and thin-skinned center. And two slices of light infantry on each side."

"I don't know if that's appropriate," Zeno protested.

But Cornelius noted that Arathia still faced his Century.

"Go ahead, Centurion," Cornelius urged.

"And why do we maintain the sausage formation?" Arathia quizzed his Century.

"Sir, if we want to question the orders from the command staff, we should become heroes of the Legion, assume leadership positions, rise through the ranks, until we reach a height where we can tell dense, meaty, and thin-skinned Legionaries what to do," the eighty men replied. "Until such time, Centurion, we will follow orders without question and embrace the sausage formation."

"General Scipio, you asked me why. We maintained the formation because you ordered it," Arathia told Cornelius. "We held it until the African Corps came out to play. Then we adjusted so we could teach them a lesson in manners."

"Colonel Zeno. Be sure the Twenty-fifth gets extra rations and coins from the sales of the wagons for their funeral fund," Cornelius instructed. Then he addressed the Century. "Twenty-fifth, I salute you."

And eighty-three voices responded with a robust, "Rah, General Scipio."

***

Cornelius Scipio, Sidia Decimia, five Junior Tribunes, and ten mounted Legionaries trotted out of Steed's stockade.

"Centurion Arathia is a good teacher," Cornelius mentioned.

"And a quality combat officer, sir," Sidia added. "General, I get placing the heavy infantry in the center for a large engagement. But forcing patrols to adhere to the formation is odd."

"I have my reasons," Cornelius told him without an explanation.

As they rode by the walls of the Trumpet of Aeneas' camp, Cornelius noticed a patrol heading for the gates.

"What's wrong with that patrol?" Cornelius asked the junior staff officers.

"It's a good defensive formation," a teen answered.

"Is that the formation I ordered?"

Another of the young Noblemen jerked his hand as if it was caught in a candle flame.

"They have the Velites spaced out ahead of the Legionaries," the Junior Tribune offered. "It is not the preferred order of march, sir."

"Go ahead," Cornelius said, "call it by the slang."

"It's not the sausage formation, sir."

The use of the term brought giggles from the sons of wealthy Roman families.

After giving them a moment of levity, Cornelius demanded, "What should a commander do?"

"They've disobeyed orders, General," a Junior Tribune replied. "The entire patrol should be put on the punishment post."

"That is an option," Cornelius agreed. "Being this close to an enemy and needing the focus of our Legions on the Carthaginian camp and not angry about a mass punishment, perhaps we could temper the penalty?"

"Half rations and latrine duty for a week, sir," another Junior Tribune suggested.

"That fits the offense. But you forgot something," Cornelius challenged.

"What's that, General Scipio?" one of the teens inquired.

"Dispensing justice from a distance means the Centurion and his Legionaries will receive the sentence from a secondhand source," Cornelius instructed. "Always strive to be the stern voice and a fair judge who looks men in their eyes. Mainly, because in a few days or weeks, you'll depend on those men to follow you into combat and to execute your maneuvers."

Cornelius guided his horse towards the gates of Trumpet's stockade. The entourage followed him, driven by curiosity about the punishment. And to hear the biting words General Scipio would deliver to the patrol that failed to follow his orders.

Act 2

Chapter 4 – Two Goats for the Glory

Two weeks later, Mago Barca and Hasdrubal Gisco peered over the short defensive wall. They sat on their mounts ahead of their bodyguard detachments as if they represented opposing armies in peace talks.

"We've been playing with the Legions for too long," Gisco complained before spitting.

The glob splattered between the legs of Mago's horse.

"If that's another way of trying to get me to agree to an assault, it won't work," Mago informed the other Carthaginian General. "They have five forts. Far too many to lay siege to."

"And how, General Barca, do you intend to feed and pay your army if we just sit here?" Gisco sneered. "We're running short of supplies and without loot, my coffers are draining like an old wineskin."

"You only look inwards," Mago advised. "Look out there. Scipio is having the same problems as us. He can't stay much longer."

"Yet, every day, he sends out patrols and we send out ours. And what happens?"

"They meet, attack, skirmish, and then retreat," Mago answered. "It keeps our infantry at their best."

"Except, the Legion patrols capture our supplies and take the wagons and livestock of our allies," Gisco pointed out.

"And that is leading us to hunger, and shortly afterwards, mutiny."

"When I commanded an army for my brother in the Republic, my strength over the Legion was patience," Mago explained. "The Republic commanders are brash, set in their ways, and predictable. Just as I sprang the trap on a Legion in the Apennine mountains, I'm waiting for the perfect moment to bring Scipio to his knees."

With a mocking salute, Hasdrubal Gisco turned his horse, kneed the mount, and trotted for his bodyguards. Behind him, Mago Barca continued to stare at the Legion marching camps. Scipio on his knees was an apt description, although neither Carthaginian officer realized it.

***

Three miles away, in Eagle Legion's camp, the ox tossed his head, the great neck flexed, and the beast's shoulder hammered into Cornelius' hip. Caught by surprise, General Scipio tripped and fell to his knees in the urine and slobber.

When his General fell, Sidia took a step forward.

"Hold, Optio Decimia," Cornelius ordered. He peered from under the ox's neck. "If the Gods are willing, I'll complete the sacrifice on my own."

Sidia squatted to better see Cornelius under the throat and inquired, "and if the Gods don't will it. Sir?"

"Then we should pack up and head for New Carthage," Cornelius replied.

With a grunt, Cornelius Scipio rose beside the animal. As he stood, the sacrificial knife slit the side of the ox's neck. Blood gushed, coating Cornelius from his face to his ankles.

Ghostly looking in a layer of ox blood, he raised his arms in the air.

"Jupiter, accept this sacrifice in the name of Eagle Legion," he yelled at the sky.

When the ox's legs folded from blood loss, and the beast fell, Legionaries, Velites, cavalrymen, auxiliary infantry, and spearmen roared their approval.

Cornelius handed the knife to a priest, and gripped hands with Gaius Laelius. Once he released the Colonel's hands, General Scipio walked to the front rank of the Legionaries.

"Let this represent the blood of our enemy," he proclaimed while patting and splashing the blood from his chest. Then he raised a dripping fist over his head and declared. "Let the might of Jupiter flow down our arms and guide our weapons. And in the morning, men of Eagle Legion, from dawn to death or to victory, let us fight together as one."

In the chaos of cheering, Cornelius marched to his mount. Sidia and a groom held the animal steady. They had learned at the first four sacrifices, horses shied away from the smell of blood.

Once mounted, Cornelius saluted and shouted, "Eagle Legion."

Sidia pulled himself into the saddle of his horse. Then he and General Scipio trotted through the gates. Once they were beyond the stockade wall, they slowed to a walk.

"Sir, are you alright?" Sidia asked.

"I never realized butchering five oxen in one day would take so much out of me," Cornelius replied. He hung his head and admitted. "I am embarrassed. The fall was unforgivable."

"No sir. It looked like you were praying with the beast," Sidia assured him. "And when you rose in a shower of blood, it was the most heroic sacrifice of them all."

Wiping away a layer of blood from his arm, Cornelius inquired, "Should I keep it on for tomorrow or wash it off."

"Definitely, a bath is in order," Sidia suggested. "The Legions need to see a General of the Republic, not a barbarian priest."

"A bath does sound inviting," Cornelius agreed.

***

Long before dawn, Arathia nudged his Optio and Tesserarius. In the sky, the stars were in their full glory.

"Get them up and fed," the officer directed. "Everyone eats. No excuses."

"Eat, Centurion?" The Sergeant questioned. "What does that have to do with getting up in the middle of the night?"

"All the Tribune told me," Arathia answered, "was this could be the only meal we get for the next two days."

"It's an assault," the Corporal guessed.

"You might be right. But that's in the future," Arathia instructed. "Right now, everyone eats."

"Yes, sir," the NCOs agreed.

While each squad would cook group meals, Arathia left the Century's area and strolled to the Centurion's mess tent.

***

Candlelight created shadows in the corners and in areas outside the pools of illumination. Even through the dimness of the mess tent, Arathia located a specific group of combat officers.

"The Twenty-fifth is rousted, Senior Centurion," Arathia reported, "and eating breakfast as ordered."

Thiphilia put a hand on Arathia's shoulder.

"Good. Now you eat," Steed's senior combat officer directed. "We're marching on the Carthaginian camp before dawn. And there's a change in the maniples."

"You're moving the Twenty-fifth?" Arathia inquired.

"General Scipio is rearranging all the maniples."

Arathia wanted to complain about the secret maneuver. But the Centurion prided himself on being a straightforward combat officer. He didn't care for politics or gamesmanship. For him, war was to win, and all his energy went to training and drilling his Century. However, being a realist, he knew spies lurked in the Legion camps and General Scipio by necessity had to hide his plans.

"Wherever you need us, Senior Centurion," Arathia assured Thiphilia.

Without further conversation, and still in the dark about the changes, Arathia went to get a bowl of stew and a stack of hard camp biscuits to soak in the watery broth.

***

Soft radiance peeled back the black of night. With the sun still below the horizon, weak light reflected downward from the sky to reveal figures on the plain. For long moments, sleepy sentries in the Carthaginian camp didn't recognize the threat. Then one, two, three and soon the entire line of sentries came to realize the situation.

"Defenders. Defenders," a Numidian cavalryman shouted. "Defenders to the walls."

He jumped on his horse and galloped around the camp calling for spearmen and infantrymen to wake up. At Hasdrubal Gisco's pavilion, aids ran to alert the General. And just as Gisco emerged from his tent, yawning, and complaining about be woken so early, an officer of the African Corps raced up.

"General, the Legion is almost at our barriers," the Lieutenant reported.

"How many?" Gisco inquired.

"All of them, sir."

"Send word to General Barca," Gisco instructed. Then to the Lieutenant, he ordered. "Assemble the African Corps and march them to the walls."

"Sir, should we give the infantrymen a moment for breakfast?" the officer inquired.

Gisco scanned the still dark camp before locking his eyes on the Lieutenant. "Don't ever challenge my orders. Now go. I'll be along to consult with General Hilles and the Captains, once I'm dressed."

The junior officer ran to alert Hilles and the Captains of the Corps, and to pass on the order to immediately assemble.

***

Gisco trotted his horse to the back rank of infantryman.

"Make way," he shouted. "Hilles, Captains?"

"Here, General," one of the commanders of the African Corps replied.

The Captains stood on boxes in the back of a supply wagon. From the height, they had a better view than Gisco on horseback.

"How many?" the Carthaginian demanded.

"All of them," a Captain answered.

Gisco stepped onto the wagon and protested, "I've heard that before and I didn't believe it then."

But the Carthaginian stopped talking. From the height of the boxes, he took in the full depth and broad front of the Legions spread before him.

"We think they want us to come out and fight," a Captain remarked.

The other combat officer added, "that's the only reason, General, we can think of as to why they aren't attacking our camp."

Hasdrubal Gisco rotated slowly until he looked back at Mago Barca's pavilion. A few messengers and cavalrymen hung around the entrance. But there was no sign of activity or a view of the patient General.

"Take the African Corps out," he ordered. "I'll have the Numidian cavalry cover your flanks until I can get the spearmen moving. And once the tips are on the elephants' tusks, I'll send them."

"You heard the Carthaginian," General Hilles instructed. "March the Corps forward."

"African Corps," a Captain bellowed, "prepare for war."

His words were passed back through the ranks. A moment later, as if waves racing for a beach, fifteen thousand heavy infantrymen responded, "African Corps, prepare for war."

The barrier at the main entrance opened and ranks of African infantrymen jogged out of the Carthaginian camp.

Hasdrubal Gisco lifted an arm and extended his thumb. Running it over the ranks of the Legion's heavy infantry, he visualized erasing the enemy's formation.

"Soon, you'll be broken, your lines destroyed, and your General Scipio dead," he whispered. Then he instructed an aid. "Send out the spearmen to flank the Corps. And get the elephants ready."

Sounding like thunder, two thousand Numidian riders galloped through the north gate. A moment later, another two thousand exited the south gate.

***

In fighting blocks, the African Corps shuffled forward to meet the Legion lines. On each flank, Legion cavalry chased Numidian riders. None of the horsemen could break free of the mounted battles to threaten the infantry in the center.

"Gisco, you've committed us," Mago exclaimed when he arrived at the wagon.

"I have. Where are your spearmen?" Gisco growled.

"You committed us without consulting me."

"Where are your spearmen, Barca?"

The animosity between the two flashed as they attempted to stare each other down. Neither won because a group of war chiefs rode to the wagon.

"Our warriors want in on this fight," one announced. "When the Legions run off in shame, we want to raid their stockade camps."

Mago Barca inhaled sharply. Then he broke off the contest with Gisco.

"Flank the African Corps. Keep their light infantry off our center," Mago ordered.

"Yes, General Barca," the chiefs acknowledged.

"We'll use the elephants to punch holes in the Legions' lines," Gisco proposed. "By the end of the day, you can write your big brother and brag about your victory."

"I don't like that Scipio dictated the terms of this fight," Mago pointed out. "I'd rather it was us who chose the day and the battlefield."

"You worry too much, Mago," Gisco proposed. "Look out there. The weight of our army is already pushing their center back."

Mago Barca watched as his spearmen ran to protect the sides of the African Corps. And as Gisco noted, the Legion center, although untouched, was stepping back. But while the center retreated, the flanks of the Legion remained stationary. Before his eyes, the straight Republic lines took on the shape of a wide lipped bowl.

"That's an odd formation," Mago remarked.

"It doesn't matter," Gisco yelled. "The elephants will soon chew through their ranks."

Thirty-two war elephants marched through the gate. Their armored tusks swayed from side to side at they walked. And as if well trained infantrymen, they spread out in a line behind the African Corps. Even Mago had to admit the sight of seventy thousand warriors gave him confidence. Then after basking in the glory of his army, General Barca turned his attention to the center of the Legion line.

"Why are they still giving ground?" he asked. "They should be holding their line."

Mago watched the mass of spearmen flood the sides of the African Corps while fighting off Legion skirmishers. Their exuberance carried the Iberian tribesmen into the gap between the Legion center and the Carthaginian heavy infantry. Acting as a buffer, the spearmen kept the most powerful ranks of each side separated.

***

Far behind the Legion center, infantryman Heren trembled. What seemed like years ago but was only months, eighteen-year-old Heren worked on his family farm. Being the youngest, he followed orders from his two older brothers. His days were taken up with digging out rocks, hoeing rows for planting, and cutting firewood. Yet, as he performed the tasks, he'd gaze at the Apennine Mountains and dream of adventure beyond the peaks. Then one day, an Optio of Legions arrived in the Caudini village. The headman of the tribe put out a call for young men and Heren skipped work to hear the NCO talk. That night, he begged his father for funds to buy armor and weapons.

"I'll never inherit land or have a chance to marry," Heren laid out his argument. "But in the Iberian Legion, I can earn pay and save coins. And if the looting is good, I'll return home wealthy."

"And maybe die on the spear of some wild man," his father countered.

"The Legion teaches their infantrymen to fight," Heren pointed out. "I'm strong and a good hunter. The Optio said I have the makings of a Legionary. All I lack is armor and weapons."

"Do I look like a Ptolemy of Egypt sitting on a golden throne?" his father challenged. Then, the patriarch softened and offered. "In the hills above the village lives an old man. He has war gear. Ask him if he'll part with the armor, shield, and spear for two goats. That's the best I can offer."

In the morning, Heren ran to see the old man and ask if he could make the trade.

***

"Veles Heren," the light infantry NCO called to his newest light infantrymen. "Are you ready?"

"Optio, I am ready."

Although well oiled, the cross-chest leather armor showed its age, as did the helmet, the plain scabbard, and the scarred oval shield. The only piece of Heren's gear not revealing its age was the polished steel spearhead fixed to a new hickory shaft.

"No matter what happens in the melee," the Sergeant warned his Century of light infantrymen, "don't show your back to the spearmen. You'll catch a spear. And a dead Veles is no good to me, the Legion, his Century, his Gods, or his family. Euge?"

"Euge. Optio," the light infantrymen responded in full voice.

"Excellent. Forward," the NCO ordered.

A rank ahead of the row of heavy infantry shields, the first wave of Legion Velites battled a mob of spearmen. The mass of Iberians might have exhausted and overrun the Legion light infantry except the Velites knew they could fight with all their strength.

The replacement Centuries pushed to the back of the fray and began pulling first wave fighters out of the melee. In quick order, the tired light infantrymen were replaced with fresh arms and legs. Conversely, the weary and hungry spearmen remained in the fight without relief.

Heren slammed his oval into an Iberian. The man stumbled back. Once at stabbing range, Heren drove his hickory shaft over the spearman's shield. After a momentary pause, the spearhead sank through the man's leather armor and into his flesh. Retrieving his spear, Heren stepped forward and hammered another Iberian shield then stabbed again. No longer dreaming about adventure, the young man from the mountains yelled as he came alive in the fog of war, and discovered he was good at fighting.

In the press of bodies, Heren came upon his Optio. Three spearmen had ganged up on him. Two shoved their spears over the Sergeant's oval seeking a double impalement of the Legion NCO.

Crack. Heren's new hickory shaft slashed down across both Iberian spears. They split as did the hickory shaft. But the sacrifice of the weapon saved the Optio. Throwing down the ruined spear, Heren drew an old sica sword and plowed back into the fighting.

Slashing and blocking, Heren cleared a circle to his front. Other Velites moved in to stand shoulder to shoulder with the youth. Together they fought until a hand tapped his neck and a voice ordered, "Rotate back."

Hyped from the combat and with his blood boiling, Heren ignored the instructions.

"Veles Heren," his Optio growled in his ear, "save some for the third wave."

"Euge," Heren acknowledged as he came off the forward line.

Again, the Legion light infantry rotated fresh men into the battle. And, as before, the hungry and exhausted Iberian spearmen faced rested and determined Velites. Heren and his Century filtered back through the rank of heavy infantry shields for a rest.

***

Once in the rear, Heren cleaned the old blade and said a prayer for the old man from his village who added the sica sword to the pile of war gear.

"If I was a younger man," the ancient infantryman had said. "I'd be off to a Legion in Iberia as well. As it stands, I'll take two goats for the war gear and the glory."

Heren sheathed the sword and began inspecting his oval shield for damages. Beside the old patches, new grooves and slits in the wood told a tale of a worthy fight.

"Veles Heren," his Optio shouted from behind him, "when you're told to rotate out, you do not stay to kill two more of the enemy. You back away."

"Euge, Optio," Heren answered as he turned to face the wrath of his NCO.

But when he saw the Optio, the man held out the old spearhead and part of the broken hickory shaft.

"Your spear saved my life," the Sergeant announced. "I couldn't in good conscience leave it on the battlefield. It's an epic weapon and belongs in the hands of a hero. It belongs in your hands, Heren. Euge?"

A roar of 'Euge and brave' erupted from the entire Century of Velites.

Chapter 5 – Told By Others

Trotting in a never-ending circular path behind his Legions, Cornelius Scipio watched the battle between his light infantry and the Iberian spearmen.

"General, can I release the Celtiberi heavy cavalry?" Sinebe inquired.

"Not yet, Centurion of Horse," Cornelius replied.

Continuing his circuit, trying to see every fight, and judging the shape of his Legions, Cornelius held himself erect and proud. Although inside, his gut cramped, and his bowels threatened to turn to water. At any moment, the Carthaginian army could break through his center and ruin his main tactic.

"Sir, should we advance the Legionaries?" Lucius Marcius asked.

"Not yet, Colonel," he answered.

On one lap Cornelius reined in and stared. A Veles out front of the center wielded a curved sword and a punishing oval shield. Once the heroic individual cleared some breathing room, other light infantryman joined him in an assault line.

"Him," Cornelius pointed out to a junior staff officer, "find out the Veles' name and unit. I want to give him and the entire Century an award."

"Yes, sir," The Junior Tribune said before galloping to the light infantry unit.

Cornelius kicked his horse into motion. Behind him, Sidia rode close by. After the personal bodyguard came twenty-four junior staff officers. Next and at different times, the Battle Commanders of the five Legions appeared. Intermixed with the others in the entourage, fifty mounted veterans from First Century maintained security around the General.

Later in the morning, Sinebe suggested, "Sir, now would be a good time to activate the Celtiberi cavalry."

Cornelius glanced over the heads of the battling light infantry, the Carthaginian spearmen, the idle African Corps, and back to the war elephants.

"Not yet, Centurion of Horse," he said again.

The General and his staff rode onward to complete the lap.

***

Since before dawn, the heavy infantrymen had been standing and waiting. The Legion light infantrymen fought for periods but recuperated between bouts of fighting. Their opponents had been in constant conflict since the first attack. And as the African Corps hadn't gotten their spears wet, they were bored, hungry, and restless.

Since before sunrise both sides had been under tension. Now, with the sun halfway to its pinnacle, the wear on the Iberian spearmen became apparent. With each rotation, the Velites pushed the spearmen back and closer to the Corps.

"Much farther, General," Sidia commented, "and your light infantry will be fighting the African Corps."

"Mago will have to order the Corps forward," Cornelius observed. "Either that or admit defeat and withdraw to his camp."

"If he does that, sir?" Sidia inquired.

"We'll follow them over the walls and butcher them," Cornelius described.

Then General Cornelius Scipio froze in the saddle. His eyes took in a group of mounted messengers coming from the Carthaginian camp. A pair stopped at the line of elephants. Others split and rode to war chiefs. And the last two trotted to the Captains of the African Corps.

"Centurion of Horse," Cornelius called.

Sinebe trotted up and saluted, "Sir?"

"Tell Captains Bekeres and Darsosin, I want a pair of elephants for my day of triumph parade through Rome," Cornelius mentioned.

"Are you releasing the Celtiberi, General?"

"Yes. Clear all but two of those war elephants from my battlefield. But hold our reserve cavalry."

"Thank you, sir," Sinebe stated before racing away.

"You're still outnumbered," Sidia mentioned.

"It doesn't matter," Cornelius assured the bodyguard. "Their spearmen are exhausted. And after the initial assault, the African Corps will crumble."

"And you'll parade through the streets of Rome with a pair of war elephants and captives from the African Corps?" Sidia guessed.

"And the heads of Mago Barca and Hasdrubal Gisco," Cornelius added. He extended his arms and announced.

"Junior Tribunes, alert the Legions. On the signal from the trumpets and flags, advance the Legionaries."

The twenty-four junior staff officers divided. Each half rode behind the center of the Legion line without stopping.

***

Arathia paced behind the Twenty-fifth Century. Just as the African Corps shuffled in place from boredom, Arathia's infantrymen scuffed the dirt with their hobnailed boots. Plus, their shoulders ached from holding up their infantry shields.

"Steady," he called to the long line. "I know this isn't our normal formation."

"Sir, this isn't a formation," the Optio advised from farther away. "This is an inspection line. Or a form of corporal punishment."

From the center of the Legion line, the Twenty-fifty had directed the retreat when the Corps first came forward. And all morning, they held their shields up to hide the ranks of light infantryman staged behind them.

"Not much longer now," Arathia told his Legionaries.

"How do you know, sir?" the Tesserarius asked. He had just returned from where their Century joined another false front of shields.

"General Scipio released the Celtiberi heavy cavalry," Arathia told him.

All morning the temperature rose. But at midday, the air cooled from clouds that partially blocked the sun.

"That's a good sign," the Optio declared. "We'll fight in the shade."

Trumpets blared and flags sent the attack signals.

"Correction Optio," Arathia reminded his NCO, "they will be fighting under shade. Our job is to act as a blocking force. No body gets through."

***

Mago Barca had been worried all morning. And the feeling didn't end when his spearmen began to faulter.

"We should pull back," he muttered.

But Gisco heard and bellowed, "Not when we have them. We'll punch through their center, let the cavalry hunt down the busted Legions for sport, and we'll find Scipio's body and take his head."

"Fine. Send the messengers to forward the African Corps," Mago conceded. "Let's finish this."

***

In the middle of the battlefield, a Corps Captain exclaimed, "African Corps, prepare for war."

"African Corps, prepare for war," the ranks called back.

Shields came off the ground, spears were leveled over the shields, and the heavy infantry took a step towards the center of the Legion line.

Then faintly, and almost drowned out by the war cries and screams of the spearmen, 'Rah' came from the sides of the Corps formation.

"What was that, Captain?" a Lieutenant inquired.

"Some kind of Latian chant," the Corps senior officer replied. "Keep your focus on busting their center."

"Yes, sir."

On the second pace, the elephants trumpeted from behind them.

"Sir, the war elephants," the Lieutenant mentioned.

"Stop paying attention to minor disturbances and direct your infantrymen through the Legion middle."

"Yes, sir," the junior office affirmed.

Then in a flurry of thumps, bronze encased tusks, and the screams of injured men, war elephants charged into the rear ranks of the African Corps and the spearmen. Driven mad by the stab wounds from the Celtiberi heavy cavalry, the elephants rampaged into the Corps and the Iberians.

During the panic at the rear, another junior officer noticed the Legion's light infantrymen had retreated back through ranks of large shields.

"Guard your flanks," the Lieutenant screamed.

But the chant of the African Corps, prepare for war, and the panicked elephants running amuck, overrode the warning. It was too late. Frightened spearmen ran from the advancing triple row of big Legion shields. They crowded into the columns of Corps infantrymen. The undisciplined Iberians fouled the Corps smooth transition from a forward attack to defending their flanks.

A moment after the Lieutenant's futile warning, assault lines of Legion's heavy infantrymen crashed into the unsuspecting sides of the African Corps. The ends of their lines folded. Men died as Legion advances cut into the formation.

Five banners appeared, marking the true locations of the Legion's heavy infantry. Cornelius' ploy of hiding his Legionaries behind Velites on the wings of his formation and using a line of heavy infantry shields in the center to mask more light infantry had fooled the Carthaginian Generals.

**

49

"That's why you had the patrols formed with light infantry always on the flanks, General," a Junior Tribune mentioned.

"That, young officer, is the nefarious reason," Cornelius confirmed. Then he pointed at Sinebe. "Centurion of Horse, send the reserve cavalry around the edges of the fighting. Use them to screen the movement of the reserve light infantry. I want the battlefield surrounded. Non capimus!"

The Centurion galloped off to organize the envelopment.

"Sir, non capimus?" Sidie repeated. "No prisoners will leave you without African Corps infantry to march in your parade."

"I got caught up in the emotion of victory," Cornelius disclosed. "Maybe we can rescue a few before this is over."

Around the sides of the battlefield, Legion cavalry cantered and unseen by the enemy, each horse towed two light infantrymen. With the help of the mounts, the gladii of the Legion closed on the throat of the Carthaginian army. And a slaughter began.

***

On the wagon in the Carthaginian camp, Mago screamed in frustration while Gisco watched with his mouth hanging open.

"We had them beaten," Gisco whined. "All we needed was to push through their center and, and. It was your tribal spearmen, Barca. They got in the way of the Corps."

"Don't blame me for your rush to war," Mago snapped. He stepped down to the rail of the wagon and mounted his horse. "I'm taking my treasury and personal guard and leaving. You can stay and die with your beloved African Corps."

As Mago rode through the near empty camp, fat raindrops began falling.

***

From a sunny morning to a cloudy midday, the weather transitioned finally to a blinding storm. Fearing a reversal of fortune hidden by sheets of rain, General Scipio shouted to a signal officer, "Sound the recall. Get our infantry and cavalry out of this."

Mud would bog down Legionary assault lines, slow the horses of the cavalry, and prevent the in and out tactics of his light infantry. And at the center of the fighting, the body of the African Corps remained intact and dangerous.

Trumpets blared and the Legions pulled back from the fighting. Once clear of the African Corps, they turned and marched for their stockade camps.

***

Cornelius positioned himself on the route to the Legion stockades. Raggedy columns of Legionaries emerged from the wall of water and marched by their General before vanishing back into the gray.

"Sir, all the Legionaries can't see you," Sidia spoke loudly enough to be heard over the thunder and pounding rain. "And you need to get out of the storm."

"Even though those located at the extreme ends have no way of seeing him, Optio Decimia, Hannibal Barca is always visible to his warriors," Cornelius shouted over the downpour. "And those who don't see him will be told, by

51

others, that their General was on the battlefield and watching."

The rain continued as did the columns of Legionaries, cavalry, and Velites flowed by. Occasionally, a combat officer would notice Scipio and offer a salute. For most of the withdrawal, however, the men caught sight of him but in their misery and the slog with rain sodden equipment, they simply trudged by without acknowledging the General.

"Two solid defensive lines," a commanding voice rose above the storm. "Keep them straight, Optio."

"Yes, Centurion," the NCO replied.

Walking in reverse, an assault line came through the veil of water. Stepping backwards while holding their shields and spears to the front, the Twenty-fifth Century maintained their battle lines.

"Centurion Arathia, isn't it?" Cornelius hailed the combat officer.

Surprised at the greeting, Arathia spun around and blinked rainwater from his eyes.

"It is, General Scipio."

"What's your duty, Centurion?"

"Sir, the Twenty-fifth has the honor of being the rear guard," Arathia bragged, "for all the Legions."

"In that case, I can rest easy knowing your Century has my back," Cornelius declared as he began to bring his horse around. Then he stopped. Pausing for a moment, he ran his eyes over the straight lines of the Legionaries. "Twenty-fifth Century. I request your permission to withdraw from the field of battle."

Stunned by the General's statement, Arathia was speechless.

"General Scipio, the Twenty-fifth will cover your departure," the Optio replied. "Rah, General Scipio?"

The eighty exhausted and soaking wet infantrymen bellowed their permission, "Rah, General Scipio."

Cornelius headed his horse towards the marching camps.

"That Century will remember their General," Sidia volunteered.

"Indeed, they will," Cornelius remarked.

***

When the command entourage entered the camp of Wings of Nortus, they expected to find the streets empty. The Velites and cavalrymen, they figured, would be under tents drying and oiling their equipment. And most were, except for a huge crowd around the livestock corral.

"Make way for General Scipio," Sidia instructed.

The crowd parted and Cornelius rode to the rope barrier.

"Captain Bekeres, I see the Celtiberi have exceeded my orders," Cornelius challenged.

"General Scipio, we captured two elephants and were herding them to the camp," the cavalry officer explained. "Along the way, the third one fell in with the other two."

"Three war elephants can only enhance my day of triumph parade through Rome," Cornelius decided. "My compliments to the Celtiberi cavalry."

Two of the elephants reared back, lifted their trunks, and trumpeted into the air. To a man, the spectators ran and the horses, including Cornelius', pranced away from the giant beasts.

"Keep the elephants healthy," Cornelius called to a group of frightened animal handlers. "They are valuable political capital."

Cornelius rode to his pavilion. At the animal holding area, the three Mahouts for the elephants calmed the beasts.

"What's political capital," one Mahout asked.

"I have no idea," a Legion livestock handler admitted. "But according to the General, that is what your elephants are. What do they need?"

Chapter 6 – A Mule Cart Isn't Fast

After cleaning up and drying off, Cornelius ate and went to bed. As soon as he closed his eyes, or so it seemed, Sidia shook his shoulder.

"I hate to disturb you, sir," the bodyguard whispered.

"Then don't," Cornelius directed.

"You'll want to get your armor on for this, General Scipio," Sidia recommended.

The idea of putting on the armor with the wet wool backing sent a chill through Cornelius' body. Then the realization that he needed to put on his armor jolted him awake.

"Report," he ordered while sitting up.

"Colonel Zeno posted scouts and began patrols after we retreated," Sidia told him. "Not long ago, an important Carthaginian and his bodyguards rode south. Right behind them, the elephants and a few wagons rolled out. And to highlight the evacuation, the Numidian cavalry rode south as well."

"That leaves the African Corps and tribes of spearmen," Cornelius declared as he slipped a tunic over his head.

"Long lines of spearmen have been seen heading north. Our Iberians said they're heading home. Only those loyal to Gisco remain," Sidia asserted. "That means, General, for now the Carthaginian camp is only guarded by the African Corps and a few Iberian tribes."

"Send for Colonel Zeno and the Celtiberi Captains."

"Sir, isn't that an odd mixture for an assault on a fortified position?" Sidia questioned.

"They aren't for the assault on the camp," Cornelius explained as he pulled the damp torso armor against his dry chest. "They're going to secure some prisoners for my march through Rome. And chase the Carthaginian Generals."

"How far do they go, sir?"

"Chase Mago and Gisco to Hades or out of Iberia, whichever comes first," Cornelius answered. "At dawn, I'm taking the rest of the Legions into the Carthaginian camp."

***

Shortly after sunrise, Cornelius stood at one of the Carthaginian Generals pavilions.

"They couldn't have gotten far," he announced. "March Eagle and Golden Cat of Deimos south. See if you can catch the African Corps, and the cavalry."

"Sir, we'll never catch those Numidian riders, they're too fast," Eagle's standard bearer advised.

Cornelius elevated his face and studied the blue sky. When he looked down, his eyes were intense and moist with passion.

"Send word to Colonel Laelius. Have him assign Eagle to a Senior Tribune. I have another mission for him."

"That decision came fast," Sidia mentioned.

"Fast is the correct word," Cornelius replied.

When Gaius Laelius arrived, he dismounted and saluted.

"I've handed Eagle off to my Senior Tribune, sir," Laelius stated. "You have another assignment for me?"

"Centurion Digitius pointed out that the Numidian riders are fast."

"It's been said the Numidians are the best light cavalry in the world," Laelius offered.

"An excellent description, Colonel," Cornelius proposed. "That's exactly what I want from you. Now, go secure a hundred squadrons of Numidian cavalry for my Legions."

"Sir, where am I supposed to find a thousand Numidian cavalrymen?"

"You're my emissary to King Syphax," Cornelius explained. "Take a squadron or two of warships and row to western Numidia. We need a treaty with King Syphax. Make sure it includes permission to land and rest our Legions on his shores when we move to attack Carthage. The thousand cavalrymen will increase the speed of our attacks. But really, they aren't as important as the landing rights."

"General Scipio, we're going to invade Carthage?" Gaius Laelius asked.

"It was one of the tasks the Senate assigned to me when I accepted the Prorogatio of Iberia title."

"You can count on me, sir."

"I know I can, Gaius," Corneluis informed the battle commander. "It's why I chose you."

No matter how good, units on foot and caught in the open were at a disadvantage. Mounted forces had the speed, the reach, and the ability to cripple or kill individual soldiers. And just as a sounder of feral pigs panicked when a pack of wolves approached, the presence of heavy cavalry caused infantrymen to scatter, making them as vulnerable as wild pigs.

"Sweep to the left then cut them in half," Captain Darsosin instructed his squadrons of Celtiberi cavalry.

After sorting out the lines of attack, the cavalry rode along the left flank of the running African infantry. Then as ordered, the riders turned right. At that moment, the expression 'cut them in half' went from the theoretical dividing a herd into two parts, to physically cutting a swatch of death and disfigurement.

Hacked and bleeding, seven thousand infantrymen raced to a hill. On the slope, they linked shields and created a barrier against the marauding cavalry.

"Keep the hill surrounded," Darsosin told his junior officers. "Other than that, hold our riders back and out of spear range. Our job is done. Going forward, we'll let the Legionaries handle them."

***

Late in the afternoon, Colonel Zeno and his Steed of Aeneas Legion marched to the Celtiberi camp. When the battle commander saw all the shields of the Corps on the hill, he inquired, "Senior Centurion. What's it going to take to dislodge the Africans?"

"We'll need to grind them down a bit, sir," Thiphilia replied. "Give me one full day. And the next, we'll crash their shield wall."

"Not that I'm complaining about your schedule," Zeno ventured while looking south in the direction used by the rest of the Carthaginian army. "How can you project victory that quickly?"

"The hill where they took refuge," Thiphilia told him, "is arid. There's no spring or stream."

Infantrymen could fight for days without food, sleep, or rest. However, deny them water and they'd collapse in two days.

"Leave some alive and their equipment in good condition for General Scipio's parade."

"They'll be plenty for a march, sir," Thiphilia assured Battle Commander Zeno.

The Colonel came from the Republic and understood the importance of a day of triumph tour through Rome. But unlike Cornelius who dreamed of leading the parade, Zeno only recognized it as a display of might, honoring Rome. Steed's senior combat officer, being an Iberian, had no real concept of a General's parade.

Yet, he didn't need firsthand experience. He only needed to know his General wanted members of the African Corps to march through Rome in a procession.

"We'll save as many shields, armor, and helmets as we can," Thiphilia pledged.

"The more the better," Zeno remarked. "And remember, Senior Centurion, they have to be in good condition."

***

58

The Twenty-fifth Century sipped from wineskins being sure the liquid dripped down their chins.

"Clean yourselves," their Optio instructed.

With wide gestures, obvious to the soldiers defending the hills, the second maniple Legionaries wiped off the excess. And while they languished in a display of plenty, ahead of them, the first maniple pushed through a forest of spears and attacked the shields of the African Corps.

The barely tested Legionaries of the first maniple pushed, hacked, and stabbed but couldn't break the barrier of the African shields.

"This is the best duty," an infantryman from the Twenty-fifth declared.

With a wide grin, he slurped from a stream of watered wine while splashing a good portion of the beverage over his face. His combat officer stopped behind him.

"Don't get too full of yourself," Arathia warned. "Tomorrow morning, we'll have a go at their shields. And you know my feelings about that."

"Sir, from the first advance to the last step back, the Twenty-fifth is committed. Let no God, man, or animal doubt it," the Legionary answered with one of the Centurion's saying. "From dawn to victory, the Twenty-fifth Century inflicts penalties, and not tenderly, on our enemies. From dawn to victory, the Twenty-fifth is committed. Rah."

"Rah, Legionary. Splash a little more vino around, make the Corps thirsty," Arathia suggested. "That'll soften them up for tomorrow."

"With pleasure, sir."

Before Arathia moved on to the next Legionary, he noticed an infantryman from first maniple fall. Bleeding, the injured Legionary collapsed in the front rank. He began kicking and forcing the Legionaries with shields on both sides, and a pair behind him to open gaps.

When an opponent across a shield wall fell, the soldier who delivered the debilitating wound normally celebrated. His reward included the honor of leading his section into the breach. But it wasn't to be on that day on that arid hill. As if a pack of street beggars, the African Corps infantrymen leaped forward, dodging Legion shields and gladii as they grabbed for water and wineskins.

"Third Squad plug that hole until first maniple figures out, they have a problem," Arathia shouted as he drew his gladius. "Forward. Follow me."

Tossing their wineskins over their shoulders, the ten Legionaries of the third hoisted their shields and raced to catch up with their combat officer. Seeing the charge of his Third Squad infantrymen with the bright red horsehair comb of the officer's helmet at the front, the Optio grabbed the squad leader of the fourth.

"Decanus. Get your herd up there and put a cofferdam around Arathia," the NCO ordered. "We will not lose our Centurion over a collection of waterskins."

On the heels of the Third, the hobnailed boots of the Fourth Squad churned grass as they crashed into the three ranks of the confused first maniple. Shoving the inexperienced Legionaries aside, the shields of the Twenty-fifth interlocked and moved forward.

Arathia kicked a Corps shield into an adjacent infantryman while stabbing the neighboring African. The violent actions tossed back three of the attackers and drew the attention of an NCO of the Corps.

"Kill the Legion officer," the Sergeant shouted.

Four African spears swept in from four directions and focused on one target, Arathia's chest. Confident against a man without a shield, only two of the Corps infantrymen stepped forward and jabbed.

"Bring it," the Centurion bellowed as he blocked the shaft of one spear with his gladius and dodged another by turning sideways. "You want some of this? Come and get a taste of my steel."

Veterans of war from a young age, the four Africans silently coordinated. On their next stab, all four spearheads would arrive at once and with authority.

The row of steel tips stared Arathia in the face. Hoping to make one of them mad enough to break the row, he challenged, "Any day now, cowards."

None moved.

For a heartbeat, the world stopped and compressed to the small standoff. Combat officer Arathia and four infantrymen from the Corps paused to inhale. The exhale would be to voice war cries, marking the death of a Legion Centurion.

***

"From dawn to victory, the Twenty-fifth is committed, sir. Rah," ten voices shouted as big Legion shields brushed Arathia's shoulders. Quicker than the blink of an eye,

Legionaries from Fourth Squad slammed the door closed in death's face. The four spears harmlessly tapped the shields.

"Rah," Arathia acknowledged. He stepped back and took in the scene around him. "How many waterskins did they get?"

"Just a couple, sir," the Decanus of Third Squad answered.

Legionaries and NCOs from the rear line of first maniple bunched up, ready to fill the break in their assault line.

"Twenty-fifth, stand by to rotate out," Arathia warned. "Third row, rotate forward on my command."

"Rotate forward on your command, sir," the young Legionaries replied.

"Third and Fourth Squads, advance and rotate out," Arathia instructed. "First maniple, forward to the assault line."

Disengaging while in contact with an enemy presented the most dangerous of any maneuver. Step back too fast and the enemy would follow the men coming off the attack line and get into the rear ranks. Step back too slow, and the rotating Legionaries would clog up the line, causing all the shields to be slanted towards the enemy, instead of facing forward. The Centurion's order to advance prevented both.

The shields of the Squads slammed into the African Corps. Stunned by the solid wall of hardwood, the Africans rocked back, and prepared to repel a forward movement. But the Legionaries withdrew their shields, stepped a half pace, and stabbed any African infantryman who resisted the bash from the wall of shields. Then the squads from the Twenty-fifth turned sideways and moved off the assault line.

Replacing them, in a smooth transition, were Legionaries from first maniple.

"What do you think of the African Corps?" Arathia inquired as he and his twenty Legionaries marched back to second maniple.

"They can fight, sir," a squad leader offered.

"That they can," Arathia confirmed. "But they're at a disadvantage."

"Because they're running out of water, sir?" an infantryman suggested.

"There is that," Arathia admitted. "But I was thinking, while I looked down the shafts at four of spears, they don't have a chant."

Without further prompting, the two squads belted out, "Sir, from the first advance to the last step back, the Twenty-fifth is committed. Let no God, man, or animal doubt it. From dawn to victory, the Twenty-fifth Century inflicts penalties, and not tenderly, on our enemies. From dawn to victory, the Twenty-fifth is committed, sir. Rah."

The six squads of the Twenty-fifth, waiting in ranks, responded, "From dawn to victory, the Twenty-fifth Century inflicts penalties, and not tenderly, on our enemies. From dawn to victory, the Twenty-fifth is committed, sir. Rah."

***

In the dark before dawn, the Twenty-fifth once again found themselves facing the hill and the African Corps. Except now, instead of their hands full of wineskins and waterskins, the Legionaries carried javelins and spears. The warfare of the mind was over, and the sharp points of combat were about to be employed.

"Century. Keep your lines straight and your shields tight," Arathia coached in a voice that was softer than one would expect. But the combat officer knew that many times the art of war required quiet confidence rather than a heart pounding speech. "Take care of the men on either side of you and they will take care of you. Rah?"

"Rah, sir," the eighty infantrymen and their NCOs called back.

Then, like the eleven other Centuries of the second maniple, they stood waiting for dawn, the trumpets, and their turn at breaking the shield wall of the African Corps.

"Centurion Arathia? Centurion Arathia?" a teamster on a small cart inquired.

"Over here," the Optio directed. "The Centurion is over here."

Pulled by two donkeys, the cart rolled between Centuries, turned towards Arathia, and stopped beside the combat officer.

"Centurion Arathia," the teamster greeted him, "I have a gift from Senior Centurion Thiphilia and a new set of orders."

"Hold up," Arathia shot back. "We missed the fight at Ilipa. I'll not miss this one. And since when does a Legion's senior combat officer have a teamster deliver orders in a mule cart."

"That's just it, sir."

"Just what?" Arathia demanded.

"It's not like you can question me about the orders, I don't know anything," the mule driver explained. "And it's not like you can expect me to race to headquarters and get you an answer. A mule cart isn't that fast. And if you leave, the sun will be up long before you can get back. And you'll miss the attack."

Even in the shadowy world of predawn, Arathia felt the eyes of his Legionaries watching to see how their officer handled difficulty and change. The effect of his calming speech before an assault on a prepared enemy hung on his next words.

"What gift, teamster?"

"In the back, Centurion."

"Optio, check it out. Now, what are the orders?"

"The Twenty-fifth is the second-best disciplined Century in Steed Legion," the mule driver reported. "And possibly the fourth best in all of Scipio's Legions."

"Skip the motivational talk," Arathia urged. "Get on with the orders."

"Ah, kiss my butt and send me to Hades," the Optio swore.

"What's wrong?" Arathia questioned.

The Tesserarius jogged to the cart and squatted beside the other NCO.

"No. Just no," he whispered. "This isn't right."

"Mule driver, what are the orders?" Arathia insisted.

"General Scipio wants captured, healthy African Corps infantrymen with pristine armor, shields, and spears," the teamster reported. "The Senior Centurion has tasked the Twenty-fifth Century with taking at least five squads alive."

"This is a combat assault," Arathia protested. "Men die from flights of javelins, stabs from spears, and gladii strikes."

"Yes, Centurion," the teamster agreed. "That's why I'm taking your javelins and spears."

"Then what are my Legionaries supposed to fight with?"

"Sir," the Optio said before grunting. Then the sound of a long, heavy pole, sliding on the bottom of the cart reached Arathia. "We have thin battering rams to break their shield wall, clubs for fighting, and nets to foul their legs. In short sir, we're now gladiators. Net men armed with clubs."

"This is ridiculous," Arathia complained.

"Please, sir. If you'll load your spears and javelins," the mule driver encouraged, "I'd like to get back to the compound for breakfast."

Arathia's chest rose and fell in deep breaths. Finally, he peered at the streaks of light in the sky and spoke.

"Corporal, have the squads bring their spears and javelins forward," he instructed. His voice carried all the frustration of a man caught between duty and what he felt was right for his Legionaries. "Optio, pass them the fishing gear. Let's get sorted out before the assault starts."

Act 3

Chapter 7 – Not in a Good Place

Only sixty of the Century's eighty Legionaries moved forward. The remaining twenty lagged behind the forward shields. They kept pace but maintained a distance.

On one end of the formation, the Tesserarius ordered, "Separate those shields."

Four infantrymen, cuddling two long beams, swung the beams back as they stepped forward. Propelled by arms, legs, and momentum, the logs snapped to the front.

Well-trained, braced, and prepared for an assault, the targeted infantryman from the African Corps was secure in his skills and his place. But when the ends of two midsized logs collided with his shield, the infantryman flew back and away from the shield wall.

"Again," the Corporal instructed.

The battering rams rocked back before powering into the adjacent shield. That infantryman lifted into the air, and as if jumping a ditch backwards, tumbled away from the defensive line.

In training, Legionaries were taught to take advantage of a single shield breach.

"A pair of you heroes, go back-to-back, get in that hole, and widen it," the instructors drilled. "Then push, like your worst day on a latrine, and widen the breach until I can march a Legion through it."

A one shield hole was a chance for glory and breaking through the enemy's defensive line. Or a death sentence for the pair of Legionaries embedded in the enemy's shield wall. A break two-shields-wide, on the other hand, was an open invitation into the enemy's backyard.

***

After the second Corps infantryman flew away, the neighboring Century noticed the wide breach and began shifting so they could pour Legionaries through the break. Before they could take advantage of the opening, a cluster of infantrymen wielding clubs, mobbed one side of the breach.

Clubbing infantrymen from the Corps, the Legionaries of the Twenty-fifth didn't rush to get behind the Africans. Rather, they bashed them with shields and beat them to the ground with clubs. And while other Centuries killed, maimed, and stomped as they drove the Corps uphill to an inevitable end, Centurion Arathia's men hesitated. They only moved upward when downed infantrymen from the African Corps were tied up. And tended to by the twenty Legionaries stationed behind the disarm-disable-and-capture line.

"This is going to be bad," a squad leader at the rear commented.

His squad, and the other squad, had left their shields at the bottom of the hill. They needed both hands to bind prisoners' wrists, give sips of water, and treat injuries.

Responding to the comment, the Decanus of the Eighth Squad glanced uphill. Bile rose in his throat. And the burning choked off the curse he wanted to lay on Senior Centurion Thiphilia for taking away their javelins and spears.

Near the summit of the arid hill, and directly above the Twenty-fifth Century, the surviving infantrymen of the African Corps gathered. Either for a last stand, or more frightening for Arathia's Legionaries, a breakout maneuver to escape the massacre visited on them by Steed Legion.

The latter seemed most likely and in response, Colonel Zeno sent the Celtiberi cavalry to the base of the hill.

"We are not in a good place, sir," the Optio remarked. "We've enemy infantry above us, and cavalrymen below. Not in a good place at all, sir."

"I am tempted to agree with you," Arathia said. "Order a fighting square. Put our nursemaids and the prisoners in the center. It might get rough, but if we're mean enough, the Corps will avoid our shields."

"It might get rough, but if we're mean enough, the Corps will avoid our shields," the NCO repeated. "That's one of your best, sir."

"That depends," Arathia venture.

"Depends on what, Centurion?"

"If our Legionaries believe it. Now form the square."

Drilled to perform quickly, the Twenty-fifth compressed into a four-sided formation. Typically, the square would bristle with spear shafts from eight squads. But two squads were needed to guard the captured infantrymen, and no one had spears.

"Here they come," the Tesserarius shouted.

From the top of the hill, a wedge of infantrymen marched downhill. The sharp, leading element, headed directly for the fighting square.

"It might get rough, but if we're mean enough, the Corps will avoid our shields," the Optio called out. "Standby to brace."

All sides of the square, in support of each other, bent their knees, dug in the foot of their rear legs, and stiffened the arms holding the shields.

The tightly packed infantrymen of the African Corps covered the ground of the hill above the Twenty-fifth, displaying their mass to the Legionaries below. On the sides, Steed Legion maneuvered into formations to contain the Corps. Squeezed in from the edges, it left only one way off the hill. And that was through or over the fighting square of the Twenty-fifth.

When the African Corps was ten paces from the Legion shields, Arathia ordered, "Century, brace."

"Rah," came back as the Legionaries flexed in anticipation of the assault.

But the African Corps stopped. A commander stepped forward and asked, "Who is in charge of this Company?"

"I am Centurion Arathia, and I command the Twenty-fifth. And we have no plans to move."

"As you will, Centurion," the African Corps' commander allowed. "From there, you can accept the surrender."

"The surrender?" Arathia inquired. "How many?"

"Why Centurion Arathia, everyone still alive. Everyone on the hill behind me. It's, I believe, around five thousand infantrymen of the African Corps."

"Why the Twenty-fifth, why us?"

"Over our shields, we noted that you and your Legionaries treated the men you captured with dignity. We trust you'll treat us in the same manner."

In the center of the fighting square, the Decanus of the Eight Squad whispered, "Senior Centurion Thiphilia, I apologize for cursing you."

***

Cornelius Scipio stood still. While his body remained immobilized, his mind raced. He wanted to join the chase for Mago Barca and Hasdrubal Gisco. Yet, he'd received requests for audiences from a number of tribal chiefs.

"A robe over a long tunic, sir," Sidia recommended.

"What?" Cornelius asked.

Thinking the General was debating on what to wear, Sidia Decimia recommended, "A robe, sir. Not your armor."

"You're thinking I should grant them a meeting?"

"It's an opportunity to solidify your hold on Iberia," the bodyguard pointed out. "Treaties with these tribes will secure more than half the territory. And put you closer to the day of triumph parade when you return to Rome."

"When you put it like that," Cornelius allowed, "how could I not meet with the Chiefs."

***

After four and a half years of war, Cornelius had subdued most of Iberia. During the multi-front campaign, he encountered Carthaginian armies and caused them to fall. As well as the outside threat, the Governor of Iberia dealt with constant tribal uprisings.

"With Mago and Gisco fleeing like children after getting caught with their fingers in a honey jar," the Chief of the

71

Vettones declared, "you, General Scipio, are in command of Iberia. The Vettones, sir, have no interest in total destruction on the swords of your Legions."

"The same, I can assure you, General, goes for the Carpetani," another Chief added. "We will abide by any treaty and trade agreement you wish to impose."

"As will the Vettones."

"The Turdules are ready to sign," the third Chief announced.

Four tribes controlled the entire south-central region of Iberia from the sea to far inland. Cornelius listened patiently as three spoke up. Then he rested his hands on the tabletop and explained, "In my experience, when three tribes talk but the fourth remains quiet, trouble comes from the silent tribe."

After his words, tension hung over the treaty table. No one drank from their glass or snacked on the refreshments.

"I lost a lot of warriors to your Legions, General Scipio," the Chief of the Turdetanes informed Cornelius. "At Baecula, at Carmona, and at Ilipa, the flowers of my tribe died on your blades. Our grandmothers cry during the day, mothers curse me in the evenings, and wives utter obscenities in my direction at night."

"Will it be war between us, then?" Cornelius questioned. "If so, I grant you free passage so you may leave in peace."

"But then you'll march on my cities, burn them to the ground, and murder my citizens," the Chief offered. "No, General Scipio, it will not be war."

"If not war," Cornelius asked, "then what?"

"War is not fought for glory, although my youngbloods believe it is," the Chief replied. "Nor is it to settle disputes of the heart or inheritance. All wars are fought over land. In order to settle the dispute between the Turdetanes and Latians of Rome, there must be conquered land. My hesitation revolves around what land my tribe relinquishes to you."

"I'd settle for a symbolic gift of land," Cornelius confessed. "Anything to make a lasting peace."

"War is a serious matter as is the conquest of land," the Chief countered. "Therefore, I surrender the land where the Rivera de Huelva and the Baetis River meet and to the west as far as you can see from the junction."

"River land?" Cornelius uttered. Then more clearly, he protested. "Good farmland is valuable. It seems a shame to use it to appease me when I have no designs on the acreage."

"Do not insult the memory of my dead warriors," the Chief challenged. "They died defending their land and their homes. To give anything less than rich farmland would belittle their sacrifice."

"I understand," Cornelius confessed. "If there is to be peace between our peoples, I demand quality land as the payment. Will you sign a treaty to that effect?"

"On behalf of Turdetanes tribe, I accept your peace terms."

"Now, while our scribes write the documents," the Chief of the Vettones declared, "we will eat, drink, and tell lies as men do in times of peace."

***

73

For a week, Cornelius entertained the four chiefs. During those days, he received reports. Carthaginian General Mago Barca had settled in Cádiz by the sea. Hasdrubal Gisco boarded a ship-of-war, and with half a squadron, rowed away from Iberia for parts unknown. And the survivors of the African Corps petitioned Cornelius for a release with a promise to pay a handsome reward.

"When you first arrived in Iberia, sir," Sidia recalled. "You had no coins, not enough Legionaries, and your future looked dim at best."

"Why are you reminding me of that?"

"Today, you are a rich man with loyal Legions, and more spearmen than you could use in three wars," Sidia listed. "You should wrap up unfinished commitments in Iberia and plan the next step in your career."

"That remark, Optio Decimia, is vaguely specific," Cornelius teased. "Let's say I'm done here. After my parade in Rome, I'll return, and we'll row the Legions to Carthage. What unfinished commitments in Iberia am I missing?"

"There are cities that turned away desperate Legionaries after the disastrous campaigns of your father and uncle," Sidia proposed to Cornelius. "Those veterans have fought for you while carrying anger in their hearts at being wronged in a time of need. Many are older and would have left the Legions except for one goal."

"To see the cities punished," Cornelius guessed. "I do owe them and my father and my uncle justice. Then we'll hold games to celebrate the lives of Publius Scipio and Gnaeus Scipio, and to salute the Legionaries, Velites, and cavalrymen who served with them. Will that appease Nemesis?"

"Your Latin God of divine retribution and revenge?" Sidia remarked. "I believe, sir, Nemesis will be thoroughly honored as will the memory of your father and your uncle."

Cornelius pointed to a junior staff officer.

"Run and collect the commander of the African Corps," he directed.

"Yes, sir," the Junior Tribune said, accepting the assignment.

A moment later, the youth raced from the headquarters pavilion.

"The African Corps?" Sidia inquired. "Why them, sir?"

"You pointed out the age of my veterans," Cornelius disclosed. "I want to see how high a price the Corps is willing to pay for their freedom."

"You're thinking of the impenetrable walls of Iliturgi and Castulo, sir."

"Like I said, it's a high price. Let's see if the Africans are willing to pay it."

"That, sir, will spare the knees, shoulders, and backs of your veterans," Sidia proposed. "But the assault on those walls will thin the number of African infantry available for your parade."

"It's a sacrifice, I'm willing to make," Cornelius admitted.

**

After the Chiefs left, Cornelius ordered most of his Legions to march for New Carthage. Both Bolt of Jupiter and Eagle of Jupiter he held at Ilipa. As well, he kept the African

Corps. And the Celtiberi cavalry to keep the African infantry on their best behavior.

When the Iberian Legions vanished into the distance, Battle Commander Lucius Marcius approached Cornelius.

"The Legions you held back are Republic Legions," Colonel Marcius noted. "And one Legion doesn't have a Battle Commander. What are you planning, sir?"

Cornelius walked Marcius away from his staff.

"I'm taking half the Africans, half the Celtiberi, and Eagle Legion to Iliturgi," Cornelius divulged.

Lucius Marcius squinted his eyes at the sun and nodded.

"When your uncle sent me away before the final battle, I swore to honor him, always," Marcius informed Cornelius. "In the months that followed, I collected stray Legionaries and Velites. Most had horror stories of how they were mistreated before I found them. Two of the worst offenders were the cities of Iliturgi and Castulo."

"Iliturgi is mine to punish," Cornelius revealed. "They invited Legionaries in and butchered them. They will pay for that violation of hospitality. If you want revenge, Castulo is yours. If not, lay siege to the city until I get there."

"The walls may hold me back, sir, but not my heart," Marcius assured him. "To honor General Gnaeus Scipio, I accept the mission."

"We'll leave in two days," Cornelius informed the Colonel.

"That'll give you time to see your Iberian holdings," Marcius suggested.

"I hadn't thought of that," Cornelius said. "I was going to use the days to pray and study maps of Iliturgi and Castulo."

"I've seen your land," Marcius told him. "It's a beautiful piece of farmland with high defensible ground to the west. You'll appreciate it when you do."

"Maybe someday," Cornelius begged off. "Right now, I need to plan the destruction of two major cities. And prepare a response to the Oretani Tribe when they find out."

Chapter 8 – How Many Ladders?

Five days after leaving their camps, Bolt Legion left Eagle Legion on the south bank of the Baetis River. The Lightning Bolt of Jupiter Legion would continue sixteen miles northward to the walled city of Castulo. Closer in, at two miles, the walls of Iliturgi made the city appear almost as far. At least, it seemed that distance to the command staff of Eagle Legion.

"The river is impressive, sir," Sidia observed. "And if we had wings, thirty-foot walls wouldn't be a problem."

"No creatures except birds and Pegasus have wings. And even among the Gods, only Mercury has them," Cornelius asserted. He continued to gaze across the wide river and up the cliff face to the stone walls. Offhandedly, he asked. "Why did you mention wings, at all?"

"I try to find the positive whenever possible, sir," the bodyguard replied. "For instance, if we had lizards, they could climb the cliff to where the walls are lower."

"First you mention the wide, fast-moving river, then the unscalable walls, and now an insurmountable cliff," Cornelius complained. "What are you getting at, Optio Decimia?"

"General Scipio, I didn't describe any of those obstacles, sir. You did," Sidia pointed out. "My comments were to stop you from staring and to get you thinking about solutions."

Sextus Digitius nudged his horse closer to Cornelius.

"General Scipio. We'll need logs to build rafts," the Standard Bearer suggested. "And once we're across, we'll split the logs and make ladders. Unless the General has a different idea, sir?"

"I'm fresh out of birds and lizards," Cornelius replied. Not understanding the reference, Digitius gawked for a moment before Cornelius added. "After we're across the river, we'll make an offering to Mercury to help the Legionaries fly over the walls."

"Using the ladders, right sir?"

"That's correct," Cornelius confirmed. He looked back at the still arriving Legion and called to the First Centurion. "Centurion Lartia. Send a runner to find Captain Micipsa. I want to get the African Corps' take on those walls before the Senior Centurion gets involved."

"Yes, sir, I understand," the Centurion of First Century said.

"I hadn't planned on asking Micipsa until you mentioned birds," Cornelius admitted to Sidia. "Some units of the Corps have birds on their shields."

"Do you think they can fly, sir?" Sidia inquired.

"Not really. But I wanted to give them the opportunity."

***

Captain Micipsa carried scars collected on his ascension from an infantryman to a leader of the African Corps. Tall and dignified, his posture fit with his narrowed and searching eyes. Almost as if he was a sleek bird of prey, the officer took in his surroundings by constant scanning.

"You wanted to see me, General Scipio?" he asked.

"Captain, I'm sure you haven't missed the monstrous structure across the river," Cornelius submitted.

"Stone walls that prominent, sir, are hard to miss."

"Exactly. I have a proposition for the African Corps. At least the half here with me."

"Our oath and pride will not allow us to fight units commanded by Carthaginians," Micipsa advised.

"The city of Iliturgi has changed sides so often, I don't think they remember where their loyalties rested yesterday afternoon," Cornelius suggested. "What I want is the best of your infantry. Prove to me you're valuable and I'll begin paying the Corps. And after my parade through Rome, I'll put you on transports and send you home."

"That, General Scipio, is indeed a proposition," Micipsa allowed. His eyes passed over the high walls once more, and he inquired. "To which side of Iliturgi will you assign to the Corps?"

"I'll use half my maniples on the north side at the main entrance," Cornelius answered. "The other half, I'll assign to the side you don't want."

"What of the cliff?" Micipsa questioned.

"I'm looking for birds, not lizards," Cornelius replied. Seeing the confused look on the Captain's face, he clarified. "It's a reference from a previous discussion. Let me know once you've decided."

"Yes, General Scipio."

As the African commander rode off, Senior Centurion Panatia galloped between members of the command staff.

"What did the murderous African have to say?" Panatia demanded. "More empty promises of gold for their freedom?"

"Not this time," Cornelius answered without revealing the proposition. "Centurion Digitius recommended swimming rafts across the river."

"A fine idea," Eagle's senior combat officer agreed. "Afterward, we can use the logs to make ladders. And if the God Sors blesses us, we'll get lucky, and the Africans will drown before reaching the other side."

"I don't suppose, Senior Centurion, I could get you to toss a bucket of water on that roaring fire of vengeance you're lugging around?"

"General Scipio, I had served in a Legion every season for twenty-three years and enjoyed success for the most," the Senior Centurion responded. "Five years ago, your uncle's Legion was caught off guard when the Celtiberi infantry ran out on us. After Numidia riders chased away our cavalry, the African Corps marched in and destroyed our undersized formations. Only a few of us escaped. To this day, I limp when I march, and every night, my shoulders ache. Thusly, sir, in no particular order, I hate Carthaginians, the African Corps, anything Celtiberi, and Numidian cavalry."

The furious nature of Panatia's revelation froze Cornelius but not Sidia.

"If you're so blinded by hate and physically damaged, Senior Centurion," Sidia questioned, "why are you with Eagle Legion?"

80

"For revenge, Optio Decimia," Panatia stated. "Plan and simple, I want pay back for my General and my dead maniple."

"And for the Senior Centurion's pay, I'd venture," Sidia proposed.

Panatia bristled and inhaled as if he was going to explode on the bodyguard. A moment later, he exhaled in resignation and addressed Cornelius.

"The truth is, General Scipio, I have nowhere else to go except Eagle Legion," Panatia admitted. "As you requested, sir, I will hold my feelings closer to my breast and treat the Africans as if…"

Noting the Senior Centurion's hesitation, Sidia suggested, "as if they were teams of stubborn mules pulling wagons of supplies you don't necessarily need but would like to have. Treat the Africans like that, Senior Centurion."

"I can't hate mules. Doesn't mean I like them, but I can ignore them and the African Corps," Panatia announced. "Now if you'll excuse me, General. I want to get the Legion started on rafts and guidelines."

"Dismissed, Senior Centurion," Cornelius allowed.

As the senior combat officer left, the Legions senior staff officer trotted up. With twenty Junior Tribunes in tow, the arrival doubled the size of the command staff.

"General, Panatia is a good officer," Fustis Lecne said, defending the Senior Centurion. "I hope he wasn't too abrasive."

"Panatia and I have reached an agreement," Cornelius assured the Senior Tribune. "I noticed he's getting on in years. How many of Eagle Legion's Legionaries and Velites are his age?"

"Of those who came to Iberia with the original Republic Legions," Lecne answered, "some are older than Panatia, and some are a little younger. But they can still fight, General Scipio."

"I have no doubt," Cornelius concluded. "I was just thinking that after the parade through Rome and the assault on Carthage, they should be released from the Legions to return home."

"That presents a problem, sir," Lecne revealed. "They left Etruria, Umbria, their homes in the Apennine Mountains, and their Sabine villages to follow the Legion to Iberia. Most have nothing in the Republic they can call home."

As Cornelius absorbed the information, yelling caught his attention. From the woods, a mule pulled a log onto the bank of the river. Moments later, two more mules dragging logs came into view.

"Sir, I'd like to be sure we get a couple of Centuries of heavy infantry across first," Lecne advised. "They'll be needed to defend our landing if the Oretani War Chief objects to our presence."

"Carry on, Senior Tribune," Cornelius granted.

Lecne cantered away and Sidia frowned.

"Something bothering you, Optio Decimia?"

"Well, General Scipio, all the talk of resigning or being resigned from the Legion is unnerving," Sidia revealed. "You see, sir, I hate farming."

"Not to worry," Cornelius assured him. "No one is putting you out to pasture. At least not until we row to

Carthage and lure Hannibal back to his homeland. For now, I hope you can swim."

"Sir, all Legionaries are taught to swim," Sidia boasted. "And after the long days of marching to get here, cooling off in the river will be refreshing."

But Cornelius didn't hear. His mind had drifted across the river to the face of the cliff and the stone walls of Iliturgi.

**

Six Centuries hiked up the access road, halted, faced the closed gates, and linked shields. The placement of the four hundred and eighty Legionaries would prevent Oretani spearmen from coming through the gates and attacking the Legion. On the ground, the infantrymen watched the top of the wall. Staying alert, they waited for the appearance of ranged weapons and the launch of spears, arrows, pellets, stones, or boulders by the defenders.

From high on the walls of Iliturgi, militiamen observed Eagle Legion's arrival. Yet, they did nothing beyond closing the gates to interfere with the long columns of infantrymen. The defenders, against all reason, allowed the Legionaries to march unmolested from the edge of the river to an assembly area outside the walls of their city.

On both riverbanks, the Velites worked to ferry supplies, raft the wagons, and swim the draft animals across the Baetis River. In all the maneuvering and transportation, few noticed and less cared that the African Corps swam the river, migrated no farther than the base of the cliff, and set up camp.

Behind the screen of Legion shields, Eagle's Senior Centurion bit down on his tongue as he watched the Africans spread bedrolls and unpack tents.

"Yesterday, I would have put Micipsa and his Lieutenants on the punishment post for separating from the Legion," Panatia complained to a pair of Centurions.

"Why not today, Senior Centurion?" one of the combat officers asked. "We know how you feel about the African Corps."

"You can't get mad at mules if their handlers are ineffective and blind to reality," Panatia uttered.

"Mules?" the other Centurion questioned.

Panatia had almost revealed his true feelings about Cornelius Scipio's use of and affection for non-Republic troops. To cover his blunder, the Senior Centurion scolded the pair of Centurions. "Don't you two have Centuries to look after?"

"Sir, they're right in front of us," one pointed out.

The senior combat officer yanked his reins, turned his horse from the blocking Centuries, and kicked the mount. As Panatia rode away from the formation, one of the Centurions said, "That was odd. The old man is usually ready to put the entire Corps up on the wood."

"That and for years, he's been talking about getting revenge on Iliturgi," the other combat officer added. "Now that we're here, he seems almost disinterested."

"Be nice," the second Centurion teased, "someday you'll be old."

They both studied the thirty-foot walls of the city for a moment, before one suggested. "If we live that long."

Cornelius trotted up the wagon trail from the river. As he rode, the General nodded at specific Legionaries, and pointed to familiar infantrymen and NCOs. In his wake, he left men bragging about being singled out by Cornelius Scipio. On a rise, Scipio positioned the horse, so he was visible to the arriving Legionaries. When most of the Centuries had reached the assembly area, he lifted his arms.

"Eagle Legion, Rah."

"Rah, General Scipio," almost three thousand voices responded.

With his arms still raised, Cornelius allowed his eyes to drift slowly over the ranks. They expected him to speak, but he didn't. After a few moments, teams of light infantrymen jogged between the ranks with eight long ladders constructed from raft logs. The ladders were hoisted on their ends, and as if stacked spears, leaned against each other for support. Cornelius moved his arms and indicated the walls of Iliturgi.

"The time has come for you to avenge the appalling massacre of your fellow Legionaries. And the treachery the city of Iliturgi would have inflicted on you, had you in your desperate flight from the broken Legions of the Scipios passed through their gates. Now, by making the city an example of your wrath, will you make this clear, for all times. No one must ever consider a citizen of the Republic, or a Legionary, marching under a Legion banner, a subject fit for ill-treatment, whatever their condition or situation. By your actions today, let this be their punishment."

A Century marched to the ladders, unstacked them, then immediately raced to the walls of Iliturgi. Slinging the ladders upward, they placed the tops against the stone blocks and started to climb.

***

The defenders had been dormant. But now, with active targets, the militia threw rocks at the men on the ladders.

Three rungs up, Legionaries felt stones and rocks bounce off their helmets and the shields strapped high on their backs. Most stones were thrown from the sides, allowing the infantrymen to absorb the punishment while ignoring the painful impacts from the ones that found flesh. A few rocks, thrown directly between the rails of the ladders, tumbled down, and smashed faces. Yet, even with bleeding noses and cut cheeks, the infantrymen continued to climb. Most blindly lifted and placed a hand and a foot, one after the other, as they scaled the wall.

By then, the militiamen had narrowed their aim to the most effective lines to defend against the assault. Using the knowledge, they called their archers forward.

Bowstrings snapped, arrows shot between the rails, and arrowheads punched Legionaries off the ladders or caused them to slide downward and into the arms of their squad mates. Without hesitation, other infantrymen took their places and began to ascend the rungs.

Seeing the wounds visited on men unable to fight back, Cornelius signaled his trumpeters. A moment later, the recall sounded.

Leaving the ladders in place, the attacking Century raised their shields overhead. After collecting their wounded, the Legionaries jogged away from the walls. To their amazement, no storm of rocks, stones, or arrows followed them.

"That is what we face," Cornelius exploded, his voice thundering over the gathered Legion. "It'll take courage and determination to scale those ladders. But Eagle Legion, like its namesake, will fly over these walls, Rah?"

In response, the ranks of Legionaries bellowed, "Rah, General Scipio."

***

Later, while the Legionaries and Velites built a marching camp in the low hills adjacent to the city, Cornelius balled his hands into fists.

"It was a costly test," he offered to his command staff. "Maybe too costly. I've just got back from visiting the wounded."

"However brutal, sir, it was necessary," Panatia said defending the action. "We've learned the Oretani have lots of rocks but less arrows. No slingers, and they're stingy with their spears."

"What does that mean for our assault on the walls?" Cornelius demanded.

"They'll defend hard in the morning but will quickly run out of arrows," Colonel Lecne said, taking the lead on answering the question. "By the afternoon, their militia will be reduced to using rocks as their primary distance weapon."

"They'll save their spears," Senior Centurion Panatia stated, "for when our Legionaries reach the top of the wall."

"How many ladders do we have for the assault?" Cornelius asked.

"There's a standard answer to that question, General," Panatia replied.

Senior Tribune Lecne cleared his throat before telling Cornelius, "More than we'll need to take the city, sir. But never enough to satisfy Soteria."

The mention of the Goddess of Safety and Preservation from Harm acknowledged the danger of attacking a walled city.

"In that case, for the benefit of our Legionaries," Cornelius vowed, "I'll offer a sacrifice to Soteria at dawn."

Although his intentions were good, General Scipio selected the wrong deity for the morning sacrifice. It would have helped if he or his staff had recognized the impact of the test attack on the rest of his infantryman. And the fact that, the failed assault drew the attention of the God Deimos - the bringer of fear and terror to men about to go into battle.

Chapter 9 – Upward to Glory

From the area at the base of the cliff, rhythmic sounds drifted to the higher elevations. In the Legion camp, Senior Centurion Panatia bristled at the almost unrecognizable pulsing.

With empty hands, the African infantrymen slapped their palms together, "Clap, Clap, Clap."

"Those Carthaginian troops are sleeping in the open and making enough noise to draw every Oretani spearmen from twenty miles around," the Senior Centurion scoffed.

Drumming followed the clapping of the Africans' hands with deep, "Boom, Boom, Boom."

"Maybe, by dawn, they'll all be dead," Panatia growled. "Their throats cut as they sleep."

With closed fists, the infantrymen of the Corps pounded their chests, "Thump, Thump, Thump."

"That's if they ever stop the racket and go to sleep," Panatia complained.

Next, sticks on hollowed out logs rattled, "Tap, Tap, Tap."

"No one will get any rest tonight," Panatia announced as he walked to a guard post. "Not with the African Corps serenading the entire Legion."

"What are they chanting, Senior Centurion?" an Optio asked.

"Hades if I know," Panatia admitted. "Probably a song about being melancholy and homesick."

***

Down where the wagon trail leveled out at the base of the cliff, and much lower than the stockade camp, the infantrymen of the African Corps clapped, drummed, pounded, and chanted.

"As sure as Hadad wars with Reshef."
Clap, Clap, Clap
"Storms and rain clash with fire and flames."
Boom, Boom, Boom
"War and rain linked like death and rot."
Thump, Thump, Thump
"As we bind a shroud with a sad knot."
Tap, Tap, Tap
"The Corps fills too many burial plots."

Clap, Clap, Clap

"At least we'll never die in a cot."

Boom, Boom, Boom

"As sure as Hadad wars with Reshef"

Thump, Thump, Thump

"Storms and rain clash with fire and flames"

Tap, Tap, Tap

"Blades and blood linked like panic and pain."

Clap, Clap, Clap

"We ask no constrain when we train."

Boom, Boom, Boom

"The Corps shields painted by bloodstain."

Thump, Thump, Thump

And death follows our every gain."

Tap, Tap, Tap

"As sure as Hadad wars with Reshef."

Clap, Clap, Clap

"Storms and rain clash with fire and flames."

Boom, Boom, Boom

A roar accompanied the final chest thumps.

Thump, Thump, Thump

***

"Are you ready Hiarbas?" the Corps Captain inquired.

Infantryman Hiarbas slapped a leather sack that hung over his shoulder by a thick strap.

"Captain Micipsa, keep the chant going, and I'll find and fix the route until dark," the infantryman promised.

"As sure as Hadad wars with Reshef."

Clap, Clap, Clap

"Storms and rain clash with fire and flames."

Boom, Boom, Boom

"You'll have the chanting for as long as you need it," Micipsa said. "Now off you go and good luck."

Hiarbas hiked to the base of the cliff and searched the face for a specific spot. Once located, he pulled an old spearhead from the sack and lifted a hammer from his belt.

"War and rain linked like death and rot."

Thump, Thump, Thump

"As we bind a shroud with a sad knot."

Tap, Tap, Tap

When the sticks smacked the hollow logs, Hiarbas pounded the point of the old spearhead into the cliff. Then he stepped on the socket, which acted as a foot peg, pulled another spearhead from the sack, and reached ahead.

"The Corps fills too many burial plots."

Clap, Clap, Clap

"You'll never die in a cot."

Boom, Boom, Boom

Hiarbas hammered in another spearhead, using the sound of the chant to cover the strikes. Then, humming along with the rhythm, he stepped on that socket and proceeded to a spot higher on the cliff. At a passable trail, cut into the face of the cliff by weather, he walked uphill until the path ended. With another spearhead in hand, he joined the chanting.

"Storms and rain clash with fire and flames"

Thump, Thump, Thump

"Blades and blood linked like panic and pain."

Tap, Tap, Tap

***

Near dark, the chanting ended. And just as a sound becomes familiar and background noise, Legionaries at the marching camp noticed its absence.

"Finally," Panatia declared as if he'd won the game.

A Centurion bent down and studied the dice and the throwing bones. They had duplicate numbers.

"In the game Tali and Tesserae, Senior Centurion," the combat officer pointed out, "all your die and bones have to have unique numbers. I'm afraid, you threw duplicates."

"It's not the game," Panatia protested. "It's the African Corps finally ending their never-ending chant."

"It is quieter," another player observed. "But, in reality Senior Centurion, I enjoyed the music."

"Hold your tongue before someone cuts it out," Panatia threatened. "And don't let the die and bones grow cold in your hands. Throw them."

***

Cornelius dressed and left his pavilion before first light. Behind him, as if a moon shadow, Sidia kept pace all the way to the livestock pen.

"Saddle the General's horse," Sidia directed, "and mine."

"Right away, Optio Decimia," a groom acknowledged.

For a moment, the horse handler looked at Cornelius as if expecting one of the General's salutations. But in the candlelight from his tent, the groom noted Scipio's upturned face and the General's concentration on the black mass of the dark stone walls. A few moments later, the handler walked two horses from the pen.

"We're ready, sir," Sidia announced.

Cornelius remained motionless as if he didn't hear his bodyguard. But while the groom became nervous, Sidia waited patiently.

"They're tall," Cornelius stated before mounting the horse.

"That they are, sir," Sidia confirmed.

The two riders trotted through the gates and passed by the defensive walls of Iliturgi.

***

In the camp at the base of the cliff, a guard called to the commander of the African Corps, "Riders coming in, sir."

Micipsa sat up and splashed water on his face before crawling out of the infantry tent. He stood erect and was stretching when the Roman General reined in his horse.

"I have room in my pavilion for you, Captain," Cornelius offered.

"An officer who sleeps separated from his men," Micipsa proposed, "misses more than their company."

"Meaning you want to know their mental state," Cornelius offered as he slipped off the horse.

"That yes, but more important, on the day of battle," Micipsa clarified, "how well the men slept and if they had appetites upon waking."

"Speaking of battle. Have you picked which wall you'll assault?"

"The African Corps will enter Iliturgi from the cliff side," Micipsa answered.

Cornelius peered over his shoulder at the blank wall. In the darkness and low visibility, the cliff face could just as well have been a cave or a hole in the earth.

"How long will it take you to scale it?" Cornelius inquired.

"The critical question, General Scipio, how long will it take your Legionaries to climb to the top of the wall?" Micipsa corrected. "Once the Corps enters the city, the defenders will pull militiamen off the walls and come for us. I don't mind helping the Legion, but I don't want to die for it."

"My Legionaries will join the battle shortly after you meet resistance," Cornelius assured the Captain. "Wait for the second trumpet blast. Then begin your climb."

The sun peeked over the top of the mountains and weak light touched the cliff face. All around the camp, voices of the African Corps chanted, and hands clapped.

"As sure as Hadad wars with Reshef."

Clap, Clap, Clap

"Storms and rain clash with fire and flames."

Boom, Boom, Boom

Cornelius noted a man of slight build with a leather sack hung over his shoulder by a thick strap. As quick as a lizard, the man darted across the face of the cliff. In moments, as if by magic or animal cunning, the man was over halfway up the face.

"War and rain linked like death and rot."

Thump, Thump, Thump

From his sack, the man pulled a spearhead and to the beat of the chant, he hammered it into the face of the cliff.

"The second trumpet blast," Cornelius reiterated before he mounted his horse. "I'll see you at the city square, Captain."

Micipsa saluted. Cornelius turned his horse to leave. And on the cliff, Hiarbas pounded in another spearhead with a "Tap, Tap, Tap."

***

The knowledge that the African Corps would draw defenders off the walls, making the Legion's assault easier, boosted Cornelius' confidence. Cantering his horse into the marching camp, he guided the animal to a temporary altar. Swaddled in robes, a pair of Junior Tribunes waited on either side of the stone slab. They bowed when the General reined in his mount.

Because Iberia was seen by the Temples of Rome as a wild and dangerous place, the Pontifex Maximus sent only a few experienced priests to the region. Of those who made the trip, most remained in New Carthage or Tarraco. Safely behind the walls of the cities, they supervised the construction of temples dedicated to their Gods or Goddesses. The shortage of clergymen serving in the Legions left Cornelius with a pair of aspiring celebrants to preside over the sacrifice.

"Today, we honor Jupiter and Soteria," Cornelius announced from horseback. "Priests. Is there anyone unwilling or incapable of honoring the Sky Father and the Goddess who Preserves Us from Harm?"

A competent priest with a grip on the mood of his parishioners would have stopped the ceremony. Then again, an experienced clergyman would have been up before dawn, walking through the camp, listening to conversations, estimating the hardiness of the infantrymen's appetite, and judging the Legionaries' attitude about the coming assault. A simple warning to Cornelius and General Scipio could have made a speech to lift the mood and bolster the spirits of his Legionaries and Velites.

"All present, do honor Jupiter, Soteria, and the Prorogatio of Iberia," the young noblemen declared.

A wave of dissatisfaction washed over Cornelius. With Eagle Legion preparing to attack a fixed fortification, naming him as anything other than a General of Legions degraded his image in the eyes of the infantry.

But the Corps was prepared, his carpenters had built hundreds of thirty-foot ladders, his Legion knew the reason for the operation, and it was getting late in the morning. Cornelius dismounted and marched to the altar.

"Today, we asked Jupiter's blessing as we climb towards his sky and deliver his thunder with our blades," Cornelius prayed. The phrasing should have elicited cheers. But none followed the meditation. Oblivious to the silence, Cornelius thought. *"What do Legionaries and Velites care about me being the Governor of Iberia? Even if I have a warrant from the Senate to raise and command Legions, the men want, no, they need a leader not a politician."*

Animal handlers brought two bulls to the altar. The junior priests displayed long knives and waited for their Governor to finish the incantation.

"May the Goddess Soteria redirect arrows away from us, block boulders, and dull the tips of spears aimed at our shields," Cornelius prayed. "For the grace of Soteria and the power of Jupiter, please accept this sacrifice."

He motioned to the two Junior Tribunes and the youths began hacking on the necks of the bulls. Rather than a dignified sacrament, the ceremony to honor a God and a Goddess became a clumsy slaughter.

"Not a good omen to start the day," Sidia commented.

"Unfortunately, not," Cornelius said. "Hopefully the assault on Iliturgi will go better than the sacrifice."

***

Throughout history, getting a battle started proved to be the hardest part of a General's day. To overcome the natural hesitation to rush into enemy blades, different cultures used rituals. The Gauls depended on intoxicating drink, and bloodcurdling war cries to get their tribal warriors to engage. Greeks compacted their Hoplites into tight ranks, gave them big oval shields and long spears, then shuffled their phalanxes forward to meet the foe. Spartans, due to their training, had no problem advancing on the enemy. Yet, they took time before a battle to groom and braid their long hair, trim toenails, and fingernails, or to exercise naked in full view of their adversaries. The display of cool confidence unnerved their enemy as much as, if not more so, than the idea of fighting the fearsome soldiers of Sparta.

The Legions of the Republic rejected shouting to build courage in the ranks or preening to intimidate an enemy. For Tribunes and Centurions of heavy infantry, discipline was preferable to uncontrolled bravado. Training and straight assault lines more effective than a staggered rush at the shields of an enemy. And, the ability to orderly rotate fresh arms and legs into a fight, beat the heroics of throwing waves of bodies against an enemy's shield wall in an attempt to break through.

Discipline and maniple control were the mainstay of the Legions. Except when the attack depended on ladders and individual Legionaries climbing face first into a barrage of arrows, stones, and rocks. Those tasks broke the procedures of the Legion. Undetected, and billowing beneath the infantry's quiet exterior were the memory of the failed assault from the day before, and the long night of thinking about the deadly climb in the morning. Compounding the thoughts, the ugly blessing of the God Deimos inserted fear in place of courage. But no NCOs, Centurions, Tribunes, or their General noticed the shift in attitude.

***

The trumpets blared.

In response, Velites and Legionaries carried ladders to the walls. Other infantrymen held shields over their heads to protect the ladder bearers. Arrows and rocks pelted them, but none breached the shield roofs. And once the rails and rungs were rested against the stone walls, the porters and their shield bearers sprinted out of range.

"Very impressive, General Scipio," First Centurion Lartia complimented Cornelius.

"Not until we have men on them," Cornelius pushed back.

Almost as if the walls were under construction, the vast number of ladders gave the impression of wooden scaffolding. However, no boards crossed horizontally between rungs. The rails and rungs only allowed travel in two directions, downward or upward to glory.

The trumpets blared for a second time.

"Eagle Legion, forward. Rah," Sextus Digitius shrieked in his high-pitched voice.

A waving of the Eagle banner accompanied his call to the Legion. Getting no response, Standard Bearer Digitius thrusted the banner higher and demanded, "Eagle Legion, forward. Rah."

Among the Legionaries, the courage of discipline had melted into pools of self-preservation, cowardice, and the inability to move.

Cornelius knew his one chance to take the city rested in a quick assault. Catching the commanders of the Iliturgi militia off guard when they realized the African Corps was already in the city depended on one thing. His Legionaries must be on the ladders assaulting the tops of the walls. Without the attack on the walls, the Corps would be massacred in the streets, and his Legion would be ruined. Until the NCOs and Centurions were replaced, and the Centuries reorganized and retrained, Eagle Legion would be useless for the invasion of Carthage.

"Not a good omen, sir," Sidia disclosed.

The trumpets blared for a third time.

But pointlessly, as no Legionaries left the ranks to claim their place on a ladder and the glory of leading the attack.

(Intentionally left blank)

Act 4

Chapter 10 – Wide, Expressive Eyes

At the second blare from the trumpets, Micipsa stood and faced the infantrymen of the African Corps.

"The city militia will be occupied defending the walls at their gates," Captain Micipsa exclaimed. "Get up the cliff and into the city quickly. Because once they realize we're in, they will come off their walls, and come for us."

For a moment, he let the gravity of their mission penetrate the minds of his infantrymen. Then the Captain drew his sword and held the hilt against his chest.

"The God Hawot will claim his share today," Micipsa warned. "Make sure at the end of the fighting, he has more of them than us."

"Praise Hawot," the Corps responded. "We'll send him their dead."

"African Corps," Micipsa bellowed while lifting his sword in salute, "prepare for war."

"African Corps," the infantrymen shouted back, "prepare for war."

Micipsa sheathed his blade, and in long strides, strutted to the base of the cliff. Before any of his junior officers could protest, he placed a foot on the first spearhead, stepped up, and began the climb to the top. Behind and below him, the infantrymen of the African Corps lined up to follow their senior officer.

Above and ahead of him, the city's militia wasn't in the chaotic state Captain Micipsa expected. Because, the Legion hadn't initiated an assault on the walls at the second call of the trumpets.

***

The third trumpet blast failed to move a single Legionary. In the ranks, Optios kicked behinds, Tesserarii shoved Legionaries, Centurions threatened sessions on punishment posts, and Tribunes strutted back and forth in frustration. But, as in every case of mutiny, group sedition bonded the mutineers together.

Ignoring the ranks of immobilized infantry, Cornelius lifted his face to the sky.

"General Scipio, I apologize," Standard Bearer Digitius offered.

"He can't respond, Centurion," Sidia told Digitius. The attempt to defend Cornelius while he thought through the situation led the bodyguard to a lie. "He's reached out to the Gods and is talking with them."

Sidia's words were picked up by the Legionaries of First Century.

"General Scipio is talking to the Gods," they reported to the men around them. In moments, Cornelius' posture and his silence were explained to an ever-widening circle of Legionaries. As word spread, the Optios, Tesserarii, and Centurions stopped harassing the infantrymen.

Hushed conversations repeated, "The General is talking to the Gods."

"What are they saying?"

"What is he saying?"

"Don't ask me. I'd never have the courage to talk with a God."

While fear gripped their hearts, making Legionaries and Velites immune to threats from their NCOs and officers, it did not replace their faith. From personal deities to family gods, to spirits that protected their Century, and idols that guided the fate of their Legion, each man held deep-rooted beliefs.

Four thousand Legion fighters stopped looking with fear at the walls of Iliturgi and gazed with curiosity at Cornelius Scipio. The man who talked directly with the Gods.

***

Without moving his head and barely parting his lips, Cornelius issued instructions.

"Sidia. When I say count, you will count to five before you move," he directed. "Standard Bearer Digitius. You will count to eight. First Centurion Lartia. You will count to ten before you and your Century move."

"Sir, I don't understand," Lartia admitted.

"First Centurion when the General gives a command, it's best to follow it," Sidia advised, "and not question him. Especially, when he's communicating with powerful deities."

On faith, the First Centurion accepted the explanation and remained silent.

***

Almost as if the Gods were pausing the scene to examine the participants, a hush fell over the Legion and the livestock. The calm extended to the defenders on the walls, creatures of the forest, and those who hunted from the sky.

"Count now," Cornelius insisted.

Confused, but following instructions, Sidia, Digitius, and Lartia said, "One."

They searched the heavens as if expecting an avenging spirit to appear.

"Two."

The pounding of hooves on the ground drew their attention to where Cornelius had been. But the General wasn't there.

"Three."

Seeing Cornelius galloping towards the wall, Lartia jerked, but Sidia's hand on his forearm held the First Centurion in place.

"Four," the bodyguard insisted.

In an acrobatic dismount, Cornelius dropped to the ground and sprinted forward to bleed off momentum. And while the horse angled away from the storm of rocks, General Scipio charged into the deluge of thrown objects.

"Five."

While Lartia and Digitius vibrated with anticipation, Sidia Decimia kicked his mount into motion. Bent low against the horse's neck, Sidia rode hard in a desperate attempt to reach Cornelius.

"Six."

Cornelius stopped at a ladder. Ignoring the stones that hit his helmet, legs, and shoulders, he turned to face the Legion. After tossing his white cloak over a shoulder, General Scipio made a rude gesture with his arm.

"Seven."

More effective than any of the kicks, shoves, or threats, the very personal insult broke through Deimos' fear. Between seeing their General in a hail of stones and his crude suggestion, the Legionaries and Velites of Eagle Legion awoke from their trance.

Sidia leaped from his horse and ran to Cornelius.

"Sir, you shouldn't be here," the bodyguard scolded him.

"Will you cover my back?" Cornelius asked.

Sidia put his small cavalry shield over the General's head.

"Eight."

Digitius screamed to the heavens as he waved the eagle banner and galloped towards Cornelius.

"Nine."

The Legionaries noticed the stoicism and scorn of Cornelius Scipio as he stood in harm's way. Then his bodyguard arrived by Cornelius' side, and now the Standard Bearer rushed to support the General.

"Ten."

Lartia dug his heels into the flanks of his steed. In response, the horse vaulted forward, leaving the rest of First Century behind. A heartbeat later, the Legion witnessed First Centurion Lartia and one hundred battle-hardened veterans dash forward.

At the sight of the support for Scipio, like threads pulled from a woolen garment, the rebellion unraveled. Legionaries from Eagle Legion flooded the open ground. Taking to ladders, they climbed. A barrage of arrows and stones launched by the city's militia flowed down the rails and over the rungs and into the faces of the Legionaries. Some fell, but others took their place as the Legion assaulted the walls of Iliturgi.

***

Four blocks from the gates of Iliturgi, across the town square, and in a doorway to a shop, an officer of the militia rested a hand on the hilt of his sword.

"Don't you worry," Lieutenant Edereta assured the cute shopgirl. "If they get through the gates, I'll be there to stop them."

The girl touched the back of his hand and winked at the officer.

Edereta leaned forward, preparing to deliver his most seductive line. But a messenger arrived and broke the mood.

"Sir, the section officer wants your reserves at the eastern end of the city," the runner rushed out the words. "There are infantrymen climbing the cliff, sir."

"Climbing the cliff?" Edereta repeated. Over his shoulder, he called to his Sergeant. "Collect the reserves and get them sorted out. We have a mission."

After the declaration, Edereta focused on the girl to see how his commanding presence affected her. She smiled. And the crinkling lines at the edges of big, expressive eyes displayed her innocence and vulnerability.

"I'll return after we throw the invaders back over the cliff," he assured her.

"Please do," she requested. "I want to hear all about it. And we can…"

Her words were interrupted. A second runner sprinted across the plaza.

"Lieutenant Edereta," the messenger blurted out. "The Major wants your reserves on the north wall. The Legion has started their attack."

Edereta froze, which confused the girl. Until that moment, the Lieutenant appeared to be brave and decisive. While Edereta remained motionless, the Sergeant shoved fifteen hundred militiamen into loose ranks. The reserves only filled a small section of the town square.

"Where to, sir?" the Sergeant asked. "Sir, which way?"

Edereta weighed a number of factors. The Major of the militia outranked the officer for the eastern sector. Advancement in the city militia was preferable to being a tribal spearmen in a border village. And for sure, there were more girls in Iliturgi. Plus, the cliff, in addition to being a formidable barrier, was fifteen blocks away. In the final analysis, the militia in the eastern sector should be able to push a few slow climbing infantrymen back over the knee wall.

"Sergeant, take them to the defensive positions at the north wall," Edereta declared while throwing his arm in the air to point the way. Then he glanced at the girl with the expressive eyes, and the pleasing smile. He flashed his teeth at the shopgirl, then saluted her, before rushing after his militiamen.

***

Captain Micipsa halted with his feet on the last two spearheads and his body pressed against the cliff. Stooped low, he reached an arm back and waved the nearest infantrymen to a stop. Above him, he heard a militiaman approach the short wall.

It wasn't a militiaman on the overlook, but the officer for the eastern sector. The Lieutenant peered at the Baetis River.

"Any sign of the reinforcements?" he asked.

Behind him, his Sergeant replied, "Not yet, sir. I expect them soon. Any sign of the infantrymen?"

Behind the NCO, fifty militiamen waited. The butt ends of their spears rested on the street and their shields lay against their hips. Although grateful to be in the east sector, and not facing the Legionaries on the north wall, they were nervous.

The militia officer tilted forward, planning to check the steep face of the cliff. He bent, leaned over the knee wall, and looked down at the Captain of the African Corps.

Acting on pure instinct, Micipsa launched his body into the air. As he lifted from the foot pegs, he extended his left arm. Years of training allowed him with just a glimpse of the militia officer's neck to latch onto the man's throat.

Suspended for a moment by the windpipe, Micipsa caught the top of the brick wall with his right hand. Then he braced his knees on the wall and pulled.

The militia Lieutenant was yanked off the overlook and dragged over the bricks. Once the man's legs cleared, the Captain of the African Corps tossed him out into space. With the falling man still issuing high-pitched screams, Micipsa pulled hard and jumped to the top of the wall. Crouching, he took inventory of the city's defenders.

**

Infantrymen, picking their way up the steep face of the cliff, were easy prey. Single file and balanced on widely spaced spearhead sockets, they could be thrown off by well-aimed rocks or brushed away by spear shafts.

Although he faced fifty militiamen and an NCO, the Captain of the African Corps didn't hesitate. Brandishing his sword, Micipsa leaped at the Sergeant.

The Militia NCO yelped and jumped back to avoid the sword. To his surprise, he wasn't stabbed or cut by the blade. Rather, he tasted the hilt, the Captain's knuckles, and blood as Micipsa drove the Sergeant backwards.

Captain Micipsa had learned long ago that he couldn't fight multiple men. Nor could he push a wounded or a dead man into enemy ranks and disrupt their formation. Uninjured, except for the busted lip, but stumbling, the militia Sergeant flayed his arms. When Micipsa released him, the NCO fell and took five militiamen down with him.

Not pausing to admire his work, Micipsa sprinted at the militiaman on the end. This time, his blade lashed out and the man fell. Then the Captain was behind the formation and the forty-four militiamen spun to face him. With their backs to the cliff, they brought their shields up, and leveled their spears over the tops of the shields.

"Who's next?" Micipsa inquired.

Angry and embarrassed, the Sergeant wasted precious moments climbing to his feet. Where he should have ordered an attack, he delayed by licking his split lip and spiting.

"You are a dead man," the Sergeant announced.

"That lip looks bad," Micipsa offered. "Perhaps we should put this on hold and discuss terms of surrender. I understand your reinforcements will be here soon."

"Surrender?" the Sergeant growled. "I'll have your head mounted over the main gate by this afternoon, surrendered or not."

Micipsa took three steps away from the formation, moving towards the city.

"You misunderstand me, Sergeant," he proposed. "I meant you and your militiamen should lay down your arms and beg me for mercy."

"Why would I do anything like that?"

From behind the formation of militiamen, a voice announced, "On your command, Captain Micipsa. The African Corps is prepared for war."

"Take them down," Micipsa directed. "No one escapes into the city."

Fifty arms snapped forward, launching fifty spears. Even at a close distance, not every spearhead delivered death or a mortal wound. A few militiamen ran for Iliturgi. Micipsa glided between them, slicing ankles and calves. And the militiamen who turned to face the infantrymen of the Corps were trampled by advancing Africans.

"Orders, sir?" a junior officer inquired.

"They have reinforcements coming," Micipsa told him. "But I don't know how many. Let's narrow their approach by burning the buildings on either side of the main throughfare."

"You heard the Captain," the junior officer ordered, "burn the city."

***

Sextus Digitius reached the top of the ladder and planted the Eagle banner on the defensive wall. On either side of him, Legionaries flowed up and over the ramparts. The fighting had moved to street level where militiamen faced moving walls of Legion shields and spears.

"Centurion, we saw fifteen militiamen go into a building," an Optio reported. "Should we go in after them?"

The combat officer looked down a cross street to see another Centuries moving deeper into the city.

"We need to keep up with the Legion," the Centurion emphasized. "Take who you need and handle it. Then catch up to us as fast as possible."

"Yes, sir," the NCO acknowledged.

"Third and Fourth Squads, follow me," the Optio ordered.

Twenty Legionaries stepped out of the shield wall and jogged to a warehouse.

"This will take time," a Decanus advised. When the Optio gave him a confused looked, the squad leaders explained. "It's a linen dying operation. There'll be sheets hanging all over the place. We'll have to flush the militiamen out, one drying line of linen at a time."

"That'll take too long," the Optio complained.

"Let's burn it," a Legionary suggested. "Set it on fire and kill the militiamen when they come out. For those who don't make it, well, they'll die in the fire. Problem solved."

The NCO peered at the backs of his Century. The Legionaries moved through another intersection as they approached the town square.

"Leave five Legionaries here to handle anyone who escapes the flames," the NCO ordered. "The rest of you, burn it, then get back to the Century."

A noticeable haze hung over the town square. Still heated from the fires, the smoke remained high enough that the combatants could breathe even if their eyes watered.

Cornelius, Sidia, Battle Commander Lecne, and First Centurion Lartia walked their horses down a side street. They had started on the main boulevard from the gates. But flames, licking out from burning structures on the east side of the road, drove them further west to a secondary street.

"Does Panatia not realize the city is burning down around him?" Cornelius asked.

"The Legion must be locked in combat with the militia and can't disengage," Lecne offered.

Scattered clusters of dead militiamen and citizens littered the roadway and the doorways. Putting a cap on the devastation, a layer of what looked to be black clouds blotted out part of the sky.

"I didn't intend to burn the city, only to punish their leaders," Cornelius denounced the destruction. "After this fire, they'll be no wealth to harvest from the ashes."

"I assumed the Legionaries would want to make a profit more than they wanted revenge," Lecne proposed. "I guess I was wrong."

A block later, they discovered why the Legion's heavy infantry remained in a burning city.

***

On one side of the town square, the African Corps stood over piles of dead militiamen. Across the square, Legionaries loomed over their own stacks of dead city defenders. And while no living bodies separated the two assault lines, the space between them was filled with almost visible waves of mistrust, loathing, and animosity. Both seemed oblivious to the flames reaching for the heavens and the smoke billowing up around them.

Fearing the start of a battle that would undue his victory, Cornelius instructed, "Senior Centurion Panatia. March your left flank down the right side of the street."

"But sir, we have them cornered," Panatia pleaded from behind the Legion line. "Let me finish the Corps while we have them trapped."

"Look around you, Senior Centurion. Before long, we'll all be trapped by the fire. Move your left flank down the right side of the street, now."

As if waking from a dream, Panatia sniffed then jerked his head around taking in the extent of the fires.

"Left flank, retreat down the right side of the street," he ordered.

Cornelius indicated the African Corps.

"Optio Decimia, kindly inform Captain Micipsa that he is clear to extract his infantrymen down the left side of the street," Cornelius directed.

"Yes, sir," Sidia agreed before trotting his horse across the square.

Because a raging fire was the greatest enemy of all, Legionaries and infantrymen of the Corps marched quickly from the town square. As if ants from different nests, they kept separated as they folded in their combat lines to form columns moving down opposite sides of the street.

When Captain Micipsa marched by, Cornelius saluted the commander of the African Corps.

"Sir, we should be going," Lartia encouraged. "The flames are moving west."

"Not until I'm sure all of my Legionaries are safe," Cornelius informed the First Centurion.

Sidia shifted in his saddle before saying, "General. You've put yourself in enough danger today. Why tempt the fates?"

After a moment to consider the question, Cornelius took a last look at the town square. Until the Oretani Tribe rebuilt the city, he would be the last person to see the bricks of the square. As he scanned, his eyes fell on a dead militia Lieutenant. He wouldn't have paid attention, except the officer's body was being cuddled by a badly wounded girl in front of a shop.

While holding the officer's hand, the girl smiled as if she and her Lieutenant were somewhere else besides a burning city. Then her bright, expressive eyes with the crinkle lines in the corners dulled as death took her.

Cornelius turned his horse and guided it between the tail ends of the marching columns. Behind him, the first blazing building collapsed onto the town square of Iliturgi.

Chapter 11 – The Agreement

"It's a fire pit, sir," Sidia suggested. "Quite possibly the largest one in the world, but definitely a box of wood, flames, and hot ash ringed by stones."

From the Legion marching camp, the General's staff could only see flare ups of flames, and light reflected off the underside of a great black cloud of smoke. The defensive walls blocked the actual view of the burning city.

"It's a waste," Cornelius remarked. "To protect a few officials, they invited in the worst of all possible outcomes."

For a time, people fled through the gates hauling a few possessions. But as the fires intensified, fewer and fewer people appeared. Eventually, no one came out, leaving the gateway from Iliturgi to spew only smoke and waves of heat.

"What about the people, sir," Colonel Lecne inquired. "Should we gather them up?"

"They've suffered enough. Let them go," Cornelius replied. "We'll march to Castulo at dawn. Maybe Colonel Marcius has found a less extreme way to punish that city."

***

The news of the total destruction of Iliturgi and the deaths of over half the population wouldn't reach Castulo until the next day. Then teary-eyed messengers from the Oretani Tribe would bring graphic descriptions of horror and sorrowful tales of the demise of entire families. But that would come in the morning.

Sixteen miles up the Baetis River and ignorant of the news, Colonel Lucius Marcius arrived at the decision to storm Castulo and burn the city to its foundations on his own. Not out of revenge, although he had good reason to punish the city. Or to copy General Scipio's approach, he knew nothing about the actions of Eagle Legion.

The Battle Commander's strong emotions boiled up from the two men sitting in the treaty tent with him.

"Really, Colonel. We're offering you a wagon of silver and another of copper," Mayor Cerdubelus protested. "All that wealth, and yet you insist on a handful of gate guards and a few old councilmen. It hardly seems worth your while."

"The militia commanders closed the gates on my Legionaries and Velites," Marcius submitted. "And the old men stood on the walls and shouted insults at them. For those crimes, they must pay."

"But you are being offered pay," Major Himilco declared. Then the Carthaginian officer showed his true feelings. "And it's more than you deserve. You arrive and demand that Castulo hand over leading citizens in the name of an old vendetta. Let me remind you, we have more than tribal militia within our walls. I command a Company of Gauls. You come at our ramparts, and we'll throw your Legionaries off the ladders and let the fall kill them."

Cerdubelus reeked of lies, and Himilco smelled of inherited superiority. Marcius knew he could make a deal with either man, individually. But together, they supported each other, limiting the negotiations to only left-hand turns. As happened twice a day now, for two days, the talks ended up where they began.

"Imagine, a couple of wagons full of silver and copper," Cerdubelus proposed. "That will make you a rich man."

"Which will do me no good when General Scipio puts me up on a cross for dereliction of duty," Marcius countered.

"Then we are at an impasse and it's getting late, Colonel," Himilco stated.

The city's Mayor and the Major stood, bowed, and left without any pleasantries.

"That went well," Marcius said.

"We need to bleed them, sir," Standard Bearer Trebellius suggested from the back of the tent. "Hurt them enough and they'll sit down and get serious."

"There's only one problem with that approach, Centurion Trebellius."

"Which is, Colonel?"

"Our casualty count will be just as high as theirs," Marcius answered. "And I don't need the blood for motivation I'm already serious."

The Standard Bearer stood absolutely still. Just when Marcius thought the conversation was over, Trebellius told him, "You're facing two different enemy units. You need to separate them and attack one at a time. Or, get a partner to distract one while you negotiate with the other."

"Are you volunteering?"

"Me, sir. No sir," Trebellius begged off. "I'd rather climb a ladder into a blizzard of arrows and spears than sit and make nice with a man of no honor. And a coward."

"You think Himilco is a coward?" Marcius inquired.

"Well, Colonel, he retreated from Mago's army. And took a Company of Gauls with him as his personal security detail."

Marcius got to his feet, reached down, and lifted his glass of wine.

"Where can I find a brave man," he pondered before taking a sip, "who can relate to a Carthaginian coward?"

"I have no idea, sir. But tomorrow is another day. Perhaps something will occur to you by then."

"It better," Marcius uttered. "Or I'll be on the ladder next to yours when we assault the walls of Castulo."

They left the treaty tent, mounted horses, and trotted to Bolt Legion's marching camp. All the way to the gates, Marcius considered the option of scaling the walls and burning the city to the ground. Then as he entered the stockade, the Battle Commander of Bolt Legion looked at the weathered faces of his veterans and decided a couple more days of negotiations wouldn't hurt.

***

Darkness faded away with the first rays of dawn. Illumination made the rutted wagon trail, heading north from Iliturgi, passable and the road became crowded. Not as in backed up like the supply wagons, but busy over the sixteen miles to Castulo. Armored cavalrymen traveled faster than Eagle Legion's infantry and wagon train. But quicker than both were the Oretani riders, who easily outpaced the Legion horsemen.

Long before the riders of Eagle's vanguard appeared, tribal messengers galloped from the riverbank and charged through the gates. Shortly afterwards, the gates closed, putting a barrier between the citizens of Castulo and the Legionaries of Bolt Legion.

"And on day three," Marcius pontificated when he heard the news, "they sealed their fate."

"Excuse me, Colonel," Bolts' Senior Centurion inquired.

"Send a messenger to the gates," Marcius directed. "Tell them if the Mayor or the Major, or both, aren't at the treaty tent when the sun is directly overhead, Colonel Marcius will not be pleased."

"Sir, wouldn't you want to used wording that implies an actual threat?" Trebellius asked.

"Don't you find it unnerving that I might be displeased, Standard Bearer?" Marcius asked.

"Yes sir, it does. You're the Colonel of Bolt and every man in the Legion works to follow your orders," Trebellius explained. "But the spearmen and shield bearers in Castulo aren't Legionaries and they don't care about your feelings, sir."

"You're correct. Stronger words are required," Marcius admitted. "Senior Centurion, amend the message and convey this – if the Mayor and the Major aren't at the treaty tent when the sun is directly overhead, Battle Commander Marcius well be annoyed. Better?"

The last word was spoken to the Standard Bearer.

"Colonel, I don't understand," the Senior Tribune confessed.

"I couldn't actually tell Cerdubelus and Himilco that in the middle of the night Lightning Bolt of Jupiter Legion will scale their walls. Once in their city, we'll murder everyone in their sleep," Marcius informed his staff. "So, I'm just annoyed. Let them drink toasts to their security and my patience."

"We're going over tonight?" Trebellius questioned.

"Unless the principles come out to talk," Marcius confirmed.

A runner marched into the Colonel's command tent, braced, and saluted.

"Sir, our scouts report that Eagle Legion will be here this afternoon," the courier reported.

"That's embarrassing," Marcius commented.

"What's embarrassing, Colonel?" the Senior Centurion asked.

"General Scipio has finished with Iliturgi, and we're still dancing around the walls of Castulo."

No one argued. How could they? Eagle had finished an assignment while Bolt sat in their camp like an overweight and blind magistrate. Stationary with no vision of which path to take forward, and an inability to move if they did.

"Supper with the General should be interesting," Marcius muttered before going outside to watch the progress of the messenger at the gates.

***

The sun topped the sky and started down the backside of the day. And while neither Mayor Cerdubelus nor Major Himilco ventured out of Castulo, General Scipio, and Eagle Legion, appeared in the valley.

As the long tail of Eagle Legion marched alongside the Baetis River, Cornelius and his staff trotted into Bolt's camp.

"General Scipio, welcome to Castulo," Colonel Marcius greeted him.

Fearing a rebuke for his lack of progress, Marcius left off any further salutations. It might have been a mistake.

Cornelius twisted in his saddle and examined the unblemished stones of the defensive walls and the closed gates of the city. A dramatic wave of his arm caused a rock to form in the pit of Marcius' stomach.

Then the Prorogatio of Iberia, the most powerful General outside the Roman Republic, proposed, "At least one of my commanders knows better than to burn down a city before we can take enough profit to pay the Legion."

Lucius Marcius had fought off Carthaginian mercenaries with a rag-tag collection of Legionaries from two broken Legions. Brawled for command once back at Tarraco so his men would be properly cared for, before battling two Generals from Carthage and their armies. He defeated both in daring nighttime attacks. And he survived a hearing by the Senate of Rome. All his prior successes had taken guts and grim determination. Standing in front of Cornelius Scipio, a man he respected, Marcius was prepared for the dressing down.

"Sir, I can explain," he offered.

Cornelius rotated his head to the front and inquired, "Why you preserved the city? Or why you haven't wasted the lives of your Legionaries trying to capture a heavily defended fortress?"

"Sir, how did you know about the defenders?" Marcius asked. Then he thought back over Cornelius' questions. "Preserved the city, sir?"

General Scipio expelled air from between his lips in a forceful manner.

"In our zeal to punish Iliturgi, we managed to kill half the population. And before extracting one silver bowl of plunder, we burned the city," Cornelius answered. "You can imagine how excited I am to find Castulo intact."

"It wouldn't have been by morning," Marcius confessed. He indicated the closed gates of the city. "Negotiations have reached an impasse."

"Let's go into your tent and you can tell me about it," Cornelius suggested. He glanced at the gates once more before dismounting. "I can't imagine the news about Iliturgi helped with the talks."

"In my experience, General, failure was inevitable," Marcius admitted as they crossed the camp. "They have a force commanded by a Carthaginian Major and a Mayor who should have been a horse trader. I could have made an agreement with one or the other. But with them playing off each other, an assault was unavoidable."

"That would be Major Himilco. How many Gauls does he have with him?" Cornelius asked.

The question stopped Marcius in mid stride. "Four hundred, sir. But how do you know about them?"

"I'm a General. It's my job to know things," Cornelius bragged. Turning to Panatia, he directed. "First Centurion send a runner for Captain Micipsa."

"I'm not sure what the commander of the African Corps can do," Marcius stated. "Since we arrived, my African infantrymen have refused to do anything. Guarding them is another reason I wasted days in useless talks."

"They're sworn not to attack a Carthaginian command," Cornelius advised. "But that won't stop Marcius from negotiating with the Major for us."

"Why would the Captain make an agreement for you, sir?"

"Between Bolt and Eagle, I have enough Legionaries to crush the Corps, right here, right now. And afterwards, to easily take Castulo," Cornelius detailed. "But I also have the power to free the Major and most of the Corps, if I choose to."

"Ships to Carthage are the price for the agreement," Marcius concluded.

"Except for a company of Corps infantrymen. I'll need that many Africans to balance the four hundred Gauls for my General's parade through Rome," Cornelius added. "They'll look good marching through the forum followed by the elephants. Or maybe after them. What do you think?"

***

Sixteen souls witnessed their last sunrise on day five of the siege. Their crosses, bold across the crown of a hill, stood as a reminder of Cornelius' words.

"*...No one must ever consider a citizen of the Republic, or a Legionary marching under a Legion banner, a subject fit for ill-treatment, whatever their condition or situation...*"

The guards who shut the gates on the fleeing Legionaries from Gnaeus Scipio's Legion felt the pull on their outstretched arms from the cross beams. And the councilmen, who stood on the walls berating the wounded and exhausted infantrymen, attempted to breathe between episodes of their heels slipping off the small footrests.

None yelled, they didn't have the energy. But all cried and bemoaned the memory of those days five years ago. And while relatives beneath the crosses wept, wagons full of silver, gold, and copper rolled into Eagle's camp. There was one consolation for the citizens of Castulo. While poorer, their city remained undamaged. Unlike Iliturgi, which was now a city of ash and bones.

Chapter 12 – Twin Guardians

Seven days after leaving Castulo, a joyous Cornelius Scipio rode through the gates of New Carthage.

"Sidia," he stated with a grin, "I've avenged my family's name. Cleared Iberia of the Carthaginian menace. Brought peace to the region, for the most part, and amassed a fortune, not only for me, but for Rome. And, I've created profitable shipping and mining concerns to keep the coins flowing. For all that, I've decided we need games to honor my father, my uncle, and my veterans."

"Very good, General. Then you'll take the festival to the Capital," Sidia teased, "and party with the Senate of Rome?"

Cornelius missed the jest.

"That is precisely what I'm going to do," Cornelius informed his bodyguard. "But I'm not a fool. I'll write to the Senate and ask them when I can hold my day of triumph. It'll take precise timing and an effort to ship the Legions, cavalry, auxiliary infantry, and the elephants to Rome for the day."

"I'm sure you'll figure it out, sir," Sidia offered. A serious expression clouded Cornelius' face, prompting Sidia to ask. "Is everything alright, sir?"

Pointing ahead, Scipio replied, "Gaius Laelius is back from Western Numidia. I'm impressed he completed the task so soon."

The Colonel stood on the steps at Temple Hill. But his face did not reflect the pride of a man who completed a successful mission.

"I'm sure, General Scipio," Sidia remarked, "his report will be informative."

***

Scribes jogged into the chamber, took notes, then ran out to send requests.

"We'll invite every Iberian chief," Cornelius declared. "Footraces, horse, and chariots races, feasting and sacrifices. Music and dancing. Medals and parades. It'll be a glorious four days of games."

"A fitting ceremony to honor your family and your veterans," Colonel Laelius offered. "But we do need to talk, sir."

"All the way back from Castulo, I've been thinking about nothing except the games," Cornelius said, putting off the conversation. "It's almost planned. Then we can talk. But I'm forgetting something, something big."

"Gladiator competitions?" Laelius suggested.

"That's it," Cornelius exclaimed. "We need gladiators."

Two scribes jotted down the need for fighters before scurrying from the temple chamber. While Cornelius conceived the contests and events, he would leave the details to others. Managers would bring Scipio's games to life, or they would no longer work for the Prorogatio of Iberia.

"Now, Colonel Laelius," Cornelius invited, "tell me about Western Numidia. What sort of man is King Syphax?"

"General Scipio, I wouldn't know," Laelius admitted. "I never got an audience. Once he learned I wasn't you, he ordered me off his beach."

"He was expecting me?" Cornelius sighed. Then brightening up, he questioned. "Should I plan on going to Western Numidia?"

"I can't answer that for you, sir," the Colonel confessed. "But I can say, you're the only man who can secure a treaty with Syphax."

Cornelius glanced at a calendar and realized he only had the winter and the first of March to hold his parade. Around the Ides of March, Rome would be considering two new Consuls. The citizens would not be in the mood for a parade by a provincial General.

"The Numidia staging area is important for the invasion of Carthage," Cornelius insisted. "I can't very well go before the Senate of Rome with a half-formed plan."

"Then you're going to Western Numidia?" Laelius guessed. "I'll ready the Iberian fleet."

"No Colonel. It's a diplomatic mission, not an assault on the people of Numidia," Cornelius informed him. "Don't look so worried, I'm not suicidal. Give me two warships with the best crews."

"When will you leave, sir?"

"Three days," Cornelius answered. "Before I'm free to travel to Western Numidia, I have to compose the perfect letter to the Senate. The Senators will want to know that I've thought of every contingency for my day of triumph, and that, the Carthage campaign is well planned."

***

On the morning of the third day, a trireme pushed off from the shoreline and rowed for Cartagena Bay. As it left the harbor of New Carthage, the Ship's Centurion ordered the sail unfurled. Between the oars and the wind, the three-banker sped over the water, heading for the sea.

"If everything works out, I should be back before the Senate's reply," Cornelius stated. Then he indicated Cartagena Bay and directed, "Centurion Tutatus, kindly take me to Western Numidia."

"Yes, General Scipio," the Ship's Centurion acknowledged. "First Principale signal *Aniketos' Challenge* that we are launching. And stand by to get us wet."

A second five-banker rested on the beach a few ship lengths from Tutatus' warship. Even though the officers could see the other quinquereme, when the oarsmen pushed it into the surf, the First Principale alerted his skipper.

"Centurion Tutatus, *Aniketos' Challenge* is afloat," he announced.

"Very well first officer, launch *Alexiares' Rampart*," Tutatus ordered.

As the officer called down to alert the Third Principale and his team of rowers on the beach, Sidia moved up to the rail.

"The two crews are like matched sets of chariot horses," the bodyguard proposed.

"How's that?" Cornelius inquired.

"Aniketos and Alexiares are the twin Gods who guard the gates of Olympus," Sidia explained. "Making the warships, by name, twin guardians."

"I've been preoccupied with the letter and hadn't put that together," Cornelius admitted. "But I like that we're traveling on *Alexiares*, the God who wards off war. And we're escorted by *Aniketos*, the unconquerable God."

"*Alexiares' Rampart* and *Aniketos' Challenge*," Sidia said. "What do you think, sir, a shield and a spear?"

The steering platform dipped as the bronze ram plunged under water. As quickly as it tilted, the keel leveled, and the warship floated free of the beach.

"First Principale, I see that *Challenge* has outpaced us by twenty ship lengths," Tutatus alerted his first officer. "Fifteen is as far from them as I want us to be for this entire voyage. Understood?"

"Yes, sir," the officer stated. The First Principale faced the bow of *Rampart* and shouted. "Second Principale. While your oarsmen were sleeping, the neighbor pinched your wife and children. And worst of all, he took your favorite dog."

From the rowing deck, a voice screamed, "Drummer, set a pace. Not a let's-go-for-a-stroll on a lover's walk. Give us something a man can bend his back to."

"Right away, Second Principale," the musician replied before the boom, boom of a drum beating a rapid cadence drifted to the upper deck.

Under power from the slapping oars, the quinquereme surged forward.

"Racing chariots," Sidia whispered.

When the two five-bankers reached open water, they saw no sign of the 3-banker carrying Cornelius' letter. And they wouldn't. The trireme had tracked northward, moving up along the coast of Iberia, on its way to Rome. Traveling in the opposite direction, the quinqueremes steered south, heading for Mojácar Beach.

***

The beach was more than adequate for two warships. Above the shoreline, on a rise, the town of Mojácar overlooked the sea.

"Not much here," Cornelius mentioned.

Tutatus pointed down the deck boards as his ship cut a half circle in the water. He held the pose as the oarsmen of the five-banker backstroked the aft to the shallows.

"You're correct, General," the Ship's Centurion confirmed. Half the crew scampered over the rails, put their shoulders to the hull, and pushed the warship onto the beach. All the while, Tutatus held his arm out, indicating the sea. "Mojácar isn't important. It's no more than a dot on a chart. Out there is what gives weight to this beach."

"The sea?" Cornelius questioned.

"Beyond the water, sir, is Oran. Home to King Syphax. Mojácar sits just across the sea from there."

"I thought it would take several days to reach Oran?"

"On a normal patrol with an average crew, it would," Tutatus said. As the other warship backstroked to the beach, the Ship's Centurion addressed his crew. "Good job, First Principale. My compliments to the crew for showing *Aniketos' Challenge* our steering oars."

"How far?" Cornelius asked.

"Never more than fifteen ship lengths," Tutatus replied, still thinking about the other five-banker. Then he focused on the question and corrected. "We'll leave at moonrise, sir. And make landfall around sunset tomorrow."

"You cheated," the Ship's Centurion from the other quinquereme accused Tutatus.

"Technology, Centurion O Mors, is not cheating," Tutatus answered.

Sidia chuckled. Cornelius snapped his head around to silence his bodyguard.

129

"Go ahead and make fun of his name," Tutatus commented. "But do it here and away from his blade."

"I apologize, Centurion," Sidia stated. "But Sweet Death commanding the unconquerable God's warship. Really, sir, it's a little theatrical."

"Tell that to the five Carthaginian ships-of-war he's sunk. And the seven men he's killed in single combat," Tutatus pointed out. Then to the Centurion of *Challenge,* the ship's commander revealed. "A larger forward sail is not cheating."

"It is cheating, if you don't tell your protector about the sail," O Mors exclaimed.

"I need the sail to protect you," Tutatus declared. "My instructors always coached us to care for the weaker ship in the squadron."

"Tonight, we'll cross the sea," O Mors reminded Tutatus. "It would be a shame if my lanterns went out."

"Then instead of following your slow boat, I'd get to shore faster."

Cornelius ducked away from the banter and asked Sidia, "How are our guests?"

"The boy and the old man are scared to death," Sidia reported.

"Tell Shuphet that I have no intention of delivering him to King Syphax," Cornelius emphasized. "For over a year, I've given him food and shelter and allowed him to train with Numidian cavalry."

"But those were Western Numidians," Sidia prompted Cornelius. "His uncle is the King of Eastern Numidia."

"And that was another expense," Cornelius said. "Paying the western riders not to kill the eastern nobleman. Remind Shuphet of him that."

***

They launched at moonrise and sailed into the night. Later, the occupants of the warships calmed, and settled into the voyage.

The rocking of the warship, the whisking sound of water rushing down the hull, a few soft whispers of Legionaries on the upper deck, and from oarsmen below, combined to create a small, small world. Contrasting with the tiny wooden vessel, the dome of stars in the heavens expanded beyond all reason.

Almost in a trance, Sidia sat next to a navigator, manning one of the rear oars.

"I've never been lost at sea," he mentioned to the navigator.

"Neither have I," the rear oarsmen replied.

"This is the first time you've crossed the sea?" Sidia gushed. "And the ship's officers left you alone on the steering deck?"

"I've made the crossing many times," the navigator assured Sidia. "The ship is never lost at sea because we're guided by the stars."

"Just by looking up?"

"No Legionary. From looking ahead," the navigator informed him. A pair of weak lights in the distance revealed the other warship. "They're navigating by the stars and to be sure we land together, we're following *Challenge*."

Slightly embarrassed by his ignorance of the sea and seamen, Sidia curled up in his blanket and tried to sleep.

"Still feels as if we're lost," he grumbled.

***

Late in the day, but long before sundown, the coast of Africa appeared on the horizon. The warships had been in a staggered formation with *Challenge* maintaining the forward position. When land came into sight, they rowed until the ships were side by side. Sailors cast grappling hooks across and hauled the vessels together. The Ship's Centurions stood at the rails calling back and forth over the short gap.

"Recognize anything?" Tutatus inquired.

O Mors answered, "It's what I don't see that pleases me."

"The buildings of Oran," Tutatus guessed. "No argument. Any idea where to beach for the night?"

"One beach along that coast is the same as any other," O Mors replied. "Short and hard on our keels. I'll take the lead."

"Shield forward," Tutatus countered, "in case we meet any ships-of-war."

"Guide us in," O Mors said relinquishing the lead.

For planning operations and the command of his fleet, Cornelius relied on experienced Tribunes. While he understood the movement of Legion battle lines on land, the placement of warships at sea baffled him. But the reference to a shield identified the thinking behind the formation. He took confidence from the professionalism of the Centurions.

"Release the lines," Tutatus and O Mors ordered at the same time, "and free us from this anchor."

132

Sailors on both ships released hooks and hauled in their lines. Using poles, they pushed off, separating the hulls. Next, the rowers dipped oars and propelled the warships towards land.

***

The shoreline was a tiny section of coarse sand which barely fit the lengths of the one hundred-and-forty-eight-foot-long vessels. Fortunately, the small cove accommodated the width of the two quinqueremes before ridges of bare stone closed in on the sides. Unfortunately, the shape granted very little flatland for the camp of six hundred oarsmen, ship's officers, fifty sailors, and Cornelius' escort of two hundred Legionaries.

"Give me lookouts on the hill," Tutatus directed the First Principale.

Off the sand, a slope of rocks climbed three times the height of a man to an exposed layer of topsoil and grass. Over the crest, the highest branches of a few local fir trees were visible, but not much else.

The cove appeared deserted with no trace of human activity. The desolation prompted Cornelius to inquire, "Are you expecting trouble?"

"Numidians are people bred to the horse," Tutatus replied. "It makes them nomadic, sir. We never know where a hunting party or a patrol will show up."

As if the Ship's Centurion was a seer, the first lookouts to reach the top shouted.

"Wait. Come back. We want to trade," the sailor called out.

A moment later, five riders appeared on the hill farther along the coast. They held an animated discussion before wheeling around and kicking their horses into motion. As they vanished, O Mors walked up the ramp.

"A very profitable day for the Numidians," he ventured. "They'll sell the news of our location to the highest bidder."

"We have a letter of safe passage from King Syphax," Cornelius reported. "Prior knowledge of our arrival shouldn't present a problem."

"Yes, sir. I'm sure it'll protect us from an attack at Oran," O Mors affirmed. "But these are Carthaginian waters."

"You see, sir," Tutatus explained. "The hunting party will sell us to King Syphax's men. And to any Carthaginian ships-of-war beached there."

"They'll be waiting for us," O Mors warned. "Your safe passage letter, sir, only counts if we make it to the beach."

"Is there any other way to get there?" Cornelius asked. "Maybe we can buy horses and go overland."

"General Scipio, getting through blockades is our specialty," O Mors bragged.

"As long as you don't mind spilling Punic blood and wrecking a couple of their ships-of-war," Tutatus described, "we're your best way to reach Oran."

"The blood of my enemy is of no concern to me," Cornelius assured the Ship's Centurions. "And while I like captured prizes, the destruction of an enemy's war machine is profitable in other ways."

"One more thing, sir," O Mors mentioned.

"Speak freely," Cornelius allowed.

"General Scipio, during the engagement, do not give me directions or question my actions," Tutatus submitted.

"No matter the situation, I will endeavor to ignore my vast knowledge of warfare at sea," Cornelius promised. "I bow to your proven techniques. But will offer prayers."

"An excellent idea, sir," O Mors said.

Sidia smirked and observed, "On land, an infantryman needs a shield and a spear for war. It appears sea battles aren't much different."

(Intentionally left blank)

Act 5

Chapter 13 – Come Out and Play

After two days of cramped sleeping arrangements on the decks of the ships, on slices of beach, or higher up on the grass, a shout awakened the rowers, sailors, and infantrymen. The darkness enticed most to ignore the loud voice and remain under their blankets.

"Get up," Ship's Centurion O Mors bellowed from the steering deck of his warship. "Rest time is over ladies. You are about to row into Hades."

"But sir," a sailor pointed out, "we can't launch in the dark and it's a long way to daybreak."

"Can you sense that?" O Mors demanded. "I can taste it on my tongue. Feel it in my bones. Smell it in the air."

"Smell what, Centurion?" Cornelius inquired from the other vessel.

"A sirocco, General," O Mors answered. "It's coming, and with it, fog to cover our approach to Oran."

"And tricky winds to foul our sails and baffle our oarsmen," a navigator pointed out.

"The same is true for the Carthaginian ships-of-war," O Mors countered. Then he yelled. "Get up and eat. We row out before sunrise."

***

The *Rampart* and the *Challenge* glided over the water. Sailors stood on the starboard side holding long poles. Between strokes of the oars, they extended the poles searching for errant rocks or the fog shrouded coastline.

"Stroke, stroke, stroke," the Second Principale of *Rampart* called from the rowers walk. "Let it run."

The oars came out of the water as the ship glided over the sea.

"It's very dense," Cornelius remarked. "I'm not sure I'd march a Legion in this soup."

"Rarely would a good Ship's Centurion venture out in a sirocco fog," Tutatus admitted.

"Aren't you a good commander?" Cornelius inquired.

"No, sir. O Mors and I are great commanders," Tutatus assured him. "Navigator, what's our location?"

"Sir, we've just passed four point," a rear oarsmen reported.

"First Principale, tuck us in against the rocks until dawn," Tutatus directed. Next, he addressed Cornelius. "We can't charge blindly into the bay at Oran. We might run aground or rip our hull on a rock. And with the wind swirling, we need room to maneuver if the sail fails."

"Fails?" Cornelius repeated.

"If the wind fails to push us to the beach, and instead drives us into the rocks," the Ship's Centurion answered. "We'll need space for our navigators to work."

From the rear, a voice called out on the second warship, "Four point. Tuck us in, First Principale."

"Four points?" Sidia mentioned to a navigator.

138

"On a chart, there are five nubs of land sticking out from the coast before the Bay of Oran," the rear oarsmen told Sidia. "On the other side of the fifth point, we'll be in the bay. And within sight of the ships-of-war."

"How do we know there'll be Carthaginian ships in the bay?" Sidia inquired.

"We don't know. But would you stroll into the site of a possible ambush," the navigator proposed, "or sneak up to the area, just in case?"

***

Where the rocky cliffs had blocked the sirocco along the five points of land, once at the mouth of Oran bay, the wind buffeted the warship.

When a strong gust shoved *Rampart* sideways, the First Principale requested, "Permission to roll the sail, sir."

"No. Fight the wind with your oars," Tutatus instructed. "Keep us under sail."

Dangerously close to the aft, the bronze ram of *Challenge* swung in an arc, nearly gutting the hull of *Rampart*. At eye level with Sidia, the foredeck officer of the *Challenge* seemed to hover on a cushion of fog.

"Shouldn't O Mors back his ship off a little?" Sidia whispered to Cornelius.

"I promised not to interfere," Cornelius uttered. "Not that I don't want to, but I gave my word."

"You also gave your word to pray, sir," Sidia reminded him.

"That, I've been doing since we launched into the wind and black fog."

***

With sunrise, the black turned to gray fog. The lighter mist covered the sea beyond the mouth of the bay while uneven currents of wind cleared the haze from the inlet. When the bow of *Rampart* nosed out of the fog bank, it became visible to a pair of vessels on picket duty. In moments, the alert was passed from the forward watch officers to the rowing officers. Dipping oars, the Carthaginian ships-of-war surged forward heading for *Rampart*.

Seeing the threat, Cornelius announced, "Tutatus, they've spotted us."

In a leisurely manner, the Ship's Centurion turned to Cornelius, and across the steering platform, recommended, "General Scipio, please confine your comments to asking the Gods for their blessings. And leave the command of my ship to me, sir."

Without waiting for a reply, the Ship's Centurion glanced at his two navigators on the rear oars and remarked, "Gentlemen, maintain your current course."

"Yes, sir," they confirmed.

Normally, distances between ships could be estimated by how many lengths of vessels separated the hulls. During an attack run, when the rams of the approaching ships-of-war threw twin rooster combs of bay water high into the air, normal didn't count.

Cornelius and Sidia gripped the rails.

"Let me loosen your armor, sir," Sidia offered. "If we go in, we can swim to shore. But not in armor."

"No, Optio Decimia. It's important that I show trust in the Ship's Centurion."

"Even if Tutatus is a madman?" Sidia inquired.

"Even if he drowns us all," Cornelius confirmed.

***

The Third Principale concentrated on the approaching vessels. From the forward deck of the *Rampart*, he could make out details of the bow officers on the pair of Carthaginian ships. He studied the signals they were sending back to their steering decks. In his hands, the Roman officer held two flags.

Back on the steering platform of *Rampart*, the First Principale also held flags. But he held them in a tight grip and showed his nerves by bouncing on the balls of his feet.

"Steady, First Principale," Tutatus coached. "Have the oarsmen stand by."

"Second Principale, stand by for evasive commands," the officer instructed.

Between the words of his Centurion, and the act of issuing orders, the first officer stopped bouncing on the balls of his feet. He landed flatfooted on the deck and rotated his shoulders to relieve the tension. It did no good.

At that moment, the Third Principale snapped his flags up and overhead. Pausing for a heartbeat to be sure the officers on the steering deck noticed the signal, the forward officer leaned to his left. The flags parted, and hung in the air, as if tree limbs bent and blown apart by a strong wind. The Third Principale held the pose even as the enemy ships-of-war adjusted to parallel courses for their attack runs.

"They're separating," Sidia warned. "Aiming to rake our oars and gouge out sections of the hull."

"Port side, power fifteen," Tutatus ordered. "Starboard, hold water."

"Port side, power fifteen," the First Principale shouted. "Starboard side, hold water."

Then as the Second Principale directed his oarsmen, the first officer turned to face aft and held his flags extended to the left. With the flags together, he held them until the foredeck officer on *Challenge* raised his flags.

***

With oars digging hard on the left side, and the oar blades on the right held in the water, *Rampart* pivoted. At the seventh stroke, *Rampart* offered the broadside of its hull to the pair of Carthaginian rams.

Sidia moved closer to Scipio, preparing to save his General. And Cornelius lifted a hand to the strap of his armor.

Before the ships-of-war reached the hull, the Roman ship completed a full half circle and Tutatus issued a new command.

"Back-it-down for five."

"Back-it-down for five," the first officer yelled.

Below deck, the rowing officer repeated the order.

Much like a cart on a hill, simply stopping didn't end the movement. Afloat, a ship would continue to slide in the water, following the momentum of the last oar stroke. As the blades dipped to back-it-down, and the oarsmen pushed on their oars to stabilize and reverse direction, the *Rampart* drifted into the path of an oncoming ship-of-war.

"Pull your oars in," Tutatus commanded.

"Oars in" the first officer called out.

"Oars in," the Second Principale instructed his oarsmen.

Still drifting, from the last strokes, *Rampart* floated to the other side of the Carthaginian. The movement caused the ships to pass almost rail to rail.

Seeing the danger, the Carthaginian Captain ordered a hard turn to starboard. But as his navigators attempted to veer away, their port side oars were sheared off by the hull of *Rampart*. Inside the hull, splinters of wood and flying shards slashed the Carthaginian rowers. Screams of agony and terror replaced the booming drum of their musician. Resembling a downed bird with a broken wing, the ship-of-war limped in a circle before stalling dead in the water.

"Push us away from that piece of trash," Tutatus orders. After a glance to his left, he instructed. "Row us to the beach."

***

Having the Roman a short distance in front of their ram, assured the second Carthaginian ship-of-war an easy kill. But they found their vessel rowing by their sister ship as it floundered in the bay. Somehow, their target had slipped to the other side and, using the first picket ship as a screen, avoided being rammed.

"Bring us about and line up for another attack," the Captain directed his rear oarsmen.

During the turn, the crew, and the ship's officers, focused on the Roman warship and the damaged Carthaginian vessel. Because they were looking in the other direction, the Carthaginian ship failed to notice *Challenge* emerge from the sea fog as O Mor made his attack run.

As if a claw on a monster cat, the ram dug into the sideboards. In a slashing maneuver, *Challenge* raked away a section of hull at water level. Before the bronze weapon pulled away, bleeding Carthaginian oarsmen fell through the gash. They drowned. Which saved them from the sight of dead comrades. And the screams of mangled friends who would also drown. But only after suffering long painful moments before the ship-of-war keeled over.

***

Rampart and *Challenge* rowed hard for the beach. As they crossed the bay, the wind filled their sails.

On the shoreline, crews from seven ships-of-war ran to launch their vessels.

"Wouldn't O Mors love that," Tutatus commented.

"Love what, Centurion?" Cornelius asked.

"To catch seven Carthaginian ships-of-war just coming off the beach," he answered. Then overcome by exuberance, he shouted at the beached ships. "Come on out and play."

"You're on a mission to get me to Western Numidia," Cornelius reminded the Ship's Centurion. He pointed at the beach. "And I believe it's right over there."

"Yes, sir, it is," Tutatus agreed. "First Principale. Roll the sail."

***

Rampart and *Challenge* carved half circles in the water and backstroked to the shallows. Rowers jumped down and pushed the quinqueremes onto dry land. With the two Roman crews far outnumbered by the seven Carthaginian ships-of-war, it might have been advisable to post a few hundred men on a shields wall between them. But Cornelius didn't have to as elements of the Numidian army arrived and set posts between the adversaries.

"For horse people, they march pretty," Tutatus observed.

In even ranks, three Centuries of heavy infantryman marched to the beach. Their formation and organization looked very familiar.

"Rome had an agreement with King Syphax," Cornelius informed him. "In exchange for trading rights, Legion instructors were dispatched to train infantry for Syphax."

"From their appearance," Sidia mentioned, "they learned the lessons well."

"Doesn't mean they can fight as well as Roman Legions," Tutatus offered, "or even Republic Legions."

"Your discounting Iberian Legions, sir," Sidia argued. "They hold their own in an assault line."

"Heart, Optio Decimia, it comes down to heart and Legion pride," Tutatus countered. "Roman Legions have hundreds of years of military tradition. The Republic Legions have less. And the Iberian Legions almost no history. Just like the Numidians."

"The Numidian infantry does have one thing none of the others have," Cornelius proposed.

"Sir?" Tutatus commented.

"Right now, they have your life in their hands," Cornelius pointed out.

Over two thousand men glared over the Numidian shields at the Roman warships. From their expressions, there was little doubt that the presence of the infantry prevented a battle on the beach.

"General Scipio, you might have a visitor," a navigator suggested.

From beyond the beach, an assembly of men in robes of rich fabric appeared. They walked their mounts onto the sand and stopped midway between the warships.

"Is General Scipio among you?" one inquired.

"I'm Cornelius Scipio. Who is asking?"

One of the men nudged his horse over until he was directly behind *Rampart*.

"I, sir, am Pelops, advisor to King Syphax. Allow me to welcome you to Western Numidia. The King is expecting you."

"If he's expecting me," Cornelius inquired. "What are the Carthaginian ships-of-war doing here?"

"Besides yourself, we are pleased to be entertaining another luminary," Pelops answered. "Also attending King Syphax is Carthaginian General Hasdrubal Gisco."

Chapter 14 – Banquet of Foes

King Syphax's compound consisted of several buildings built around a central park. His winter residence, with a balcony overlooking a section of gardens, took up one side of the green space. A building with offices for magistrates and the barracks for his personal guards occupied the opposite side. On one end of the park, a cluster of isolated cottages for visiting dignitaries filled a half-acre of ground.

The location of the cottages forced dignitaries to stroll through the park to reach the other end. There, they entered the King's reception hall and banquet room. After a walk through the trees and flowers, the visitors arrived refreshed.

At the seven entrances to the King's park, Numidian infantrymen stood sentry. Trained by Legion officers and NCOs, the guards were as deadly as any foot soldiers in the region. The one drawback to their effectiveness came from their placement. Because the King mandated privacy for himself and his guests, the sentry posts were designed to keep undesirables out and not to maintain vigil on the interior of the park.

On the night of the feast, a million stars dotted the sky. Their combined light created pale shadows in the park. Along the walkways, between the trees, trellises, grape arbors, and flower beds shapes were simply lighter versions of the same background. For predators and eyes trained to identify movement, the phase of the night held few secrets. Yet at moonrise, the brighter illumination would generate contrast. Dark recesses standing apart from solid objects produced deep shadows, creating black holes, appropriate for hiding assassins.

**

Inside the banquet hall, a servant filled a glass. He crossed in front of adjacent couches to the next table. While the servant filled a glass there, Hasdrubal Gisco lifted his glass. He took a sip, beamed a smile in the direction of the King, and saluted him. By deliberately excluding the occupant on the neighboring couch, he demonstrated his dislike for Cornelius.

"King Syphax, you are to be congratulated on your choice of wines," Hasdrubal Gisco purred.

"You should appreciate them," Syphax told him. "They're from Carthage."

"Aha, no wonder it's so refreshing," the Carthaginian acknowledged, "it's a taste of home."

"Have you been away long?" Syphax inquired.

"Six long months," the Carthaginian answered.

"And you, General Scipio," Syphax questioned, "how long have you been away from home?"

Cornelius took a sip from the glass and made a face.

"My preference is for a full-bodied red. This wine, while tasty, is very sweet," Cornelius observed. "As far as home, it's been three years since I've seen my wife and children. But there were matters in Iberia that required my attention."

Gisco flinched at the meaning of the remark. He'd enjoyed the wine during dinner, and the distance from the Roman. But afterwards, out of some sick sense of humiliation, King Syphax had placed the General from Carthage and the General from Rome on adjoining couches. For Gisco, the wine had gone from a source of enjoyment to a way of drowning his discomfort.

"At least we aren't sharing a table," Gisco thought.

"What was that Hasdrubal?" Syphax inquired.

Realizing he'd spoken out loud, Gisco tried but his tongue refused to form a lie. Then, as if possessed by an evil spirit, he slurred, "Why do you Romans care about Iberia?"

***

Cornelius rested the glass on the table, stretched his neck, and gazed at the ceiling.

"Why do we Romans care about Iberia?" he repeated. "Let me start with the obvious. Twelve years ago, your

Hannibal Barca crossed the Alps and invaded our northern territories. He brought spearmen, cavalry, and livestock from Iberia. At the Trebbia River, his light and heavy horsemen routed our Legion cavalry and almost captured a Consul of Rome."

"I've never heard that," Gisco admitted. "All we were told was the Legion riders fled in fear."

"We did not flee in fear," Cornelius insisted. "It was an orderly retreat."

"You sound as if you were there," Syphax pointed out.

"I was in that battle," Cornelius assured him.

"What I should have asked earlier, General Scipio," the King of Western Numidia proposed, "how long have you been at war?"

"Almost half my life," Cornelius answered. "But we were talking about Iberia, not my chosen profession. Iberia, like my Roman Republic, represents opportunity."

"In that vein, Scipio, Carthage represents opportunity," Gisco challenged, "as well as east and west Numidia, and the Greek states."

"That, General, is where you're wrong," countered Cornelius. "My test for an opportunity is what countries will flock to your banner, fight alongside of you, and accept payment in promises."

"That could be said of any country," King Syphax insisted.

"Hannibal Barca is in my Republic commanding mercenaries from other regions," Cornelius proclaimed. "And in Iberia, I gathered fighters from local tribes as well as from Greece, Numidia, and Macedon. And why did they come? For payment in promises because Iberia is an opportunity for taking land and building settlements. Carthage isn't. If I took my Legions to Carthage, few if any foreign units would join me."

"Because Carthage is strong," Gisco boasted. "And we always find a way to win."

A moment after the statement, Sidia stepped close to the couch and touched Cornelius' shoulder. Silent communications passed between them.

"Optio Decimia. We're going to be awhile," Cornelius told his bodyguard. "Go stretch your legs."

"Yes, sir," Sidia confirmed before marching to the exit.

"Carthage is like an island. A wealthy, well defended island, but one just the same," Cornelius described. "After picking through the bones of the city, there's not enough land to settle debts nor metals to dig up to pay off mercenaries."

"That's an insult," Gisco protested. "It's like saying my wife is ugly."

"Is she?" Cornelius asked. Gisco flexed as if to come at Cornelius. But after a moment, he settled back, and smirked. Cornelius offered. "It's a good thing you remained on the couch. Or we'd have had a replay of the battle at Ilipa."

"Generals please," King Syphax urged, "we're here for a social evening. Not a knife fight. Let's talk of other, less arousing, subjects."

***

In the park, Sidia drifted down a side path. While inhaling the fragrance of the vegetation and enjoying the fresh night air, he stretched his back and swung his arms. A

150

little ways down the garden path, he reached under his chest armor and opened the left side buckles. As he turned around to head back to the banquet, he dropped his helmet and the armor beside the path. On the next step, the armored skirt and his under tunic fell to the dirt. Yawning loudly enough to be heard down the center of the garden, he strolled towards the door to the King's hall. But the Legion bodyguard never reached the threshold. Somewhere between the edge of the park and the doorway, Sidia Decimia vanished.

***

The grape arbor over the central walkway offered good concealment. Between the climbing vines on the tall structure, the narrowing of the path as it passed under the trellis, and the deep shadows, the two assassins felt confident of quick kills.

In robes with hoods to break up their silhouettes, the pair stood in the shadows next to a wall of grapes. At their sides waited their unsheathed sicas, while their eyes watched the path. All that remained to complete their assignment was the Latian victim and his bodyguard.

A twig snapped and both killers braced while looking around. When nothing followed the sound, they relaxed. Then, a thud on the other side of them caused tension to grip their bodies. But no other noises followed, and their muscles loosened. A twig snapped farther away and one of the killers leaned forward. Either he was attempting to find movement in the dark or to hear better. In either case he didn't catch sight nor sound of a potential foe.

But while the killer didn't, Sidia did. And two heartbeats later, a man-beast rushed through the park. As primitive as a mountain cat and bearing the marks of the Goddess Mefitis, the War Chief slashed the throat of one and hammered the other to the ground.

"The Hirpini people have hunted in mountain forests for a thousand years," he whispered to the dazed assassin. "Trees and leaves are but ways to track our prey."

Reaching down with both hands, he twisted the killer's neck. Not until the head faced the wrong way and the bones in the neck snapped, did the War Chief release the dead man's head.

From around the garden, footsteps disturbed dirt as they converged on the grape arbor. Sidia sheathed his Legion dagger and picked up one of the long-curved knives.

"Good weapon," he acknowledged before fading back among the trees and the trellises.

***

Cornelius took a sip of wine and watched over the edge of the glass as Sidia returned. For everyone at the feast, he appeared as he had when he left. Armored with a gladius on one hip and a legion dagger on the other, the bodyguard strolled to his General and stood behind the couch.

"Our path to the cottage is clear of pests," Sidia whispered to Cornelius.

Hasdrubal shot Sidia a sharp look as if the bodyguard had interrupted an important discussion.

"Scipio. To what do you attribute your gains in Iberia?" Hasdrubal inquired.

Cornelius stretched and yawned to display his boredom with the topic.

"It's not so essential for you Carthaginians to inquire how your Iberian province was lost," Cornelius speculated. "As it is to consider, how you plan to hold onto your city in Africa."

Hasdrubal paled and his hand shook. The bare truth and naked insult should have driven the Carthaginian General from the banquet. But he remained on his couch as if glued to the fabric.

"King Syphax, it's been a long day," Cornelius informed the King, "topped with a delicious meal. But I am exhausted. If you'll excuse me."

"I understand. Take your leave, General."

"Thank you," Cornelius acknowledged.

Partway to his feet, the garden door opened, and a Numidian Captain rushed in.

"We've had an incident in the garden, sir," the officer announced. "For the safety of your guests, we've arranged escorts."

"That sounds serious, but your timing is impeccable," Syphax offered. "General Scipio was just leaving."

The Captain of the Guard saluted Cornelius. Sidia stepped behind Scipio, and they started towards the doorway. But Hasdrubal Gisco rolled off his couch and staggered to the door ahead of them.

"King Syphax, I'll take my leave," Hasdrubal slurred.

Once the Carthaginian and the Captain of the Guard had vanished through the doorway, Syphax declared, "Too much wine is not an excuse for bad manners. I will see you in the morning, General Scipio."

"I look forward to your visit, sir."

***

Late in the morning, Cornelius sat at a table under a shade tree. With his eyes closed, he prayed for a positive outcome from his visit to western Numidia.

"General Scipio," Sidia notified him, "King Syphax is heading this way with a handful of guys in fancy robes."

"Advisors, Optio Decimia," Cornelius instructed.

"The manner of dress does not make a man wiser," Sidia stated.

"There is that," Cornelius admitted.

Syphax stopped farther down the garden pathway. After a quick conversation, the King approached Cornelius alone, leaving his advisers out of hearing distance.

"Even at my invitation and protection, you're very bold to come here and openly taunt General Grisco," Syphax observed. He sat at the table and searched Cornelius' face. "I'm trying to decide if you are your father or your uncle."

"I came to your lands, not as a traveler, nor as a reprobate who idles his days away on the beautiful shores of Iberia," Cornelius answered. "I am a Roman Governor and I willingly departed from a newly subdued province. A General who left his Legions behind. And keep this in mind, with only two warships, I crossed over to Africa and entrusted myself to you. In a region controlled by my enemy, I gambled my life on your control and authority."

"Hasdrubal warned me to be cautious about your ambition," Syphax revealed.

154

"It's the Carthaginian, Hannibal, who ravishes my Republic," Cornelius pointed out. "I'm not waging war on Africa. My grievance is with Carthage. It's their General Barca who provides shelter to foreign fighters who hate Roman law. What I need from you, King Syphax, are landing rights for staging my supplies for the invasion of Carthage."

"And no doubt, you'll want two thousand Numidian cavalry," Syphax added.

"It's said the Numidian cavalry are the best light cavalry in the world," Cornelius proposed. "What General would turn down such a generous offer?"

"A little of Publius Scipio with a healthy dash of Gnaeus Scipio," Syphax decided. "But mostly, Cornelius Scipio, you are very much your own man. You have the beach rights and the cavalry."

Syphax stood and glanced at his advisors to let them know the King was moving.

"Thank you, sir," Cornelius acknowledged. "With our business concluded, I trust you won't take offense if I slip away in the dark."

"With two warships against seven ships-of-war, I'd consider you a fool to launch in daylight."

"I thank you for the hospitality, King Syphax," Cornelius said loudly so the advisors could hear. "It'll be good to get back to Iberia."

Once the crowd moved away, Sidia eased forward, "Sir, was it a good idea to let the advisors know we're leaving soon? Some of them are sure to tell General Gisco."

"The Carthaginians will give chase," Cornelius assured him. "Except while they row west, we'll sail east. "

"We're going to East Numidia, General, to trade Shuphet for some goodwill?"

"Yes. Now let's figure out how to get us to the beach, unseen."

Chapter 15 – Margin of Authority

Three hundred miles east of Oran, and five days after meeting King Syphax, *Rampart* and *Challenge* launched from the beach at Bougie. Under a ceiling of low clouds, they stroked into the Gulf of Béjaïa.

"Shuphet seemed pleased to be home," Sidia offered. "And King Masinissa was happy to have the son of his sister back."

"The trip wasn't a total loss," Cornelius said without enthusiasm. "We've several bags of silver and copper. But I didn't get a treaty with East Numidia."

A gust of wind rocked the quinquereme. In the distance, the sky dipped to the sea with misty fingers.

"Heavy clouds," Cornelius observed. "Looks like rain."

"Good signs, sir," Tutatus claimed. "We're halfway between Carthage and Oran. The weather is a blessing. It'll keep the Carthaginian fleet off the water."

"For good reasons," Cornelius proposed. "They don't want to get stuck at sea in foul weather."

"Neither do we, sir," Tutatus assured him.

At midday, the sky went black, and rain started falling. *Rampart* and *Challenge* located a small cove and backed onto the beach.

"The storm should pass by this evening," Tutatus estimated.

Contrary to the assessment by the Ship's Centurion, the warships were parked for four days as rain and wind lashed the inlet and the beach. For the oarsmen, ship's officers, Legionaries, and passengers, the days passed without problems other than discomfort. In New Carthage, however, panic set in at the possibility that the Governor of Iberia had been lost at sea.

***

Junius Silanus took the stack of correspondence, lifted it from the desktop, and dropped the sheets of parchment on the floor.

"There, that's better," he sighed.

The wooden top was empty except for a single piece of parchment. On it were neat rows of numbers.

"Senior Magistrate," a scribe reported, "we have Chiefs from three more tribes in the city. And sir, they want to know when the games will begin."

Six additional clerks came in, each with a question and a piece of bark paper.

"Send them a cart of wine and beer. That should keep them occupied until I get this figured out," Silanus instructed. "And if the Chiefs press you, tell them the games will start any day now."

"Sir, our storehouse is getting low," another scribe mentioned. "At this rate, there won't be enough beverages for the games."

Junius Silanus was a rich man, but also a thrifty one. If he put up his own coins for the games, and Cornelius turned up dead, Junius would have to absorb the cost. After a moment to consider tossing away a fortune to memorialize Cornelius Scipio, he decided.

"It seems the entire world wants my silver," Silanus complained. "Put out the word to vendors that we're buying beer and wine. But make sure the quality is good before we pay."

A scribe shuffled forward and placed a bark sheet over Silanus' accounting parchment.

"What's this?" the Senior Magistrate inquired.

"A list of sacrificial animals needed for the festival and the feasts, sir. The animal herders want to get paid."

With a sinking feeling in his stomach, Junius Silanus signed the bill of lading.

"Anyone else?" Silanus inquired.

Five scribes extended requests for payments.

***

Sixteen days had passed since Cornelius Scipio left New Carthage. In the morning, Junius Silanus sat on the balcony of his villa. From the elevation, he could see over the defensive wall of New Carthage and out across south harbor. Although the sun had just come up, merchant ships rowed in from Cartagena Bay.

"Where did they spend the night?" he pondered. "Did they anchor and wait for sunrise? Or navigate through the darkest hours?"

As he reflected on useless considerations, two warships rowed to the entrance of south harbor and began patrolling.

"Nice to see the fleet is in good order," he mumbled. "Now, if I could only say the same for the games."

A servant brought him a platter with small honey cakes, pieces of fried lamb, and a pitcher of water flavored with vinegar. As he ate, Junius noted two quinqueremes row in from Cartagena Bay. Indecision stilled his arm, leaving a cake suspended between the platter and his mouth. Should he rush to the duty Legion's headquarters, or check on the defensive catapults, or remain on the balcony and see what developed?

Realizing rash actions would yield nothing positive, the Senior Magistrate of Iberia took a bite of the sweet cake. While chewing, he watched the patrol ships intercept the pair of quinqueremes.

***

At the entrance to south harbor, Ship's Centurion Tutatus stepped onto a rail and shouted at the nearest patrol vessel.

"You were slow in getting your oars in the water," he scolded. "If I was a pirate, you'd be sunk, and I'd have captured New Carthage before you finished the swim to shore."

"If I had been lost for two weeks," the commander of the patrol vessel proposed. "I wouldn't be so quick to offer advice."

"We weren't lost," Tutatus said defending the overdue arrival. "We were delayed by a storm."

"That's the excuse every novice Principale uses for being lost."

Tutatus stepped down from the rail.

"First Principale get us to shore," he directed. Then under his breath, Tutatus grumbled. "Novice Principale, my foot. It was a storm."

Shortly after rowing into south harbor, a detail of Legionaries gathered General Scipio's bundles.

"Will you rest today, sir?" Sidia inquired.

"No. After a bath and a shave, I'm going to see Senior Magistrate Silanus. I want to know how the games are progressing."

***

In his office, Junius Silanus paced the floor. Through the window, he had a view from Citadel Hill of the city and the defensive wall to the south. But he didn't look out. All his thoughts and movements were closed in on one worry.

For years, he'd been the voice in Cornelius Scipio's ear warning about overspending. There was no question that Silanus' constant nagging, and his keen oversight, kept the Iberian campaign going through lean times. But now, the sandal was on the other foot.

"Senior Magistrate," Cornelius announced as he strolled through the doorway, "I trust you are well, are in possession of a strong constitution, and are full of vigor."

"From your appearance, General Scipio, you have obviously thrived during your ordeal," Silanus observed. "May I offer you refreshments?"

He indicated a pitcher of wine.

"It wasn't much of an ordeal," Cornelius confessed. "Wet mostly. And while I failed at East Numidia, I did get a treaty from King Syphax. But I want to hear about the preparations for the games."

Silanus picked up the accounting sheet from his desk, which had grown considerably longer than the original, and handed it to Cornelius.

"Under my watch, and I take full responsibility, I have authorized an enormous sum of coins for the games," Silanus confessed. "If you feel it's unjustified, I will offer my resignation."

Cornelius took the parchment and began reading the long list of expenses. While studying the items, he sat, then waved Silanus to the seat behind the Magistrate's desk.

"This adds up to a tremendous sum," Cornelius acknowledged. "An amount greater than I expected."

"As much as I tried, I couldn't keep the cost down."

Cornelius picked up the pitcher and poured two glasses of watered wine. He handed one to Junius, took a sip of his, and returned to reading the list.

"Fifty transport wagons and teams of horses?" Cornelius inquired.

"It was pointed out, that veterans limping along the route would slow up the parade," Silanus explained. Saying the reason for the expense out loud caused him to cringe. "Plus, the wagon beds will help display them to the crowd."

"Fifty wagons to elevate the veterans and keep the parade moving?"

"When you put it like that, I may have been a little extravagant," Silanus admitted. "I imagine there are places you can cut."

"I imagine there are, but I won't. Not a bronze coin, nor a single wineskin will be slashed," Cornelius assured him. He shook the list at Silanus. "You taught me to track my expenses and to be responsible, at least on parchment. And I taught you to spend on important items regardless of the cost. You learned the lesson well."

"That's a relief, Prorogatio of Iberia," Silanus disclosed. "Because the sacrifice of the bulls is tomorrow at first light. We didn't know if you would be coming back."

Cornelius took a sip, swirled the wine around in his mouth, and swallowed.

"It hurts to think I might have missed the games celebrating my father, my uncle, and my veterans."

"Alive or dead, General Scipio, you wouldn't have missed the games," Silanus advised. "Because, had you failed to return, you would have been celebrated as the fourth honoree of the festival."

***

The sun came up over the hills bordering Cartagena Bay. Naked and bloody priests accompanied the dawning of the first day. They sprinted from the bleeding bulls, transferring red blessings to the attendees. Shouts of warning greeted the holy men as they sprinted into the crowd. And although people feigned avoiding the priests, everyone in their path sported the impression of a bloody hand, arm, or shoulder print.

"Certainly, Jupiter and Mars will look down on us this day with favor," Cornelius exclaimed. Colonels from the eight Iberian Legions stood with their General. "Gentlemen, together we command over thirty-two thousand highly trained infantrymen, another twenty thousand spearmen, fifteen thousand horsemen, and eight thousand specialists. We are truly the most powerful force outside the Republic."

"With our numbers," Gaius Laelius suggested, "we could go after Hannibal."

"We will," Cornelius assured him. "But not in the Republic. Hannibal has attracted too many foreign allies. Attack him and he'll draw more to his side. However, attack Carthage, and Hannibal will have to return home to protect his people."

"When, General Scipio?" Colonel Nabars asked.

"I've secured spaces for supply depots on western Numidia," Cornelius told him. "The plan is to move on Carthage right after my day of triumph parade through Rome."

Sidia noted a signal from the walls of New Carthage.

"The messenger trireme is back from Rome, sir," the bodyguard informed Cornelius.

"Surely this is a blessed day," Cornelius declared. "Colonels, please enjoy the festivities and do mix with the Iberian Chiefs and Kings. While you perform the official duties, you'll excuse me. I absolutely must know what the Senate thought of my proposal."

***

Cornelius arrived at his office long before the message traveled from the harbor to Temple Hill.

"I could have stayed and entertained the Iberian Chiefs," he complained.

"I'm not sure, sir, if that would have been a good idea," Sidia warned. "Watching an agitated and distracted Roman Governor would not have done much for your reputation among the Chiefs."

"Am I that bad?"

"Truly, it's not my place to pass judgement on my General," Sidia begged off.

"That bad?"

"I'm afraid so, sir."

They waited long enough that the smell of smoke from the cookfires drifted to the temple.

"The butchering of the bulls is over," Sidia pointed out. "By this evening, there will be plenty of sacrificial meat for the feasts."

A courier appeared in the doorway and braced.

"General Scipio, a message from the Senate of Rome, sir," he announced.

"Bring it here."

A heartbeat later, Cornelius unrolled the scroll, read a section to himself, and sneered.

"Optio Decimia. Take the duty Century and round up my Battle Commanders," Cornelius directed. "Bring them here all at once. I don't want to do this again."

"Bad news, sir?" Sidia asked.

A scorching glare sent the bodyguard from the room. Once Sidia had gone, Cornelius allowed his hands to shake with frustration.

***

Not long after he left, Sidia escorted the Battle Commanders into the room. The Colonels and Senior Magistrate Silanus lined the room, forming a semicircle around their General. None spoke, and in response to the silence, Cornelius didn't look up from the scroll as he read.

"*Citizen of Rome, Cornelius Scipio, also known as the Prorogatio of Iberia, and the General of Iberian Legions, we trust this letter finds you well and in excellent health,*" Cornelius began. "*We, the Senators of Rome, feel the need to remind you that you are not a Consul of Rome nor a Proconsul, a past Consul of the Republic. In your limited capacity as a Governor, you were extended a benefit. That of being allowed to create and command Legions in your area of authority. Thus, the title of Prorogatio of Iberia was granted to you due to the distance from the Republic, and the danger to the interests of Rome in Iberia. There is little doubt that your success is noteworthy. However, as a Prorogatio, you have no authority beyond the margins of Iberia. As a citizen, you are not to negotiate with Numidia leaders, Gauls north of Iberia, or plan a foolhardy attack on Carthage.*

Your day of triumph parade is denied. Your plan to challenge Carthage is beyond all reason, and your audacity at suggesting either puts your sanity in doubt.

Additionally, should you attempt to bring your Legionaries to Rome or to the Republic, you, your commanders, the Legionaries, and any auxiliary units will be charged with treason, arrested, and crucified. Signed, the Senate and People of Rome."

A hush hung over the assembled commanders as their General let the missive slip from his fingers. Then in a savage gesture, Cornelius swept the scroll over the side of the desk and allowed it to drop to the floor.

"We know how much you wanted the day of triumph," Silanus mentioned.

Cornelius held up a hand to stop him.

"I have one goal in life, and that is to meet and defeat Hannibal Barca in battle. To do that, it seems, I have to return to Rome and wage a new kind of war. One I dislike, but in light of the message from the Senate, I am duty bound to wage."

In place of the scroll, Cornelius unrolled a large piece of parchment.

"This is a map of the plot of land I received from the Turdetanes Tribe. As I can't take my veterans home, I will build them a home here. And when I get to Rome, I'll send Latin families with sons and daughters back to fill out the population."

"Sir, we've had a few migrants from the Republic move here and settle in towns," Lucius Marcius pointed out. "But no Roman colonies have ever been established outside the Italic peninsula."

"In that case," Cornelius began before stopping to think for a moment. "I will call the colony, Italica. As a salute to the former home of my veterans, the Italic peninsula."

***

The Senior Magistrate and the Colonels shuffled out of the room. Each had reassuring words for Cornelius as they filed by. When the office was empty, Sidia pointed out a window at New Carthage.

"You've built a legacy in Iberia, sir. You have Legions and auxiliary forces, both sworn to you and not sworn against you, which in some cases is just as good. And three massive elephants. You'd give this up to go into politics?"

"I built all that for a reason," Cornelius explained. "But the Senate won't allow me to use the assets. So, I'll come at it from a different direction."

"How different?" Sidia inquired.

"I'm shipping the elephants, the Gauls, and any Legionary who wants to volunteer to Silicia," Cornelius told him. "They can train there until I have the authority to build them into Legions. Which reminds me. I need a Legion instructor who can devise training techniques to help the maniples deal with Hannibal's elephants. Any suggestions?"

"Just one, sir," Sidia replied. "Senior Tribune Jace Kasia."

"Good choice," Cornelius agreed. "Send a letter to Crete and offer him a contract. Tell Jace no requirement is too demanding, or price too high, for a Cretan archer."

(Intentionally left blank)

Act 6

Chapter 16 – Market Days on Crete

Dawn found Neysa Kasia sorting vegetables. From her cart to the wooden stands, she arranged the asparagus, carrots, leeks, radishes, and the peas. Green, purple, green, white, then the green peas, chickpeas, and finally, she placed the yellow peas in the last bin. Pleased with the ordered shapes, and arrangement of colors, Neysa glanced around.

Market day at Eleutherna brought farmers from surrounding farms, tradesmen from distant towns and cities, and craftsmen from their workshops. With one craftsman in mind, she looked at the road descending from the city searching for Jace. But her eyes drifted to the field on the other side of the road. And although she fought the emotion every market day, the memory of her brother dying while protecting her flooded back, and her heart broke all over again.

"Neysa, can we talk?" As if her nerves weren't frayed enough, an intrusion into her memories by her traitorous brother-in-law sent a violent shiver through her body. He insisted. "Really. It's been years. Can't we just talk?"

"Dryas. Jace will be along shortly," Neysa warned him. "He promised not to seek you out or cause trouble. But if he finds you bothering me, he will kill you."

"I just want to talk," Dryas Kasia pleaded.

"That talk should have happened before you pointed us out to the Rhodian spearmen," Neysa suggested while turning to face him. "The talk should have been before you had my brother killed, and my life and Jace's threatened. Go, now."

"But you're the only family I have."

"It's a sad tale, I know," Neysa conceded. "The barrel maker's daughter used you to help her father then rejected your advances. Let me check the balance of a rotten, faithless, broken heart, against the life of my brother and the years of exile for my son."

"I get your point," Dryas Kasia said. Abruptly, he turned and strolled away.

Dryas resembled her dead husband so much it hurt. But where her husband had been a Cretan Archer and an honorable man, his younger brother lacked integrity. And he was pushy, so pushy that he rarely gave up easily. The thought brought a smile to her face and Neysa looked back at the road from Eleutherna.

Waving, she called, "Jace. I'm set up over here."

Tall and broad shouldered, Jace Kasia lifted one hand from the pole. Behind him, the fresh carcass of a fat boar rocked from the one-handed grip. Over his other shoulder swung a large bundle. And across his back, he carried an archer's long pack with bows and quivers strapped to the leather bag. The three items would have caused a normal man to stagger under the weight.

Ignoring the heft of his load, Cretan Archer Jace Kasia waved at his adopted mother, adjusted his stride, and strutted to the vegetable stand.

By midday, the crowds prevented vendors from seeing each other across the aisles. Voices rose and fell, and smoke climbed gently into the sky from food sellers and craftsmen requiring heat to display their art.

Neysa piled vegetables on top of a basket filled with meat, bread, and trinkets made of bone, wood, and metal. She accepted a few coins and thanked the shopper.

"It can't be done," a man challenged from behind Neysa.

"This hunting bow already has," Jace insisted. "Look at the skin. Unless the pig stood on its hind legs and invited me to place an arrow in the middle of its stomach."

The vocal man knelt and inspected the boar skin for more holes. He located one arrow hole and poked a finger through it.

"Well, I'll be," he admitted after a moment.

"Buy a hunting bow and you too can be a pig slayer," Jace offered. "I'll throw in a chunk of roasted pig and five arrows if you buy right now."

The man pulled out a purse, opened it, and handed Jace a stack of coins. He left with a quality hunting bow, a handful of arrows, and a chunk of roasted pork.

"Did you really kill that boar with one arrow from that hunting bow?" Neysa inquired.

Jace pulled another hunting bow from a bundle. As he flexed the bow to loosen the wood before stringing it, he winked at his mother.

"This one right here," he lied to her. "One arrow and the monster fell dead,"

"You didn't by chance use you war bow to put an arrow in its eye first?" she questioned. "You know, so a second hole didn't show in the boar's skin?"

"Me?" Jace said slapping his chest as if insulted. He flexed the hunting bow behind a knee and attached the bowstring. Then he announced to the crowd. "One arrow from this excellent hunting bow and this monster of the forest fell dead. Come see for yourself."

**

The morning ended and the crowd thinned a little. But where the earlier shoppers were after staples, the afternoon customers looked to buy in quantity or were searching for specific items. And, sadly, a few attendees to the market were young animals searching among the vendors for entertainment.

"Vegetables," a young man sneered. "How about you, old lady, cut me a piece of that pork."

From behind her back and under her robe, Neysa slid a knife from a sheath.

"Your manners are bad, and you probably smell worse. But I don't want to get that close," she asserted. "If you want pork, you'll have to convince my son that you weren't just rude to his mother."

The young wolf whistled. In response, three juvenile cubs pushed through the crowd to attend him.

"What have you got?" one asked.

"This farmer refuses to cut me some pork," the leader growled. "I say smashed vegetables are in order."

The four moved towards the stand, Neysa stepped forward to defend her produce, and Jace dropped a bow and moved to defend his stepmother.

From behind the four thugs, a slim young man with broad shoulders inquired, "I have a question. Have you ever fought in a fighting circle?"

Jace stopped midstride and backed up to where he dropped the bow.

"What a bizarre question," the troublemaker commented. While his statement appeared to be the start of a conversation, he waved for his three underlings to spread out. Then he drew a knife and asked. "What's a fighting circle?"

The arrow threaded between the leeks and radishes and lost elevation on the far side of the stand. Because of the short draw, the arrow lost most of its speed. But when the arrowhead smacked the blade of the knife, there was enough momentum to strip the knife from the young wolf's hand.

"I just saved your life," Jace announced as he lowered the bow.

"You shot me with an arrow," the troublemaker accused him. "But you're a lousy bowman, because I'm still standing."

"You wouldn't be," Jace warned him, "if you attacked a Cretan Archer with a naked blade."

The young man with the muscular shoulders made a come-at-me-motion with his hands. Realizing they faced a trained mercenary, the four ran through the crowd and vanished.

"Can I offer you a slice of pork, Archer?" Jace asked.

"Sounds like an adequate payment for services rendered," the archer decided. As he walked by Neysa, he bowed, and said, "excuse me, ma'am."

"By all means," she allowed. With a twinkle in her eyes, she added. "We don't see many Cretan Archers around here."

"We're just passing through," he told her.

"Where are you heading?" Jace inquired while handing him a slice of juicy pork.

"King Phillip the Fifth of Macedonia has declared war on the Island of Rhodes," the archer replied. "I was with a file at Knossos. But they're a trading partner of Rhodes and my people are from Olous. I can't very well go against my own kind."

"Eleutherna is the wrong direction if you're going to Olous," Jace suggested.

"But it is halfway between Knossos and Chania," the archer stated. "And Chania is where I'm headed. I'm sure you'll see a few Rhodes loving archers passing through on their way to Knossos."

While chewing, the Cretan Archer scanned Jace's wares. He paused at the hunting bows and admired the craftsmanship. Then he noticed Jace's long pack, the quivers, and the war bow.

"Threading a soft-released arrow through piles of vegetables and hitting a knuckles width of steel is an almost impossible shot," he ventured. "Your name archer?"

"File Leader Kasia of Lieutenant Gergely's Company," Jace replied. He assumed the young archer would have no idea of the validity of the claim. The title referred to a position from twelve years before.

"The escape from Lake Trasimene," the archer blurted out. "I thought you'd be older, sir."

"How do you know about Lake Trasimene?" Jace asked.

"Instructor Gergely uses you and the Cretan dance to demonstrate what archers can do to restore order in a broken formation," the archer replied. "You, heroically standing on the arrow cart, directing files of brave archers to open the escape route. I still get chills thinking of the lecture."

The events were more happenstance than heroic, and the escape less bravery than slipping away through the trees. But Jace wouldn't spoil the archer's memory or Acis Gergely's rendition.

"It was a long time ago and not a profitable day," Jace admitted.

"Come with us to Chania," the archer suggested. "I'm positive you could get a contract from the city."

"I don't think so," Jace turned down the offer. Although he glanced at his long pack with affection.

"Then you're a Rhodes lover," the archer spit out.

For a heartbeat, Jace almost revealed the massacre of a Rhodian patrol by him and his mentor, Zarek Mikolas, as proof that Jace was hardly a lover of Rhodes. But he held that knowledge and presented another as evidence.

"I would be very careful of my tongue, if I were you, Herd," Jace chastised the young archer. By referring to him as Herd, an archer student, he exhibited dominance as a File Leader. "The field across the road is where my teacher, Zarek Mikolas, was killed by Rhodian spearmen. And seeing as you've forgotten your oath of brotherhood, and your manners, walk away. Because young archer, you aren't the only one who learned to battle in a fighting circle."

Realizing he had allowed his emotions to insult a Master Archer, the young man marched away. After he vanished into the crowd, Neysa Kasia walked to Jace and rested a hand on his upper arm.

"He was only defending his choice," she offered.

"I know that," Jace confessed. "My outburst had more to do with my confusion than his insinuation."

"Because you want to go to Chania and fight?" she asked.

"What I want to do is go to Knossos and offer my services," he answered. "Mostly because Macedonia is an enemy of Rome. And that makes King Phillip my enemy. But I have no contract nor contact in Knossos. So, mother, you're stuck with me."

"My heart is reassured," she whispered. "However, I fear my Cretan Archer is growing weary of life on a farm."

"What did you say?" Jace asked.

"Nothing. Nothing important."

***

In the evenings of market days, the vendors intermingled. Typically, they gossiped, caught up with distant friends, and told stories of outrageous customers. That evening on the first day of market, the normal chatter gave way to talk of war.

"Phillip of Macedon will row his fleet in and butcher every Cretan standing against him," a farmer suggested.

"He'll have to search the entire island to uncover them," another farmer countered. "With Olous and Ierapetra shoving everyone in line, what city's left to stand against him?"

"There is Knossos," a metalworker offered.

"Archers are fleeing the twin harbor," a basket weaver stated. "I saw five of them today, all heading for Chania."

"Perhaps tomorrow we'll see some going in the other direction," a clay worker mentioned.

"The Macedonia army is one of the best. No city can stand against them," a harness maker remarked. "I don't see why anyone would go to that doomed city."

"Because they're Cretan Archers," Jace told the group. "And if the city of Knossos offers employment, archers will accept."

The talk went late into the night before the gathering broke up and they went to their individual stalls. Between traveling to the market, hawking their goods all day, and staying up late, most vendors slept late.

Dawn found Neysa and Jace at breakfast. After the meal, she straightened her display and added more vegetables to the stand. At the same time, Jace assembled a pair of stools.

"What are you going to do today?" she inquired. "You sold all your hunting bows yesterday."

"I am going to sit on one of these stools and tell fortunes," Jace told her.

"In all the years of watching you grow, I never once saw any sign of you being a seer," she admitted.

"It's not a vision you would recognize," Jace replied, "nor approve of."

Although busy on the first day, by the second, the market was overflowing. Families from outlying villages and towns arrived for a day or two of shopping, trading, and visiting.

"Come sit across from me," Jace invited the eldest of three brothers, "and you could earn a silver coin."

When the older brother hesitated, his younger brothers pushed him forward.

"Go ahead and try," they urged.

"What's it going to cost me to earn a silver?" the eldest inquired.

Jace snapped two fingers up. Suspended between them was a shiny silver coin. "I have silver, do you have three coppers?"

"What do I have to do to win the silver?"

"Just sit across from me and let me guess when you'll stand up," Jace told him. He reached out and patted the other stool. "If I guess wrong, the silver coin is yours."

"Are you going to push or hit me?" the young man questioned. Seeing how close the stools were, he added. "Or kick me?"

"I promise not to touch you," Jace assured him. Because of the spacing between the stools, when the man sat, his knees almost touched Jace's knees. Jace dropped the silver coin on the ground between them and announced. "I've looked into your eyes, and I can see you are a brave man."

The younger brothers yelled their agreement and jumped up and down.

"Easy money, big brother," they exclaimed. "Easy money."

The man dropped three coppers on top of the silver, crossed his arms, and challenged, "When will I stand up?"

"Before the count of four," Jace replied.

Reaching back, he grabbed his hunting bow and an arrow with a nasty looking triple-bladed arrowhead. After fumbling with the bow and arrow, he notched the arrow, pulled the bowstring, elevated the bow overhead, and launched the arrow straight up into the air.

The two younger brothers screamed, "Duck. Get away."

But the eldest sat still, watching Jace. In four heartbeats, the arrow came down and stuck in the ground behind the bowman.

"Ha, if that's all you have," the brother told Jace, "you've already lost the silver."

After retrieving a second arrow, Jace said, "Two." And dropped the arrow. After scooping it off the ground, he notched and launched the arrow towards the heavens.

Zip-Thwack!

The shaft appeared in the triangle formed by their legs.

"I think I have the range," Jace mumbled.

The older brother's legs began to shake. Only pride and the need to impress his younger brothers kept him on the stool.

"Two more and you walk away with the silver," Jace informed him. As he notched the next arrow, he added. "Congratulations. And three."

Zip-Thwack!

A hand's width from the other shaft, but closer to the man's crotch, the arrow quivered in rhythm with the shaking of his legs.

As soon as Jace reached for the fourth arrow, the legs began to bounce. From bouncing to standing to running, the older brother shouted as he approached his siblings, "He's insane."

From the crowd, five pairs of hands began to clap before separating from the crowd of onlookers.

"An excellent demonstration of fifth year Herd bow practice," one observed.

Jace watched the five approach. Each had a long pack on his back, and they moved in the smooth well-balanced strides of Cretan Archers.

"If I was to hazard a guess," Jace greeted them, "I'd say you were traveling from Chania to Knossos."

"Yes, sir. We heard about you on the trail, and we wanted to meet you," one replied. "And to ask a favor."

"I'm not going with you to Knossos," Jace told him.

"We didn't think so, File Leader. What we wanted was to leave our packs at your stall while we enjoy the market."

"Stack them near my pack," Jace directed.

Moments later, the five archers vanished in the crowd. Jace raised his arms to call out another candidate for the silver coin challenge when a sixth Cretan Archer appeared.

"You can leave your pack over there," Jace directed. "The rest of your File is around somewhere."

"Not my File," the Archer corrected. "I'm looking for Jace Kasia."

"I'm Kasia."

"Acis Gergely sends his regards," the archer informed Jace. He extended a small scroll. "An important client has requested your services. Acis said to tell you the pay is excellent and the job easy."

"Have you ever taken an easy job?"

"Not ever," the archer answered.

Chapter 17 – The Sea Wall

Unrolling the scroll, Jace read.

Archer Kasia,

When last we spoke, you were heading home for a rest. Hopefully, you are rested. An opportunity came to the agoge today and you are my archer of choice for the contract.

Admiral Cleonaeus of the Rhodian Navy has requested an archer with traditional military experience. The situation is as follows. Spartan and Celician pirates and ships-of-war from Macedonia are attacking merchant vessels out of Athens, Knossos, the coast of Paranomia, and the Island of Rhodes. At sea, the pirates are the responsibility of the Navy. There is, however, a harbor on the island of Folegandros used by allied merchants. Your assignment concerns the harbor at Karavostasis on Folegandros.

The job is simple. Greek spearmen were sent to Karavostasis to defend it. Unfortunately, they are inexperienced and commanded by a young officer. Admiral Cleonaeus of the Rhodian Navy needs to hire a man to train the force and improve the defenses at the harbor. You are my choice.

Signed,

Acis Gergely, Captain of Cretan Mercenaries and Trainer of Archers

***

"Suppose I don't want the contract?" Jace remarked.

"Gergely said you can go to the Island of Folegandros," the messenger explained. "Or go back to the Republic, or anywhere else in the world. But you cannot remain in Eleutherna. No archer can, it's a neutral city."

"In that case, it was nice of Captain Gergely to think of me for the contract."

***

The two-harbor town of Knossos retained some of its bygone glory. The walls still towered over the deeper harbor. Although, a few sections had fallen, and others were bowed and threatening to tumble. The height intimidated, even if the blocks were now more of a home to weeds and bird nests than stout ramparts.

Jace walked by two warships from the Island of Rhodes. They rested on the sand of the beach harbor. To reach the deep harbor and the docks, he needed to enter the city.

The gates were unhinged and being repaired by carpenters while stonemasons worked on rebuilding the gate columns. Looking around, Jace saw that a lot of the older homes and buildings were deserted. At one, he stopped to look through a doorless entrance.

"Can I help you?" a city militiaman asked. "Perhaps show you to the archer quarters?"

Turning, Jace put his back to the derelict building.

"No. I need the Rhode's Navy office," Jace told him.

"On the left by the ramp to the harbor," the militiaman directed. Then he warned. "Don't let me catch you loitering or stealing."

"Aren't the archers here to defend the city?"

"Some are and some aren't. We can never tell which is which."

As he walked towards the ramp, Jace congratulated himself. Not volunteering to defend Knossos, with or without a contract, appeared to be the right choice.

***

In the office of the Rhodes Navy, Jace faced a suspicious Lieutenant.

"There are more than thirty islands in the Cyclades," the naval officer noted. "Why Folegandros?"

"I imagine it has to do with its location," Jace answered. Then he thought that a naval officer would already know about Folegandros. It'd be hard to ignore a safe harbor for ships sailing from the Island of Rhodes on a western track. The harbor provided shelter before they turned northward to Athens. Jace changed his reply from accommodating to confrontational. "Admiral Cleonaeus hired me to help with the harbor's defenses. If there's a problem, you should take it up with the Admiral."

"There are warships on escort duty heading for Thira in the morning," the Lieutenant reported. "I'll task one with diverting to Folegandros. Does that suit your needs?"

"Lieutenant, it's not my needs," Jace reminded the officer. "It's what pleases Admiral Cleonaeus."

***

Jace had experience with Republic triremes. And from where he stood, there was little difference between the Roman and Carthaginian three-bankers and a Rhodian trihemiolia. Except, the forward beam swept upward farther,

183

there were several more oar holes, and the hull appeared to be slightly wider.

"This, Archer Kasia, is a true ship of war," Captain Zenon boasted.

"Sir, it pretty much resembles a trireme," Jace observed.

"I've got twenty-six more oarsmen to a side than the triremes. And with the extras, the rowers in my engine section can double up on some oars."

"Fast?" Jace guessed.

"Especially in combat," Zenon told him. "My crew can come about to an angle of attack before most vessels can start a turn."

"Given that, sir," Jace questioned. "If your ship is so fast, why can't you keep pirates away from your shipping?"

The Captain spit on the beach and sneered, "the pirates from Cilicia and Sparta row in liburnas. They're faster, lighter, and more agile than triremes."

"And Rhodian trihemiolias," Jace added.

"Like the other three-bankers, my oarsmen have to push a massive piece of bronze through the water. The liburnas don't have the weight of a ram. Stow your gear under the steering platform. We'll launch after the transports finish loading."

Jace walked up a ramp and crossed the deck to the steering platform.

"Where are you heading?" a navigator inquired.

"Folegandros. To work on the harbor defenses."

"That's only a morning run from Thira," the navigator told him. "No more than twenty miles. We'll be in sight of land one way or the other."

"That's good, right?" Jace asked.

"Better than the run from Knossos to Thira," the man informed Jace. "For that sail, we'll spend a better part of the journey at nights on the open water."

"Couldn't you island hop or go around to avoid traveling the sea at night?"

"The islands of the Cyclades are across the Sea of Crete," the navigator told him. "There's only one way to reach them. And that takes a couple of days on the open sea. Of course, we'd be faster if we weren't shepherding them."

Four large transports tossed off lines and drifted away from the docks. With midships resembling bowls set adrift, their wide bellies restricted the vessels' progress through the water. Deck hands walked oars fore-to-aft, marking the slow rate of movement.

"I see what you mean," Jace commiserated.

***

The two warships launched when the four transports reached deep and darker water. Even with the head start, shortly after dipping their oars, the trihemiolias caught up with their slower charges. Next, as if they had rehearsed the maneuver, the six ships turned right, lowered, or raised their sails depending on the configuration of the mast, and proceeded along the coast of Crete.

"I thought the islands of the Cyclades were north of Crete," Jace mentioned. "We're sailing east."

"On land, you follow trails beaten into the earth by people who passed that way before. On the sea, you can't see the trails. But ships before ours have left us knowledge of the pathways," the navigator said. Jace studied the land sliding

185

by the right side of the warship and shook his head. Seeing the archer's confusion, the rear oarsmen offered. "On the sea, wind and current are the secrets to getting where you need to go."

"I can barely feel the wind. And, the currents are invisible," Jace pointed out. "How do they help you?"

"Wind comes down the eastern slope of Mount Ida, rolls across the beach, and crashes into gentle sea winds coming from the north. On the beach at Knossos, you notice a breeze at your back. But off the coast, the mountain winds split the air, creating flows to the left and to the right. We're sailing on the right-hand wind."

"As an archer student, my teacher had me study maps," Jace remarked. "And I know, if we travel far enough eastward, we'll end up at Cyprus."

"I said wind and current," the navigator explained. "When we reach Smenou Bay, we'll turn north and ride the currents that come around the end of Crete."

The navigator took a hand from the rear oar. He used the hand to simulate the current coming around the end of the island and its flow northward with a westerly direction. It appeared as if he was signaling directions on how to get to a location. Jace scanned the empty horizon, and for obvious reasons, couldn't find any landmarks. Not being a sailor, he lacked the knowledge of wind and currents.

"Two nights at sea?" Jace questioned.

"Just pray it doesn't get overcast," the navigator warned. "Without the stars we could be lost at sea. Or worse, in the darkness, our lanterns could attract the children of Kato."

"The Goddess of sea life," Jace ventured. "What's wrong with a few fish?"

"And the mother of sea monsters," the navigator cautioned. "Draw the attention of any of her children, and we're dead. Someone should make an offering of silver to Kato."

"I could make a sacrifice to Kato asking her to bridle her children," Jace suggested.

"Always a good idea," the navigator agreed.

Jace walked to the left side of the warship and tossed a silver coin into the water.

"What's the archer doing?" the second navigator inquired.

"Making a sacrifice to Kato for us," the first answered. "He's praying for the Goddess to keep the monsters in the deep overnight."

"Doesn't he know we'll reach the island of Thira before dark?"

"I lied to him. But you know, we'll take all the blessings we can get."

***

Jace, not being a sailor, had no idea he'd been told a sea tale by the navigator. It wouldn't occur to him until near sunset when the convoy struck their sails and rowed to a small, crescent shaped island.

"The winds were favorable and the currents strong," Captain Zenon declared. "Tomorrow, Archer Kasia, we'll drop you at Karavostasis harbor."

"Thank you, sir," Jace acknowledged.

When Jace cast an accusing glance at the aft oarsman, the man shrugged in a noncommittal gesture. The Cretan Archer accepted that he had been tricked into donating a coin. The sacrifice was for the benefit of the crew and that didn't bother him. However, by throwing away a coin, he had gone against the Cretan code of earning a profit every day. And that bothered him.

***

The navigator had been right about one thing. They were never out of sight of land. From dawn when they rowed away from Thira, Jace had a view of the rocky hills of the crescent shaped island. And just as Thira faded, a larger mass appeared over the bow.

"Folegandros," Captain Zenon announced. "We'll drop you on the rocks. And go about our business."

From midship to the aft, rowers held water with their oars until the warship slowed. The forward rowers on the port side pulled their oars in board. The vessel drifted and softly nudged against a low course of stones. Jace stepped off the rail and onto the harbor wall. He turned and saluted Zenon.

"Stroke section, back us into deep water," the Captain directed.

A moment later, the Rhodian warship backstroked into the center of the harbor, pivoted expertly, and rowed away.

"You can leave your bundles right there," a voice directed. "You won't be staying."

Jace glanced over his shoulder to see three spearman standing on a dirt slope behind the wall.

"And why would I do that," he inquired.

"We don't want any criminals or pirates on Karavostasis," one told him.

"You must be the local militia," Jace started to greet them.

"You don't get to make inquires, here," the spearmen scolded. "Lieutenant Diceärch said all strays are to be confined to the inner harbor."

"Criminals and pirates?" Jace questioned. "If that's your mission, I'm afraid you've failed."

"What are you talking about?"

"Come see for yourself," Jace invited them.

He pointed over the wall at the water some nine feet below. Pirates used liburna vessels. And while the deck of the Rhodian warship had been even with the sea wall, a liburna could easily slip in below eye level.

The three rushed down to the wall. As they moved, Jace dropped his long pack.

"Where are the pirates?" one demanded.

In giant side steps, Jace scooted behind the first spearman. An elbow from Jace in the man's lower back knocked the breath from him. Silently, he toppled over the edge. Just as the first hit the water, Jace hammered the second in the back of his head. Confused by the blow, the dizzy spearmen fell from the stone wall. Screaming before he plunged into the water, he drew the attention of the third. When the final spearman half turned to check on the other two, the Archer's foot kicked him off the wall.

Bent over and looking down, Jace questioned, "Where can I find Lieutenant Diceärch?"

From the water, one of the three tossed back threats, "I'll kill you for this. You'll die on my blade."

"Never mind," Jace assured him. "I'll find the Lieutenant myself."

***

Near the town square, Jace asked directions. A moment later, he found the location described by a craftsman.

At an angle never planned by the builder, the awning cantered to one side. As shoddy as it was, the roof provided relief from the heat and glare of the rising sun. In the shade, three men lounged on reed chairs, their legs extended and heads resting on the chairbacks.

"In a moment, three of your spearmen will come charging up from the harbor," a stranger notified the trio. "I suggest you get them under control."

None bothered to look at the speaker.

"Or what?" one demanded.

"Or Ill put them in the dirt and let you nurse them back to health," Jace answered.

The promise of violence made the three men sit up and pay attention.

What they faced was an archer. With four arrows clutched in the fingers of his bow hand, and a fifth shaft notched on the bowstring, he stood relaxed. The loaded, but undrawn, bow rested alongside his hip.

"A sailmaker said I could find Lieutenant Diceärch under the awning," Jace said. "Is he here?"

"I'm Lieutenant Diceärch. What three men are coming?"

"I imagine they're the spearmen you assigned to the harbor."

From down the slope, a man cursed as he jogged. With him were the other two spearmen. Except, in their anger and need for vengeance, they had forgotten something.

"This is about to get ugly, Diceärch," Jace alerted the militia officer. "They left their shields at the harbor. And trust me, spears against my arrows are not a fair contest."

"There's only one of you. And six of us," the Lieutenant challenged.

Zip-Thwack!

The arrowhead cut through the skin and skimmed the top of a man's thigh bone. Exiting his inner thigh, the arrow cut the woven reeds, allowing the shaft to pass halfway through the bundle of the chair's seat. The extra movement drew more of the arrow through the puncture wound. In its journey, the shaft stripped muscle and flesh as it passed through.

"Five against one," Jace reported as he drew a replacement arrow from his quiver. "Want to try it with four against one?"

Screaming, the man pinned to the chair gripped his cramping thigh.

"Shut up," Diceärch ordered him. The officer stood and marched out from under the awning. "You three stop right there."

"But Lieutenant, he threw us in the harbor," one complained.

"He kicked Sergeant Sarpedon off the wall," the other divulged. "We saw him do it."

Sarpedon pointed his spear at Jace and declared, "I am going to kill him."

Things were escalating and getting out of control fast. The young officer held up his hands.

"Hold on, we need to discuss this," he suggested.

"Sergeant, you made two mistakes," Jace called to the NCO. "You thought your superior numbers at the harbor would prevent me from attacking. And you left your shields behind."

Sarpedon's face redden, and his cheeks puffed up. No doubt in preparation for delivering curses reflecting on the archer's lineage before promising a violent thrashing. But a scream from under the awning drew his attention.

"What's wrong with Corporal Ambrus," the Sergeant inquired.

"The archer put an arrow in his leg," Dicearch replied. "Let's all calm down and focus on helping Ambrus."

"What about the archer?" Sarpedon growled.

"We can talk about his demands after we bandage the Corporal's leg."

"That, Lieutenant Dicearch, is the first smart thing you've done since you and your spearmen arrived on the island," Jace told him.

"What are you talking about?" Dicearch asked.

"You haven't improved the sea wall, set up watch towers," Jace listed, "fixed this embarrassing awning, or trained your men to defend against overwhelming odds."

"Overwhelming odds," Sarpedon repeated. "What do you know about our training?"

"There are three of you and you're wet," Jace pointed out. "I'm dry. If there were three of me, and I wanted, you'd be dead."

An ear-splitting scream came for Ambrus.

"Who are you?" Dicëarch asked.

"Admiral Cleonaeus hired me to improve the harbor's defenses," Jace answered. "And to train the spearmen he sent here to defend the harbor."

"If you're here to train us," Dicëarch questioned. "Why did you assault Sergeant Sarpedon and wound Corporal Ambrus?"

"Rule number one," Jace lectured. "When facing a superior force, intimidate with violence. It'll pause your enemies and make them question their commitment to the fight."

"What now, sir?" the Lieutenant inquired.

His choice of sir showed a swift change in attitude. Perhaps too swift, Jace thought. But he didn't know the officer and let the idea go.

"The Corporal needs attention," Jace advised. "Do any of you have medical training? Can you even sew a straight line?"

No one spoke up.

"Rule number two. Treat your wounded quickly," Jace explained. "It'll help them heal faster and get them back to work sooner. Plus, a man well treated will be loyal and he'll trust his leaders. And, for the rest of the squads, they'll know you'll take care of them if they get wounded."

"Will you teach us to care for our wounded?" Sergeant Sarpedon asked.

His bluster, it seemed, was replaced by his concern for Ambrus. Yet, the turnabout made Jace suspicious. In training and in the Legions, he'd experienced many sleepless nights.

Until he felt safe enough on the island to sleep through the night, he'd remain guarded.

"Yes. And we'll start with stitching up the Corporal. Who has vinegar?" Jace asked.

Chapter 18 – The Priest of Zeus

Corporal Ambrus sat on a stump overlooking the harbor. With his injured leg propped up, he took streams from a wineskin to ease the throbbing. In front of the NCO, eight spearmen bound beams together, creating support structures for a watch tower.

"Straighten that leg," Ambrus instructed. He winced as if giving the order reminded him of his wounded limb. "If it's angled on the ground, when you lift it into position, the stand will be tilted."

Down the hill and off to the right of the harbor, Sergeant Sarpedon grabbed a spearmen. He shook the man while turning him to face the harbor wall.

"That stone will fall and take the rest with them," he complained. "Get back there and restack it."

Elbowing his way through the line of spearmen carrying stones, the offender reached the stone he had carelessly placed. After reseating it, he went to fetch another. All along the harbor wall, flat rocks had been layered to raise the height of the sea wall.

Higher on the slope, behind the watch tower construction site, Jace Kasia indicated the sea wall.

"That's coming along nicely," he commented.

"But the stacked stones won't support weight," Diceärch protested. "If anyone tries to climb on them, they'll fall into the harbor."

"That's the point," Jace remarked. "Rule number 3, Lieutenant. You pick the battlefield. Let your adversary deal with the obstacles you've identified. Don't let it be your men attacking through their barriers."

"Between the stones on the sea wall and the split rail fence narrowing the path from the beach," Diceärch listed, "I can see how we're defining the battleground. But why the tower? We can see a lot of the harbor from here. Is there a rule for the tower?"

"Be aware of your surroundings," Jace answered. "Know where the main body of your enemy is, and if he's sending out flankers. Plus, you might get fixated on the main attack force coming off the beach. The man in the tower will see more. He'll warn you of what's coming behind the first wave, or what's coming up behind you, or closing in from the sides."

"Rule number four, always have extra lookouts in every direction," Diceärch ventured. Next a shadow fell over the young officer's face, and he concluded. "We should make a sacrifice and ask the Gods to bless our fortifications."

"You can if you want," Jace begged off. "I'm going to check on the patio under the awning."

"Hold on, Archer Kasia," the Lieutenant said. "All of my prior commanders sacrificed for everything. From dawn to morning, noon, afternoon, evening, and night, they prayed and burnt things in the name of the Gods. But not once in the three days since you've been here have you mentioned, or suggested, an offering to a God or Goddess."

"Artemis," Jace replied.

"Why do you mention Artemis?" Diceärch asked. "She's the Goddess of wild animals and the wilderness."

"Artemis is also the Goddess of hunting, archery, and the moon," Jace said. "For a Cretan Archer, the Goddess Artemis, and our war bows, keep us safe, fed, and employed."

"That explains it," Diceärch declared.

"Explains what?" Jace asked.

"Why the sentries report seeing you walking around the town at night," the Lieutenant responded. "You're sacrificing to Artemis at moonrise."

"Something like that," Jace lied while using the back of his wrist to hide a yawn. As he started to walk away, Jace encouraged. "But you go ahead and sacrifice to your personal God for the harbor defensives."

"Not me, Archer. I don't honor any God or Goddess," Diceärch uttered. "Or owe homage to any temple."

Jace stopped in mid step. Cretan Archers were taught the Gods and Goddesses of many lands. The knowledge helped the mercenaries blend in with the cultures of their employees. And while bowmen uniformly honored Artemis, any worship of other Greek Gods was a personal choice. Jace adhered to no other deities save Artemis. Although when he served with the Legions, he practiced the paganism of the Latins.

Looking into the Lieutenant's eyes, Jace attempted to see if the officer was jesting. Realizing he wasn't, Jace invited, "Tell me why."

***

Dicearch peered left and right to be sure they were isolated from the spearmen and his NCOs.

"I'm from Neroula. A small agricultural village several miles from the port of Methoni," he described. "You may have heard of Methoni. Homer mentions the port city in the Iliad. According to him, a woman named Chryseis was taken by King Agamemnon. But her father was a priest of Apollo. Backing his priest, no matter the situation, Apollo sent a plague amongst the Greeks besieging Troy. Would you expect anything less than death and disease from a God? Anyway, a prophet figured out the cause of the plague. Fearing retribution, the prophet wouldn't tell Agamemnon the reason unless Achilles promised to protect him."

"Your rendition of the epic poem is rather hard on Apollo and his priest," Jace suggested. At the comment, the Lieutenant smirked. Seeing no remorse for the slanted retelling, Jace urged. "Go on with your story."

"Achilles vowed to protect the prophet and Agamemnon was told that the cause of the plague was the capture of the priest's daughter. The King returned Chryseis to her father. For revenge, Agamemnon took a war prize from Achilles, a woman named Briseis. Angry at the loss of honor and the confiscation of his plunder, Achilles refused to fight. To appease his best warrior, Agamemnon offered him bribes. One bribe was the city of Methoni. Oh, when Achilles finally

197

decided to fight, Zeus held him back to save Troy from being sacked. More useless meddling by a God."

"You're angry with religion because of a poem," Jace concluded.

"That's just to explain where I'm from," Diceärch told him. "My view of temples and priests comes from a more personal experience."

"I'm listening," Jace assured him.

***

"In my ninth year, after an argument with my grandfather, my father went to Methoni, joined the Messenia navy, and rowed away on a warship."

"It's for the best," grandfather explained. "After the death of a wife, a man needs time to adjust. A taste of war will help him appreciate what he has at home. Now, lets you and I go irrigate the olive trees on the southern edge of the grove."

"Work was grandfather's solution to everything," Diceärch said with a chuckle. "Our family had a three-acre grove of mature olive trees. From irrigation, to draining, pruning, harvesting, pressing, and packing the fruit in salt water, olive trees demand work. So even if there were no problems, there was always a lot of work. Besides, the grove left little time for self-reflection. And where it didn't help my father, the work helped me get over the loss of my mother."

The Lieutenant's face softened, and he stood a little straighter.

"A month after father's departure, grandfather climbed to the top of an old tree. A branch snapped, the ladder twisted, and he tumbled from limb to limb until smashing headfirst into the ground. Near midday, I found him and the crooked ladder. His neck and left arm didn't look right. After rolling him onto the ladder, I picked up one end and pulled. Despite my will and desire, I could only manage ten steps before collapsing."

***

Diceärch kicked a stone. It flew a few feet before skipping down the slope towards the harbor.

"But each time I fell, I stood, lifted the end of the ladder, pulled, and prayed. Kratos, God of strength, might, and power, give me might so I can drag my grandfather home. Ten steps and I fell to my knees. Kratos, grant me the strength to carry my grandfather home. Ten halting paces and down I went. God Kratos, please."

The Lieutenant spit on the ground in a violent display as if attempting to punish the soil.

"When I reached grandfather's house, my knees were bloody, my shoulders ached, and my legs trembled. But I managed to pull the ladder inside and roll grandfather onto his bed. He wouldn't or couldn't speak to me. Only his eyes moved as they filled with tears. Work was the answer for every emotion. Not sobs, or moans of sorrow, and certainly not tears. I had never seen him cry. Frightened by his helplessness, I ran from the house."

***

Taking a stream of wine, the Lieutenant's breathing slowed. Although Jace suspected Diceärch didn't realize it, he had been panting as he talked.

"In my desperation to get help, I ran down the lane. Olive trees flashed by and at the end of the grove, my feet took a rarely used path. Bushes brushed my arms as I ran up

199

the hill to a shrine of Zeus. Perhaps, the Gods had finally awakened to my plight. They were directing me, showing me where to find help for grandfather."

***

He squatted and rested a fist on the ground to steady his stance. And for a moment, Diceärch's face revealed his youth. Open and trusting, almost as if he was once again a nine-year-old boy, seeking a savior.

"A cleric and two men stood on the steps of the shrine. Shouting, I dashed to the Priest of Zeus. Dropping to my knees, I clutched the hem of his robe, and begged, please, please help grandfather."

"Who are you?" Xanthus, the Priest of Zeus, inquired.

"My grandfather owns the olive grove on the lower slope," I gushed out. "He's fallen and I fear he's seriously injured. Please come, please help."

"We will. But first, we need to ask the Ruler of the Gods to intercede on behalf of your grandfather," Xanthus declared. Taking my arm, he guided me up the steps. As we came level with the floor of the shrine, the priest asked. "Do you have a sacrifice for Zeus?"

"I don't understand," I admitted.

"It's tradition, when asking for blessings from a God, to offer food. I see you are without a pack. Some offer spices. Alas, I see you have no spice bags," Xanthus cooed. "A gift of coins for Zeus is also acceptable."

"I have two bronze. I use them to weigh down my coin purse," I told the priest. "Without the coins, the purse would flop around and get hung up on an olive branch."

"Such an embarrassing sacrifice," Xanthus scolded. "Suppose I add two gold coins to your two bronze coins."

"Would that be a worthy offering to Zeus for grandfather?" I questioned.

"It will suffice for a sacrifice to Zeus," Xanthus proclaimed. "You can pay me back later."

***

"I remember little of the ceremony. Only that it seemed to last all afternoon. When it ended, Xanthus and I left the shrine. At a maddingly slow pace, we strolled around the hill to the lower ground. Even on the straight and level lane of the olive grove, the priest shuffled in half steps."

Diceärch launched himself upward. In a snap, he stood erect with his fist raised as if prepared for a bout in Apollo's sport. But he wasn't going to box, it was him reliving the memory of a boy in trouble.

"The open door to grandfather's house didn't alert me," he related. "I ran out so fast, I didn't remember if I closed it."

Far from the threshold, Xanthus grabbed my shoulders, and spoke loudly, "When we get inside, I'll examine your grandfather, and of course, pray for his health."

"I couldn't figure out why he suddenly became so animated. Then two figures burst through the doorway. Each held a fat coin purse. My mind filled with visions of my injured grandfather defending his hoard. In a moment of clarity, before I ran into the house, I noted one of the thieves had a knife sheath outlined in silver rivets. But then I was inside and beside grandfather's bed. Taking his limp hand in mine, I felt for but detected no life in his veins. He was dead. Through tears, I noticed his cocked neck was straightened."

201

"Have you coins for Charon, the ferryman of Hades?" Xanthus asked. "Your grandfather will need to pay a fee to be carried across the river Styx."

"I have some," I looked to the cabinet where grandfather hid his savings. The wood was broken, and the coin purses gone, "but the thieves took the coins. Did you see them? Did you know them?"

"I saw only shadows run from the house," Xanthus replied. "But now we have an existential emergency. You have no coins for the burial wrap, no coins for the ferryman, no coins for the ceremony, nor coins for the grave diggers, and you owe me two gold coins. How do you propose to pay?"

"What if I dig a hole and bury grandfather myself," I pleaded. "Won't that be enough?"

"It is said that Charon couldn't take the deceased across the river to Hades until they have received a proper burial," Xanthus almost whispered to relay the gravity of his speech. "What you propose will doom your grandfather to an eternity of wandering the earth as a tormented spirit."

"My eyes drifted to grandfather's body as if he would sit up and give me guidance. But he didn't. Looking to the Priest of Zeus, I asked what I could do to assure grandfather reached Hades."

"Do you have parchment and ink?" he inquired. "We can draw up a bill of sale for the olive grove. That will cover the cost of everything. For your signature, you'll grant your grandfather access to Hades. And thanks to you, he'll drink from the river of forgetfulness and be free of pain and regrets forever."

His nostrils flared and Dicearch inhaled as if he was an angry bull.

"A greedy cleric is always a problem," Jace pointed out. "I can appreciate your dislike for the priesthood and the Gods. Maybe if you purchase some land and plant olive trees, you'll find peace."

"The theft of my family's olive grove isn't why I hate priest," he replied. "That and my revulsion for the Gods came six months later."

***

"Xanthus gave me a job in the grove," Dicearch continued the tale. "For irrigation, draining, and pruning the olive trees, he paid me two bronze coins a week. Almost charity, for a boy, he said. Whenever he left the sanctuary and came off the hill to inspect his olive grove, the Priest of Zeus walked between the trees praying."

Digging a heel into the soil, the Lieutenant created an indention. Rocking the foot back and forth, he deepened the hole. When he pushed his foot, the hole became a short trench.

"Most crops will use all the water you can get to the rows," Dicearch explained while pouring wine into the foot trench. "Olive trees are different. They like sandy soil, a little moisture, but never a deep soaking. After a heavy rain, the excess water needs to be drained away from the grove. Grandfather had been in Hades for six months when a storm blew in. All night, heavy rains came down. Before dawn, as grandfather had taught me, I took a hoe to the lowest area and cut a trench. Once water began to flow, I followed the source, extending the trench. It's dirty, but necessary work. At a low spot, I positioned myself in the muddy water and began digging a new channel. The hoe hit a rock and the blade splashed into the puddle. Catching a face full of water, I blinked to clear my eyes. In the haze of my vision, I saw an image."

***

Gently, as if covering seeds in a garden, Diceärch shoved dirt into the trench. Next, he tapped the soil flat with his foot.

"Under the limbs of an olive tree, an image of my father watched me. Not believing my senses, I returned to lengthening the drainage trench."

"Where's your grandfather?" the spirit demanded.

"The voice drove a stake into my heart. Joy and pain swirled in my mind. I dropped the hoe, then dropped to my knees. And I told him the whole story as I knelt in the mudhole."

"You are a fool," he screamed. "Wait here."

"He stomped away, and I remained on my knees in shame. Had he really returned home? Slowly, I peered at his muddy footprints. Next, I pushed out of the mud and chased after father."

"A boy's legs in mud are less efficient than an angry man's stride. I didn't see him when I reached the lane. Not even on the path up and around the hill. But when I reached the top, I saw my father and Xanthus standing nose to nose at the bottom of the steps.

"It's my family's olive grove," my father shouted.

"Here at his shrine, all things belong to the Ruler of the Gods," Xanthus countered. Then his voice softened, and he advised. "Let's go into the sanctuary and discuss this like civilized men. Come friend, we will make this right in the name of Zeus."

"My father's arms and shoulders dropped as the fight eased from his body. On the first step, a temple guard ran up behind my father and stabbed him in the back. Not once but four times. With each thrust of the blade, I watched the knife sheath with the silver rivets bounce against the guard's hip."

"The will of Zeus is done," Xanthus announced from the top step. "Burn the body. Then find the son and kill him too."

***

Dicearch smiled and told Jace, "I collected my father's armor and weapons from the house and fled to Methoni. Even though I was only ten years old, because I had my own armor, sword, and spear, I was able to hire on to a warship as an oarsman."

"A man with reason to hate will always hate," Jace commented. "I'm going to check on the awning repairs. By the way, did you ever return to Neroula?"

"A couple of years ago, for a short visit," Dicearch replied. "It was a hot summer night and hotter still for the Priests of Zeus."

"I hope you found satisfaction in the vengeance. And are finished burning temples."

"Mostly. These days, I build altars after I finish a sea voyage."

"An altar?" Jace questioned. "To which God?"

"Two altars," Dicearch corrected. "One dedicated to the crime of *Asebeia*, to celebrate the desecration and mockery of

205

divine objects. And, a second altar, devoted to *Paranomia*. It's my way to call attention to the delusional beliefs of priests and their followers."

"You are a committed heretic, I'll give you that," Jace stated.

As he hiked to the patio under the awning with the intention of taking a nap, the Archer pondered a question. Not about the Gods but concerning if he should be teaching the secrets of warfare to an unstable man. With that thought in mind, Jace Kasia changed direction. He marched through the small village, heading for the shrine of Poseidon high above the harbor.

Perhaps the view would give him clarity and maybe he'd draw some inspiration from the shrine.

"You can pray," Zarek Mikolas suggested. Jace shifted the deer carcass, leaned forward, and used his free hand to push upright. Once on his feet, Jace staggered under the weight of the fresh kill. Slowly, he moved forward along the mountain trail. Behind him, the Master Archer explained. "You asked Zeus for a clear day for the hunt. And the Goddess Artemis for the game, the arrow, and the aim. But now, as your sweat under the load, you want the Goddess Nephele to bring clouds to shade you. And you pray for the God Kratos to lighten the load by giving you strength. Isn't that an insult to Zeus for the clear day and to Artemis who sent you the big deer?"

"Should I not pray at all," Jace inquired.

"Prayers like wishes, and like decisions only work when you act on them," Zarek advised. "Get through the task first. Then if you want you can sacrifice and thank the Gods who earned it."

Jace reached the shrine of Poseidon, turned around, and peered down the long slope at the harbor. Farther out, he noticed sails powering a cargo transport across the water. Then from the side, a long, low vessel appeared. It headed directly towards the merchant ship.

(Intentionally left blank)

Act 7

Chapter 19 - Skills for the Unstable

Jace touched the altar. Although not given to strict adherence, he wouldn't temp the Gods by ignoring Poseidon. After his fingers brushed the surface of the altar, he left the shrine and sprinted downhill to the working parties. A moment later, the coastal trader changed course and headed for Karavostasis harbor.

"Don't," Jace pleaded as he ran.

The race to safety by the merchant ship raised no concern for the archer. The harbor, and the spearmen, were there for the safety of merchant ships, as shelter for damaged vessels, and to act as a retreat for outnumbered warships. The trading vessel was welcome to the security of the harbor. The raider, on the flip side, required a different kind of reception.

"Don't," Jace repeated. But the pirate ship mimicked a sheep dog as it cut to port, increased stroke rate, and attempted to head off the trading vessel. The maneuver made the Cretan Archer groan. "I should have left the harbor defenses for later. Right now, I'd give a hefty chunk of my pay to have the days back. A few days of weapons practice with the spearman would be comforting."

Rowing wise, the raider dipped thirty-six oars which propelled the sleek liburna quickly across the water. The coastal trader had three sailors walking long oars up and down the deck on each side. Except for two factors, the dash to the harbor should not have been close.

In an attempt at stealth, the raider depended solely on oar power. And while the merchant ship had only six oars, the vessel traveled with its mainsail full of wind. In this case, the movement of air against the fabric of the sail won out over strokes in the water by oars made of fir trees. Another difference between raider and trader rested on the skills of their captains. When the merchant skipper noticed the raider vessel, he took quick action and ordered a change in course. Hesitation by the pirate commander made their turn late, giving the trader a head start to the beach.

***

"We have a coastal trader coming in," Jace alerted Diceärch. "Hot on his tail is a liburna raider."

"Sarpedon. Get everyone armed and to the beach," the Lieutenant directed.

"Hold up, Sergeant," Jace said making a correction. "Give me ten men above the sea wall and send another ten to the shoreline. I want that trader out of the water and up on the beach. Let's see if the raider is willing to come ashore and pay a blood price to claim his prize."

"That only leaves me fifteen in the shield wall," Diceärch complained. "The liburna's crew is thirty-six oarsmen and who knows how many warriors."

"Then your fifteen spears better be ready. As fierce as Spartan Hoplites, and their shields as steady as a rock wall," Jace described. "Rule number five, Lieutenant, assume victory and project confidence. Make your enemy question if he wouldn't rather be anywhere else except facing your spears and your wrath."

"Rule number five," Diceärch mumbled with no passion or conviction. Despite his misgivings, he ordered. "Sergeant. Ten on the hill, ten in the water, and fifteen at the harbor fence."

"Yes, sir," the NCO said. The lack of enthusiasm was obvious in his lackluster response.

"Sarpedon. Let me make you an offer," Jace suggested. "Demonstrate confidence for your men. Strut back and forth in front of the shield wall and challenge the raiders to come and taste your steel, I'll give you something you really want."

"The only thing I want Archer," the NCO told Jace, "is to bash in your face."

"Done. You'll have your shot. Be ferocious when facing the pirates, and when this is over, you and I will step into the fighting circle."

"What's a fighting circle?" the unsuspecting NCO asked.

***

Two ship lengths separated the coastal trader from the pirate. But the merchant vessel needed to reach the beach and be hauled out of the water to be safe. All the raider required was to get close, throw a grappling hook, and drag the trader back into deep water.

"She won't make it, Kasia," a spearmen stated.

On the fore deck of the raider, a pirate twirled a rope overhead. On the end of the line, an iron hook spun faster and faster. Once they were within a half a ship's length, he'd release the rope, free the grapnel, and hook the merchant ship.

"Let's make some space," Jace replied.

"Do you expect us to dive over the wall, swim out, and delay the liburna with our bare hands," another asked.

The Archer placed a shaft on his war bow and notched the arrow.

Zip-Thwack!

The arrow arched across the sky, nosed over, and flashed down to the pirate with the hook. Entering the side of his neck, the shaft sent a splash of red into the air. During the upsurge of the blood, the rope swung around and cut the splatter in half. As the two sprays of blood fell to the deck, the uncontrolled hook whipped out over the water. The rope tightened and yanked the wounded sailor. He toppled over the rail and followed the grapnel into the bay.

As the pirate and the hook splashed into the harbor, Jace answered, "No, spearman. I expect you to throw stones at the pirate oarsmen on the starboard side."

While Jace's ten spearmen began chucking rocks over the sea wall, a voice at the harbor fence bellowed, "Come taste my steel, you, pieces of filth. You come into my harbor, threaten one of my traders, and expect to just leave. Come ashore and show me if you are men or bottom feeding crabs."

Jace chanced a look. The fifteen spearmen behind their Sergeant were braced, steady, and appeared as threatening as their NCOs words were condescending. The Cretan Archer pulled an arrow from his quiver and selected his target.

Zip-Thwack!

At the bow of the raider, a pirate attempted to pull his injured shipmate and the hook out of the water. He paused in mid pull, grunted, then sprawled on the deck. The arrow shaft, through his back, pierced his heart. The rope slipped through his dying fingers and the hook sank to the bottom of the harbor.

***

From powerful strokes used in an attempt to catch the trader, the raider vessel made a yaw to the left. The break in the rhythm by the right-side rowers put them out of sync with their opposite numbers. The awkward turn allowed for even more rocks to rain down on the oarsmen. From nearly catching the trader, the pirate vessel lost ship lengths.

On the beach, sailors jumped into the shallows, and along with the ten spearmen, they heaved the merchant ship out of the water. Once the coastal trader was high, dry, and safe, the crew ran to get behind the shield wall.

"Come taste my steel, you, pieces of filth," Sarpedon yelled at the retreating pirate vessel. "Where are you going? You're spineless jellyfish. Come back and fight me."

Seeing their fellow spearmen standing proud and defiant in the wall of shields, the ones assigned to bringing the trader ashore ran to get their shields and spears. In moments, the wall increased by ten shields.

Frozen in a stance with his sword held down, to the front, and ready, Diceärch watched the raider row out of the harbor. Even when the pirates were out to sea, the Lieutenant, the Sergeant, and the spearmen remained postured for battle.

213

Jace and his team of stone throwers jogged to the harbor. The ranks of shields and spears still spanned the opening in the wooden fence. No spearman, NCO, nor their Lieutenant gave any indication that they planned to break the formation. Behind the spearmen, the crew of the coastal trader huddled, still recovering from their flight to safety.

"They had you outnumbered nearly two to one," the merchant captain stammered. "Yet, you faced the Spartan pirates without flinching."

When Diceärch failed to answer, Jace offered, "these are handpicked Aetolian warriors. To them, Spartans are goat herders."

"If not for these brave men, we'd be dead, our ship taken, and cargo lost. Thank you. Thank you."

Diceärch snapped out of his trance but ignored the merchant captain.

"Cretan, Archer, rule number five," he uttered.

"They did seem, sir," Sarpedon admitted, "that they wanted to be anywhere but here."

"It's a poor commander who will throw loyal men against a shield wall for a coastal trader," Jace pointed out. "Especially a solid wall of shields held with authority."

"What else do I need to know?" Diceärch asked.

"Only two more rules. Plan your escape route before engaging with an enemy," Jace replied. He pointed out to sea, using the retreating raider as an example. "And finally, learn the correct moment to break contact with an enemy."

"That's evident," Diceärch proposed. "When you're losing the battle."

"If you wait that long your spearmen will be overwhelmed. You start withdrawing when you stop winning, but before you start losing."

"How does a commander know when he starts losing?" the Lieutenant asked.

"Mostly luck, at first," Jace stated, "but the good ones learn."

When Jace paused for too long, Diceärch inquired, "And the bad commanders?"

"They end up dead. Dismiss your men, Lieutenant. Good job all around."

***

The next morning, two ranks of fifteen spearmen waited for their officer. Uneven and wiggly, the lines displayed their lack of formal training. Sergeant Sarpedon occupied a spot in front of the detachment while Corporal Ambrus sat off to the side.

"What are we doing here, sir?" Sarpedon inquired.

Diceärch marched across the patio, passing under the newly repaired awning. As he approached the formation, he told the NCO, "Archer Kasia said we're running shield drills today."

"He's going to slip out of his deal with you, Sergeant," whispered a spearman in the first rank. "You can't trust a Cretan."

"After yesterday, I'm not as hot to push in his face," Sarpedon informed the speaker. "But I am tempted to punch the next spearman who speaks out of turn."

Diceärch peered around the village, up the hill to the shrine of Poseidon, and to either side of the high ground.

Not finding the Archer, he scanned downhill to the harbor. After examining the fishermen and their boats, he studied the rocks on top of the sea wall. Not once did he spot the Archer.

"Perhaps, Kasia has forgotten his orders for the spearmen to stand in ranks," Diceärch pointed out. "Or he ingested too much wine last night. Both could account for him missing the formation."

All the Lieutenant could do without the Archer was dismiss the spearmen. Before he gave the order, a voice spoke from behind him.

"Say, Lieutenant, the Archer sent this," a fisherman remarked as he approached from the harbor. "Where do I put it?"

The man had a basket of sand balanced on one shoulder. While he waited for directions, five more fishermen hauled loads of sand to the formation.

"What am I supposed to do with sand up here?" Diceärch asked.

"Sir, I imagine if Kasia wants sand," Corporal Asebeia offered, "you could have them dump it into a pile. And let the Archer sort it out later."

***

The six baskets of fine white sand formed a cone with a circular base. Jace appeared on the shoreline then climbed the hill. As he approached the formation, Diceärch noted that the Archer's hair was wet.

"I apologize for being late, Lieutenant," Jace said. "I felt like a swim before shield training."

216

"We have thirty men with their shields ready to begin," Diceärch informed him. "Do you want to get dressed before we start. Maybe in your armor or at least a tunic?"

Jace bent over and studied his linen undergarment for a moment.

"Nope, this is appropriate," Jace said. He walked to a spearman and took the man's spear. Then, pacing a few steps from the sand pile, the Archer put the spearhead in the dirt and drew a wide circle. Once done, he returned the spear. "I need five men to trample the sand pile flat."

"Is this part of the shield training?" the Lieutenant asked.

Five men marched through and over the pile until the sand flattened.

"No, it's preparing the fighting circle," Jace answered before looking at the Sergeant. "You might want to take off the armor. When grit gets under it, it'll rub your flesh raw."

"Only if I'm on my back," Sarpedon asserted.

"Or on your face," Jace countered. He walked around kicking down high spots. Then he addressed the spearmen. "A battle can be a thousand warriors wide or as simple as a five-man assault. But for a spearman or a soldier, the number of participants is meaningless."

Jace walked the edge of the sand pit all the way around.

"This is too big for you, but it'll serve as an example of me controlling my space," Jace bowed to Sarpedon. "Sergeant, you want revenge for the kick that landed you in the harbor? Here's your chance."

Sarpedon marched to the edge of the fighting circle still dressed in his armor.

"No sense taking it off for a few punches," the NCO proposed.

"Everyone, twist at the waist and imagine a circle around you as defined by your shield arm," Jace instructed. "That's your area to control and this is mine."

Jace took a position in the center of the circle and waved Sarpedon forward.

"The man across from you doesn't simply want to get by you," Jace warned the spearmen. "He wants to hurt you."

Sarpedon hopped forward, swinging both fists at Jace's head. Dropping to his knees, the Archer drove a shoulder into the NCO's knees. Off balance, Sarpedon toppled backward. He tried to kick Jace, but the Archer's arms encircled his legs.

Standing while controlling the Sergeant's knees, Jace flipped him over and pulled him to the center of the circle.

"What did I just do?" Jace asked the spearmen.

"You took him off his feet," one answered.

Another spearman offered, "You flipped him over."

From the side of the formation, Corporal Ambrus answered, "you moved back to the center of your circle."

Holding a bucking, angry man proved too much of a distraction. Jace lifted the Sergeant off the ground, swung him around and released him. Sarpedon flew a short distance, before bouncing out of the fighting circle.

Jace returned to the center of the sand.

"What am I doing?" he inquired.

"You're waiting for the next attack," a spearman suggested.

Lieutenant Diceärch declared, "you cleared the threat from in front of you and returned to your place in the shield wall."

"This is my circle," Jace preached. He moved his arms to indicate the border of the sand. "Other circles don't concern me. If he's outside my circle, the fighter in front of me doesn't concern me. Why?"

"For the same reason you didn't follow up on the assault of Sergeant Sarpedon," Diceärch replied. "Because your shield in the defensive line is more important than, what?"

"More important than personal glory," Jace told the Lieutenant. "I can't control a circle a hundred shields from me. All I can do is allow my shield to stabilize the circle on my left and the circle on my right."

Sarpedon sat up and shook his armor.

"Sergeant. Are we done?" Jace asked. "If not, I'm still in my circle."

"We're done, weapons master," the NCO said using a term of respect. "The sand is already beginning to scour my flesh."

"Now that," a spearman noted, "would be a horrible way to die."

***

To everyone's surprise, Diceärch picked up a shield and took a spot in the defensive line.

"Your circle overlaps the circles of your neighbors," Jace described. He walked down the line while talking. Then in a flash, his foot shot out and he kicked a gap between a pair of shields. The spearman and the Lieutenant were thrown back by the surprise attack. Adding to the assault, Jace hammered each man with an elbow as he walked between the shields. "I'm now behind your shield wall. That's a problem."

The snarl alerted Jace to trouble. Ducking as he pivoted, he dodged the spear tip. Continuing the turn, he brought a knee up behind the shield that tried to smash him to the ground. It caught Diceärch in the hip and drove the Lieutenant sideways before he tripped and collapsed.

Confused by the outbreak of real violence, the NCOs and spearmen gawked at their officer. Jace ran to him and sat on the Lieutenant's chest.

"Diceärch. It's alight. It's a drill to make your spearmen more efficient," he cooed. "Nothing personal. Breathe deep. Inhale and let it out slowly. There that's better. Maybe Lieutenant, you should just observe."

Standing, Jace took the officer by the arm and helped him to his feet.

"I let my temper get the better of me," Diceärch proclaimed. "No harm done, Archer. Continue with the training."

But even as his words were pleasant, there was a challenge in the undertone of his speech. And hatred simmered behind the Lieutenant's eyes.

"Second rank step forward," Jace instructed. As the spearmen moved up, a troubling thought crossed the Archer's mind. Had he just taught war skills to an unstable and possibly insane officer? Shoving the idea down, he addressed the spearmen. "Your circle is your home. Protect it and defend it from every threat."

Softly, and unheard by most of the spearmen, Diceärch muttered, "Your home, protect it and defend it from every threat."

Chapter 20 – Pack of Wolves

Several weeks of training, and after the realization that Diceärch was slightly mad, the day dawned bright and clear. And while the villagers and fishermen were up and going about their tasks, one man slept late.

Jace woke to sunlight streaming in under his door. Typically, the Archer rose before dawn. But the long days of drilling the spearmen on shield and spear techniques left him exhausted. Being bruised and weary to the bone triggered a memory.

"You take a commander's coin, and you give value," Zarek Mikolas had taught. *"You don't have to like the client, approve of his war, or his personal hygiene. You just have to hold your nose and do the job."*

"All these years, I thought you meant body odor," Jace confessed to the ghost of his mentor. "Instability of the mind can stink as much as the inside of a crusty pile of cow manure. And yes, I know Master Mikolas, I've slept half the day away."

Jace dressed in a tunic, and his combat sandals, then he opened the door.

Diceärch's body filled the doorframe.

"Good morning, Archer Kasia," the Lieutenant greeted Jace. "You know, we have actual bedrooms closer to the harbor."

Diceärch refused to give ground, leaving the two men chest to chest in the doorway.

"I can't believe you've been waiting to talk to me about my choice of sleeping quarters," Jace suggested. Gently, he placed a hand on Diceärch's chest and moved him away from the threshold. "There must be another reason for your visit to my humble room."

When Jace first arrived at the harbor town, he worried about being attacked by spearmen because of his rough treatment of them. To resolve the issue of safe sleeping accommodations, he located a storage room. It possessed no windows, but provided a sturdy, if ill-fitting, door. The only problem, the doorway faced the hill on the upper side of Karavostasis. From the room with the door open, he had a good view of Poseidon's shrine but none of the harbor.

Rather than entertain Jace's query, Diceärch asked, "I didn't scare you, did I?"

In reply, Jace revealed his skinning knife and spun the tool on the palm of his hand.

"If you had, we'd be stitching you up and sewing closed the hole in your tunic," he informed the Lieutenant before slipping the skinner back it its sheath. "Why are you here?"

"I understand the need for a tight shield wall," the Lieutenant began, "and coordinated spear thrusts. But when the Spartan pirates arrived, all they saw was a small line of stationary shields and one loud NCO. Yet, it was enough for them to back away. Why?"

They strolled into the village, heading in the direction of the drill field. Once among the buildings of the tradesmen and fishermen, aromas from cookfires drifted through the streets.

"Hunters don't fear a snarling pack of wolves," Jace lectured. "The demonstration of noise and fury are to make their quarry run. Once the prey flees, the pack can take it down from behind. Unknown to your spearmen, their fear, and the words of their Sergeant, gave the impression of seasoned warriors. Their stance resembled soldiers, waiting for an unsuspecting prey to step in front of their shields."

"Is there a rule for that?" Dicearch inquired.

"No more than hide glue is listed as part of a bow," Jace told him. "You have the riser, the limbs, the bow string, sinew, and bone. But few will list hide glue."

"Hide glue?" Dicearch questioned. "I don't understand."

"All the shield and spear training and field maneuvering will amount to nothing when you encounter a strong enemy force," Jace explained. "Unless your spearmen have discipline. Discipline is the glue that holds shields together in combat and allows spearmen to advance into enemy steel."

"The drills will install discipline," Dicearch ventured. "How could it not?"

"Situational control is a basic requirement of any company," Jace stated. "But the control will break when the situation goes bad. And it will, Lieutenant, after the first clash of shields. Discipline needs to become ingrained. From how they form up, to how a unit crosses the drill field before and after practice. Every moment they're on duty is a chance to practice discipline."

"That's extreme," Dicëarch pushed back. "I've been around Hoplites for years and no phalanx marches outside their formation. Name one group that does."

"Spartans, Cretans, and Romen Legionaries," Jace listed. "You asked and I answered. Now, I'm getting breakfast before we begin today's drills. Join me?"

***

To Jace's amazement, under direction from their officer, the spearmen began marching together. Before and after drills, and when a ship arrived in the harbor, the sailors witnessed five spearmen marching in a line to greet the vessel. Dicëarch had embraced the rules and applied the glue. Shortly after requiring discipline from each spearman, the drills became more intense and the movements sharper.

"Your spearmen are as good a unit as I've seen since leaving Iberia," Jace complimented the Lieutenant. "I pity the pirate ship that beaches here."

"I don't. I crave the opportunity," Dicëarch admitted. "When Admiral Cleonaeus brought us here, he made a promise. If we grew our skills and protected the harbor, he'd transfer us to a marching army. A place where we can win honors and get rich. That's certainly not here."

Jace scanned the small harbor village, the bare rocks at the highest point of the island, and the white beach at the lowest. He had to agree with the Lieutenant, nobody on Folegandros was getting rich.

"Then again," Jace remarked to Dicëarch before walking away, "no one on the island is getting shredded in an assault line."

The Lieutenant failed to respond. He either didn't hear or he didn't care.

***

Three days after their talk, an Egyptian warship backed to the beach. The crew was greeted by ten spearmen marching in a tight formation.

Dicearch puffed up his chest and announced, "My spearmen look disciplined."

"And dangerous," Jace added. "Look at the reaction from the Egyptian Marines."

On the deck of the warship, lines of shields and spears appeared on the aft deck.

"We should get down there before we cause a small war with an ally," Jace recommended.

"If we must," Dicearch scoffed.

***

Jace and Dicearch marched to the beach. A moment after they arrived, fifteen Egyptian Marines rushed down a ramp and formed three ranks on either side of the walkway. Following them, came a man sporting a prodigious beard and wearing brightly colored robes.

"Welcome to Karavostasis, sir. I'm Lieutenant Dicearch. Is your vessel in need of repairs or supplies?"

"Nothing for *Ra's Brightness*, Lieutenant. As for myself, I am in need of shade," the Egyptian replied.

"We have an awning and can provide refreshments," Dicearch offered. Then he inquired. "Your name, sir, and the nature of your business on the island?"

"Admiral Radames of Pharaoh Ptolemy the Fourth's Royal Navy," the naval commander told him. "As for my

225

presence on your island? I'm meeting with representatives from Athens, Rhodes, and Pergamon. I take it from the empty harbor that I'm the first to arrive?"

"You are the first, Admiral. If you'll accompany me."

Diceärch guided Radames and the fifteen Marines to the patio. Before Jace moved, the ship's First Officer called from the steering deck, "Where do we construct the Admiral's pavilion? The Admiral prefers to be away from the other attendees."

"There's not much flatland for a large tent on the island," Jace replied. "And below the layer of topsoil, it's rock."

"No problem," the ship's officer assured Jace. He called across the deck of his warship. "Give me a shore party with picks."

When thirty oarsmen, each with a bucket and a digging tool, reached the sand, Jace led them to a spot above the village.

"This will give you privacy," Jace commented. "And a view of the harbor."

An Egyptian officer staked out the perimeter of the pavilion. Shortly afterwards, thirty men began chipping away rock to create a flat, level base for Radames' pavilion. Higher on the hill, the shrine of Poseidon oversaw the work.

***

Late in the afternoon, a quinquereme with Hoplites positioned on the upper deck backed to the shoreline.

"This is getting old," Diceärch whined.

He and Jace along with fifteen spearmen waited on the beach.

"You and your spearmen are building a reputation as a top unit," Jace countered. "And not just for Rhodes. You're being evaluated by the Egyptian. When Radames leaves here, he's going to Cilicia to escort a transport of mercenaries to Egypt. You could fetch a hefty price if you went mercenary."

Diceärch denounced the idea, "The Nile desert has no appeal for me."

A ramp dropped and an Athenian dignitary marched down the ramp. Behind him, twenty infantrymen marched off the five-banker and lined up behind him.

"Admiral Radames is waiting, sir," Diceärch told the Athenian.

They marched uphill to the town and Jace mentioned to the Captain, "We've a spot for your tents, sir. Above the village and away from the Egyptians."

"Good. I don't want to be any nearer to those royalists as I want to have politicians in my lap. I'll send citizens to survey the site."

"Democracy is an unnatural order of things," Jace thought before directing. "Have your engineers follow me, Captain."

***

Dawn found the separate camps performing rituals. The Egyptians prayed to Ra their Sun God in mass. Their uniformed deep chants carried down to the village and across to the Athenian camp.

Rather than group prayers, Priests from Athens beseeched the Goddess Soteria for the safety and salvation of the crew and deliverance from ills and accidents. In that camp, they listened respectfully, which kept the ceremony solemn.

"So far, no problems," Jace remarked when Diceärch came around the corner of the building.

"Except that," the Lieutenant commented. He held up a hand and spread his fingers. In a loose manner, he pointed to the chanting worshipers, those listening to their cleric, and several fisherman at the shrine of Poseidon. "Those are always a problem."

Hoping to cheer the officer, Jace offered, "Maybe Admiral Cleonaeus will arrive today. He might have a new position for a Lieutenant who can command a garrison that knows how to handle representatives from different countries."

"A palace guard is almost as bad as a temple guard," Diceärch declared. "Come on, let's get away from this *paranomia*. I'll buy you breakfast."

Standing, Jace waved for Diceärch to lead the way. As they walked, the Archer pondered the observation.

"Calling the morning rituals *paranomia*, meant the prayers were a form of self-delusion," Jace puzzled out. Then he concluded. "The description seems a little extreme even to me, a mercenary from Crete."

"It's a truth," Diceärch said defending his use of the word.

***

The trihemiolia shot into the harbor. With all oars splashing, the warship from Rhodes appeared to temp the fates and challenge the dimensions of the harbor. Yet, just a few ship lengths from shore, oars on the starboard side held water while the port side rowers muscled out powerful strokes. The vessel pivoted, then backed to shore until the keel gently nudged the shoreline.

A large man appeared between the rear oarsmen. He scanned the harbor as if inspecting the facility.

If not for the lookout tower, the island garrison would have been caught off guard by the rapid arrival. But the early alert allowed Diceärch to get fifteen spearmen, marching in perfect unison, to the beach.

"That's Admiral Cleonaeus," Diceärch informed Jace.

"Our benefactor," Jace responded.

"Benefactor infers benefits," Diceärch sighed.

The big Rhodian marched down the ramp and accepted Diceärch's salute.

"I see you've added to the sea wall," Cleonaeus said. "That makes sense. And I like the watch tower. But why the rail fencing on the beach?"

"It's to channel the enemy into our spears, Admiral."

Cleonaeus circled Diceärch and walked down the row of spearmen.

"I'm impressed with your garrison, Lieutenant Diceärch," the Admiral announced.

"Sir, I'd like to present Archer Kasia from Crete," Diceärch offered. "And I'd like to talk with you about my next assignment."

"See my secretary for your pay, Cretan," Cleonaeus instructed. Then the Admiral focused on Diceärch. "When I found you, Lieutenant, you were a Marine rower on a patched together, barely serviceable trireme. At present, by all appearances, you're an excellent garrison commander.

Why would I ever move you from here? And now I have to go wrestle with an Egyptian and an Athenian before the Pergamon arrives and wrecks the conference."

The Admiral and five Rhodian Marines hiked off the beach.

"I'm sorry, Lieutenant," Jace proposed. "Maybe he'll see things differently in the future."

"There's nothing for me here," Diceärch growled. "I've got to get off this rock and earn my fortune."

Jace recognized the desperation in his voice but thought nothing of the mention of a fortune. When a man owned land and lost it, he'd spend the rest of his life trying to replace the property. Why should Diceärch be any different?

"You go check on your guests," Jace encouraged. "I'll show the Rhodians to the drill field. They can pitch their tents there. That'll leave the other side of the village for the Pergamons, if they ever get here."

"Thank you, Jace," Diceärch said, calling the Archer by his first name for the first time.

***

Jace directed the crew from the Rhodian warship to their camping spot. Once they were busy setting up, he looked around for Diceärch. But the Lieutenant had vanished.

"Probably in the conference," Jace decided. Feeling hungry, he headed for the village, muttering. "Someone has to be cooking."

He'd taken ten steps towards the town when the spearmen in the watch tower shouted, "Ships coming in. Two. One a liburna. The other a five-banker. Duty squads to the beach."

Spearmen poured for the doorways of the house the garrison occupied. In a rehearsed manner, they fell into proper rows. Sergeant Sarpedon arrived, still strapping on his armor. Then, Lieutenant Diceärch walked out, accompanied by Corporal Ambrus and his three squad leaders. Two joined the ranks while the other took his squad to the sea wall.

"They don't need me anymore," Jace admitted. "I'll collect my pay and head home to the farm."

Then he remembered, he couldn't go home.

**

After a lazy turn, the quinquereme came about and backstroked to the beach. Slower and undermanned, the liburna rowed directly to the beach. By then, a ramp dropped from the five-banker and a man descended.

"I'm Tadhg, where's Cleonaeus?" he demanded. The Pergamon commander wore battle armor with fresh blood on the plates.

"Sir, he's in the Egyptian pavilion," Diceärch pointed up the hill before inquiring. "What about the two-banker, sir."

The Pergamon snapped his head around as if he'd forgotten about the liburna. "Pirates were accosting a merchant ship. We dissuaded them by killing their Spartan Captain and most of the crew. Those able to hold an oar we put to work. The rest, we fed to the sharks."

"I'll secure the ships, sir," an officer on the warship notified the commander.

"You do that, first officer," Tadhg replied. He strutted up the hill without a single Marine bodyguard.

**

A ramp dropped from the liburna and Pergamon seamen walked off the vessel. Realizing more rowers were on board, Jace and Diceärch went up to investigate.

The two-banker extended one hundred and nine feet in length and stretched sixteen feet wide with double rows of oars on each side. And every foot of the ship displayed blood stains as well as scatterings of body parts. If the sight wasn't enough to show the ship had recently seen battle, the twelve cut and bleeding men still at their rowing stations, solidified the tale.

From the bottom of the ramp, a voice demanded, "How many of the scum are alive?"

"We had twelve on the oars, for all the good they did us," a rower reported.

An instant later, the first officer from the Pergamon warship appeared on the ramp.

"What do you two want?" he sneered.

Diceärch rested a hand on his sword and took a step towards the Pergamon. A hand restrained the Lieutenant.

"These men are injured," Jace pointed out.

"So what? They fought and the better ones died," the first officer stated.

"We're taking them off this vessel," Diceärch announced. "You can have them back, once the garrison has nursed and treated them."

"We weren't told Karavostasis harbor was being guarded by scroll-reading clerics of the healing Goddess, Aceso," the first officer smirked.

Figuring Diceärch would attack the man for the insinuation, Jace stepped in front of the Lieutenant. But, this time, Diceärch's hand restrained Jace.

"A little vinegar, some stitching, food, wine, and rest, and they'll be ready to pull your oar," Diceärch said with a wink.

"Fine take them, for now," the first officer asserted. "Come to think of it, while your being good little priests, why don't you scrub the liburna clean for me?"

Jace braced for the clash between the Lieutenant and the first officer.

It never came, but Diceärch did say, "Of course we will."

In the rush to get the wounded pirates off the ship, Jace didn't have a chance to question Diceärch. Even when the injured were in the barracks house and being sewn up, Jace was too busy suturing wounds to ask. Only when the twelve were bandaged and sleeping did Jace track down Diceärch. Outside, the Greek officer leaned against the house.

"I have to ask Lieutenant, why didn't you put the Pergamon on his butt?" Jace inquired. "The spearmen aren't even my men, and I don't mind being called a cleric. But I was sorely tempted to knock the teeth out of his arrogant mouth."

"It's this way, Jace," Diceärch informed the Archer, "we aren't a pack of wolves."

"I don't understand," Jace confessed.

"There was no need, Archer Kasia, for a demonstration of noise and fury," Diceärch told him before hiking to the harbor.

Jace remained in the afternoon sun, pondering the meaning of the Lieutenant's words.

Chapter 21 – Two Altars

Jace accepted his payoff from Cleonaeus' secretary and a warning about how much the Admiral hated mercenaries. After the coins, an order came to get off the island as soon as possible. Plus, instructions to relinquish any responsibility for the spearmen and their Lieutenant. The island community, however, consisted of a small number of permanent craftsmen, the families of fishermen, and four warships of rowers, Marines, and sailors. The geography made it difficult to avoid mixing in the affairs of the garrison.

By the second day of the conference, Jace wandered the beach, watching the ship's carpenters replace broken boards and benches. As he walked by, he noticed crewmen soaking cotton and hemp fibers in pine tar. Then, with the sloppy sealant on the edge of a wide chisel, they hammered the caulking between the planks of the hulls. When he reached the liburna, he discovered spearmen from the garrison doing the work.

One of them told the tale, "Lieutenant Diceärch explained that his spearmen needed to practice sealing hulls. The idea delighted the Pergamon first officer. As a result, the ship's officer allowed us to caulk and waterproof the liburna. After washing and cleaning the interior of the ship, of course. What the Pergamon didn't like was the Lieutenant's refusal to allow him to check on the wounded pirates."

"But he's probably not worried," another spearmen suggested. "We imagine before they leave the island, he'll pick the healthiest pirates for the rowing crew on the two-banker prize."

"And leave the weakest here for us to deal with," the first spearman whined.

***

All five ships received the carpentry, the caulking, and sail repairs. At the end of day two, the ships were seaworthy and ready for their Admirals. And while the shelves in the shops of the harbor village were empty, the merchants and craftsmen were richer from Pergamon, Athenian, Rhodian, and Egyption coins.

"You've certainly embraced the roll of a hosting commander," Jace complimented the Lieutenant when he met him in the village. "Where are you going now?"

"To see the Egyptians," Dicëarch replied. "The village is sending wine and beer to each compound as a thank you. I want to judge if they prefer beer or wine. Then I'll check with the Athenians."

"That's your second circuit of the compounds today. I'm impressed with your dedication," Jace said. "How are your patients?"

An odd expression flashed across Dicëarch's face, and he started to say something. But he changed it to, "they're still weak and hurting."

"That's understandable."

***

Agreements were reached and plans for mutual defense against Macedonia, and the Seleucid Empire were signed. To mark the treaties, the Admirals declared a celebration for those who took part in the negotiations. As it happened, the festivities coincided with the distribution of the beer and wine from the merchants on the island.

To avoid bad arrow flights from shaking hands due to inebriation, Cretan Archers limited their intake of alcohol. As a result, Jace carried a mug of vinegar water as he strolled through the village. Seeing a few spearmen wheeling a barrel of wine, he intercepted them.

"Are you heading to the Pergamon compound or is all that wine going to the Rhodians?" he inquired.

"Neither, Archer," one told him. "Sergeant Sarpedon said men on duty tonight shouldn't miss the party. This barrel is for the harbor crews."

"Not that it's any of my business, any longer," Jace teased. "But go easy on the juice of the grape, if you have duty this evening."

"Lieutenant Diceärch ordered us to refrain from drinking," a spearman told Jace. "He said we'll celebrate later."

"Very wise of him," Jace acknowledged.

While the Archer continued his stroll through the village, the spearmen wheeled the giant cask towards the harbor.

**

Until late in the evening, the sounds of revelry sprang from the compounds. Voices screamed into the night as each attempted to outdo the other. Fueled by wine and beer, and a healthy dose of pride, the Pergamon, Athenian, Rhodian, and Egyption oarsmen, Marines and sailors attempted to out yell each other. Eventually, drink and exhaustion took its toll and silence fell over the island.

Jace went to his storage room, barred the door, undressed, and dropped onto his bed. In the morning, he'd need to pick a destination and pay for passage on one of the warships. He discounted the Island of Rhodes based on Cleonaeus' feelings about Cretan Archers. After being in Rome, he felt no calling to see the city of Athens. And from reports by other Archers, the Egyptian sun baked men, and hot winds blew sands into the food and the gear. Which left Pergamon as his first choice. He'd need to see the first officer of the warship in the morning.

***

It felt as if he'd just closed his eyes when cries of "fire, fire," came through the old door. The alert snapped Jace awake.

After slipping on a tunic and sandals, he sprinted to the exit. Throwing the beam off the brackets, the Archer shoved the door. It didn't move. Next, he slammed a shoulder into the boards. The structure rattled but held. Then he became aware of smoke in the air.

Taking advantage of the ill-fitting door, he battered the bottom of it with the locking beam. The boards splintered, providing a gap. As Jace wormed his way through, he dislodged a pair of logs that were braced against the door.

High on the hill, the shrine of Poseidon lit up as it burned. Being too far away for the aroma to reach him, Jace spun and looked up. Hot licks of flames crawled across the roof over his room and the building behind it.

"Someone didn't want me to leave the island alive," he grumbled before racing back into the smoke-filled room.

Grabbing his hunting bow, the war bow, and two quivers of arrows, Jace carried them outside. Two more times, he ventured into the burning building. It took that many trips to retrieve the war hatchet, his Legion armor, helmet, gladius, work clothing, a pair of hobnailed boots, and finally, three empty leather bags. When configured in a long pack with a couple of bundles, he could easily move the gear. Loose, the items required four trips into the acid stench.

In the flickering light from the blaze, the Archer examined his belongings. The pile reflected the fire light, and his transient life as a mercenary. Someday, he would change his situation. But at this moment, the only thing for sure was he wouldn't be staying on the island. Sounds of people battling the fire came from around the building. Jace ignored them and began packing his gear.

Whoosh - the butt end of a spear swished through the air. Using years of training and an Archer's reflex, Jace threw himself to the side. Even as he rolled away, the shaft cracked the side of his head.

"Here's one," a Pergamon Marine bellowed.

Running feet announced the arrival of more Marines.

"What do we do with him?" one inquired.

"Admiral Tadhg wants any of the garrison we can find," another said. "I guess we carry him there."

Two Marines grabbed the stunned Archer by his arms and hauled him towards the Pergamon compound. Jace's belongings remained behind in an unguarded pile.

***

Beyond the light of two burning buildings, the compound depended on torches for illumination.

"Stand him up," Tadhg directed. "Get to your feet, Cretan."

Between the Marines holding his arms and despite his unsteady legs, Jace managed to remain erect.

"You owe me for a prize vessel," Tadhg declared. He balanced Jace's coin pouch on the palm of his hand. "Your pirate comrades set fire to the town and got away with my liburna. But you didn't."

"Sir, I don't know what you're talking about," Jace stammered.

"Cleonaeus said he hired you to train the spearmen and Lieutenant Diceärch," the Pergamon commander alleged. "And you did. But you neglected to teach them loyalty. But that's no longer your problem. Soon, you'll see your last sunrise. I intend to hang you by the neck from dawn to death."

"Sir. There was no discussion of theft," Jace pleaded, "nor piracy, nor arson."

Tadhg bent forward and Jace smelled the sour wine on the man's breath.

"But there was murder," the Pergamon whispered. "Foul and inhuman murder."

"Admiral, I haven't the foggiest notion of what you're talking about," Jace told him. "Please, let me explain my job."

"No, let me explain," the first officer of the Pergamon warship threatened. He stepped forward to stand shoulder to shoulder with Admiral Tadhg. "Twelve men, injured and helpless, are at this very instant burning alive along with the barracks house. Is that what your job was? To teach the garrison to be merciless."

"I think the Priest of Zeus had that covered before I got here," Jace uttered.

Mistaking the mention of the God as a plea for his life, Tadhg sneered, "Praying to Zeus won't do you any good."

Jace shook the Marines off his arms, shifted his feet, and stood straighter.

"Have you found two new altars?" he asked.

Grasping for a distraction, Jace hoped the question would cause confusion and delay the execution. It was the only thing that came to mind.

"What are you talking about?" Tadhg questioned.

The confusion part seemed to work. But would it stay the hanging?

***

From outside the circle of light, spears and shields rattled as a group of men moved in the night.

"Admiral Tadhg, permission to enter your compound," a voice called from the dark.

"Come into the light, Egyptian," the Pergamon allowed. Then he asked. "Have you found any of the garrison?"

The Egyptian Admiral marched into the light. His bodyguards formed a line behind him, but they maintained a distance from the Pergamon Marines.

"None have been seen since last night's festivities," Radames answered. "But we do have two curious issues."

"Will I have one, right here," Tadhg bragged about the capture of a member of the garrison. "And in a nod to irony, at daybreak I'm going to hang him for the murder of the twelve pirates who survived my attack."

"That is one of the issues," Radames disclosed. "The building collapsed, but we can't find any bodies. It appears the building was empty."

"Then where are the twelve pirates?" Tadhg inquired.

"We don't know," the Egyptian admitted.

Mumbling low, Jace offered, "Rule number two."

"What's that, Kasia?" Tadhg challenged.

"Rule number two, sir. Treat the wounded quickly. It builds loyalty and trust in your command," Jace told the Admirals. "Based on that, I don't think you'll find any of Lieutenant Diceärch's spearmen or the pirates on this island."

"Perhaps not. But in the morning, we'll row out and capture the lot of them," Tadhg promised.

"I don't believe you will, sir," Jace claimed. "Rule number six. Plan your retreat before you begin losing. Diceärch will know where he's heading. And be aware of your pursuit. He didn't burn your warships, did he?"

"That would have raised an alarm and awakened the compounds," Radames pointed out.

"But trying to kill me by burning my quarters," Jace proposed, "setting fire to the barracks, and turning Poseidon's shrine to ash, didn't alert everyone?"

The two Admirals remained silent as they considered the reality of Diceärch and his crew escaping with the liburna. And the mystery of the Lieutenant's scheme.

"You said two issues," Tadhg remarked.

241

"Yes," Radames responded. "We found two new altars near the sea wall. But none of the Priests can figure out who they're dedicated to."

Radames and Tadhg returned to their baffled silence.

"I do," Jace announced.

"Let's go see if you really do," Admiral Tadhg proposed.

***

In a strange twist of fate, Jace went from being a condemned man, to being the vanguard for Admirals Radames and Tadhg and their bodyguards. On the way to the harbor, the Admiral from Athens and his guards joined them. And finally, Cleonaeus and his Rhodian soldiers merged into the march. In the weak light of dawn, the procession appeared to be a top-heavy combat patrol rather than a committee intent on investigating an oddity.

The altars were rustic and hastily built. Using stone from the sea wall, Diceärch had created four columns. Between two, he placed the blades of broken oars to create two unique altars. Ceremonial candles on the flat of the wood had long since burned out.

"None of the priests can tell who they were built to honor," Radames admitted.

Four clerics stood around the shrines. With their arms crossed and faces set in serious expressions, the priests tried to give the impression of scholars deciphering a spiritual mystery.

Jace circled the unknown altars nodding and murmuring to himself. Finally, he lifted his arms towards the rising sun as if he'd uncovered the significance of the altars.

"Admiral Tadhg. Can I assume my impending death has been put off indefinitely?" Jace inquired while holding the pose.

"It has, Archer," the Pergamon answered. "But I'm keeping the coins to offset my loss of the two-banker."

The theft of his coins to make up for Dicearch's theft of the ship hurt. Not just Jace's purse, but his honor. A Cretan Archer swore to earn a profit every day. He'd done weeks of work at the harbor for nothing and that went against his code. But what could he do? Archer Kasia had no friends or allies on the island. Or did he?

***

"God Ra. Speak to me," Jace prayed to the Egyptian Sun God.

"The Cretan Archer wisely implores Ra for an answer," Admiral Radames proclaimed. "All praise Ra."

The Egyptians in the crowd raised their arms to the sun and called out, "Praise Ra." None prayed louder than Jace Kasia.

"For good or evil, reveal to me, great God Ra, the true meaning of these altars," Jace submitted.

Jace's arms began to quiver. Soon tremors raced up and down his body. They increased in ferocity until the Archer's legs failed. His knees bent, and he fell on his face in front of one altar. Twisting his head, Jace's eyes peered up at the underside of the broken oar.

"No," he screamed while backing away on his hands and knees. "No. God Ra, protect me."

Four Egyptian Marines rushed forward, creating a protective barrier around the Archer. Jace Kasia was no longer without allies on the island and for that he bowed his head in gratitude.

***

One of the Priest got down on his knees and studied the underside of the altar. His face went pale. An arm came up and he shoved over one of the columns. The altar collapsed.

"Burn it," he screamed. "Burn them both. Face down so as not to offend the Gods."

Admiral Tadhg swaggered over to the ruined altar and snatched the oar blade from the rubble.

Carved into the wood was one word.

"*Asebeia*," he read. "What Godless soul would build an alter honoring sacrilege and blasphemy?"

Admiral Cleonaeus kicked the other board free, picked it up, and read the back.

"*Paranomia*," he announced. "Who would build an altar to self-delusion?"

Another of the priests answered, "A man who plans to destroy temples and murder the celebrants of the Gods."

"Ra, save us," Jace exclaimed.

The Egyptians echoed his prayer, "Ra, save us."

***

Once released by Admiral Tadgh, Jace hiked to his quarters where he left his gear. Not only was the building burned down, but his belongings were gone. With over twelve hundred oarsmen, Marines, and sailors on the island, it wouldn't have taken long for the gear to vanish.

Jace patted the skinning knife on his hip, the empty coin purse on the other side, and gave a nod towards the sun.

Admiral Radames' First Officer had mentioned his Pharaoh was hiring mercenaries. Hopefully, his newfound friends, the Egyptians, would give him a ride to Cilicia where the blades for hire were gathering.

"It would be nice," Jace complained as he strolled down the hill, "if I had a sword or a bow to sell."

(Intentionally left blank)

Act 8

Chapter 22 – Archer for Hire

In dimensions and numbers of rowers, the Egyptian warship fell somewhere between a quinquereme and trihemiolia. But its battering ram sat at sea level rather than below the water line. With less resistance, the ship was faster. Adding to the speed of *Ra's Brightness*, the upper deck of the Egyptian warship sat higher over the waves. The deep hull allowed for more of its two hundred and fifty oarsmen to be located in the engine and the stroke sections.

"At this height," Jace remarked, "you can put arrows into the top deck of most ships-of-war."

"Javelins," the first officer said. "We haven't used arrows for a year now. Ever since the Pharaoh pulled our archers and sent them to the army."

Jace Kasia and First Officer Midhat stood on the fore deck discussing how Jace would pay for his passage to Cilicia.

"Combat archery requires volume over accuracy," Jace explained. "If we had bows, I could teach your Marines to clear an enemy's deck. Afterall, arrows are cheaper than javelins."

"We don't have either," Midhat snapped. "You'll need to come up with something else besides an easy instructor's position to pay for the ride."

The ship's carpenter came up from the rowers walk and acknowledged the officer and the passenger with a nod.

"I heard the conversation from below, sir," the carpenter informed Midhat. "We have bows and reed arrows. Except the bows were left behind because they're broken. And the arrows because the archers had too many. I've been meaning to ask if I could use them for firewood. We need the storage space."

"Appoint me assistant carpenter," Jace suggested. "I can help with repairs. And when we beach for the night, I'll work on repairing the bows."

"Do you need help, Bassem?" Midhat asked the carpenter.

"First Officer, it's a wooden ship," Bassem pointed out, "and with every stroke of the oars, we're trying to pull it apart at the joints."

"For now Kasia, you'll work as a helper for your passage. If the Bassem will have you," Midhat directed. "I'll tell Admiral Radames we might have found a position for you."

Midhat strutted towards the aft while the carpenter eyed Jace.

"Have you worked with wood?" he questioned. "Do you know anything about tools?"

"I'm a bower. That limits my experience to connections this big," Jace replied. He held his thumb and fore finger parallel to each other. "About the size of a limb on the riser of a bow. Speaking of bows, I'd like to see the weapons."

"Later. Right now, you'll have to scale up," Bassem warned Jace. "We've a forward frame timber loose at the keelson. We need to figure out how badly it's damaged. Forget the bows, you may be carving a new frame timber for the rest of the voyage."

They dropped off the side of the upper deck and used the bracing for the rowers benches to reach the walkway.

"Yo carpenter," an oarsmen called out. "We all added to your fishing pond."

The inexperienced or the weakest rowers on the ship clustered around their section leader. Never far from their oars, the Bow relaxed while the sail did the work. At mid ship, the muscular Engine section gathered as did the experienced oarsmen of the Stroke in the aft of the warship.

"Someday Bow, you'll grow up to be real oarsmen," Bassem sneered. "Maybe even become a Stroke. As for now, be grateful I bother coming into the children's section at all."

Insults followed Jace and the carpenter as they shimmied into the gap between a bench and the walkway. Under the rowers walk, the carpenter located a long hemp cable. He slapped it several times to check the tension. The tightly twisted strands of the cable didn't move or shake under the assault.

"You warrior types never realize what it takes to keep a warship afloat," Bassem commented. "This is the hypozomata. The cable keeps tension on the raised fore and aft keels."

"One could say it's as tight as a strung bow," Jace ventured. "Except a bowstring keeps the bow curved. But the ship's not bent."

"Without the hypozomata, the tall ends of the keel would lean outward in rough weather. Hit us with a stiff wind and a broadside from a big wave and the frame would separate. But even in good weather, the weight of the fore and aft sections, without the tension cable, would dip and bend the center of the keel upwards. There's your curve. And once a warship is hogged, it never rowers properly again. That's why six times a day, I check the hypozomata and keep two spares."

Going lower into the ship, the carpenter stepped onto a beam. Jace followed. Below the top lumber was the massive beam of the keel. Where the keel provided a stiff backbone for the warship, on top of it, the keelson connected with the frame timbers to create an internal shape for the hull boards.

The ship rolled and water rolled up the keel, climbed the keelson, and washed over their feet.

Deep water in the bottom of the hull presented a problem. It shouldn't be there. At least not in enough volume that a wave sloshed over the keelson. Water collected in most of the bilge area, but only in one section did it become, as the oarsmen called it, a fishing pond.

The carpenter bent over and shoved his hands into the water. Then the ship rolled to the side, the water shifted, and splashed his thighs. Bassem's knees flexed and rode out the mini wave. Jace, unaccustomed to life on a ship, fell into the pond.

"Excellent, you're already wet," the carpenter observed. "Feel the connection and tell me if the tip of the frame timber has snapped off or has simply moved out of alignment."

Positioning his feet on either side of the timber, Jace reached into the water and gripped the frame timber where it joined with the keelson. Although tight, the archer managed to wiggle the connection. After struggling for a moment, he lifted a broken dowel out of the water.

"The connection is solid," Jace announced. He displayed the broken peg. "But without the pin, I'm afraid the frame timber will slip off the beam."

Bassem pointed to other frame timbers where they appeared to butt against the beam.

"Jace, they aren't rammed against the top beam," he described. "We Egyptians invented a proper joining system. The end of each frame timber is squared off. And a matching square hole, called a mortise, is chiseled into the side of the keelson. Fitted together, they make the strongest connection of wood possible. But to keep them stable in rough weather, we pound a dowel through the mortise and tenon joint."

From an apron, the carpenter handed Jace a tapered peg and a hammer.

"Pound this in and leave the extra length exposed."

Between sloshing waves, Jace hammered the peg into the hole. Once done he handed Bassem the hammer and asked, "Can I see the broken bows now?"

"You can see them. But first, you need to bail the pond water out of the bilge. I'll have sailors begin lowering buckets to you."

***

That evening, after caulking the hull boards over the repaired timber, Jace dug a round hole in the sand, lined it with smooth rocks, and built a blazing fire in it.

Admiral Radames approached the small pit and noted, "that's a bad cookfire. The heat is too concentrated, and the narrow opening won't allow the warmth to spread to your bedroll."

251

Jace held up an Egyptian war bow. A splintered upper limb dangled from the weapon. Keeping the piece from falling off were strands of tendon and several coats of hide glue.

"Sir, I don't have a bedroll," Jace reminded the Admiral. "As for the fire pit, I need hot water in the center and warm water around the edges. Hot water is how I'll melt the hide glue and disassemble the bows. But I don't want to soak the wood. I'll use a variety of heat in the process."

Jace placed the broken bow on a pile of other useless bows, picked up a borrowed copper tray and placed it over the fire. The heat from the round pit only hit the center of the tray. Next, he filled it with water.

"And that's all it takes to fix a broken bow?"

"I'll remove the damaged and the undamaged limbs. The strongest ones will be scoured, shaved, and fitted to a different riser," Jace described. "And once I add tendons, bones, and brush on coats of glue, the bows will be ready for service."

"How many weapons can you salvage from the defective bows?" Radames questioned. "And is it worth the effort?"

The phrase defective bows revealed the history of the unusable weapons. Jace picked up two with broken limbs from the pile. Moments after examining the similar damages, he asked, "Admiral, did your Marines try to learn the bow without instructions?"

"We deal with more pirates around islands and coves than we do enemy ships-of-war on the open sea," Radames answered. "After the army took my archers, I thought to replace them with Marines. But when my infantrymen practiced, the wood on the bows splintered. It's apparent the archers left them behind because there are defects in the construction."

"Admiral, give me three bronze coins," Jace directed.

"I don't know why I'm doing this," Radames admitted. He reached into a purse and lifted out three coins. "Here. Why did I hand you the bronze?"

"Sir, you've just hired a bower, a bow trainer, and a Cretan Archer to teach archery to six of your Marines," Jace informed him.

"You think you can repair six bows from that pile?"

"No sir. I can create seven bows from the pile," Jace told him. "The seventh is for me, plus three bronze coins a day. Do you agree to the terms?"

The Admiral blinked in confusion for a moment, then a smile crossed his face.

"I see now why Cleonaeus hired you to train the garrison at Karavostasis," Radames commented. "And how you were able to teach an insane Lieutenant the ways of war."

Technically, Admiral Cleonaeus didn't hire Jace. Archer Kasia was given the contract by Acis Gergely. But Jace didn't feel the Egyptian officer needed so many details.

"In the end, Dicearch proved to be madder than I figured," Jace confessed. "If you ever want to go after him, hire me as a guide."

"Because you're a talented Cretan mercenary?"

"No, sir. Because while I taught Dicearch everything he knows," Jace responded. He held a broken bow over the tray and let the steam melt the hide glue. "I didn't teach him everything I know."

"I'll send over six Marines to help you."

Radames hiked across the sand to the cookfire where his ship's officers were camped. Behind him, Jace twisted the broken limb, stretching the soft, warm, and damp glue. A moment later, the splintered limb came loose from the riser.

"Today, Master Mikolas, I earned a profit and secured a new contract," Jace mentioned to the ghost of his mentor. He selected two limbs and a riser from the pile and chanted. "May this war bow keep me safe, fed, and employed."

***

Under the sun of a new day, Jace stood while his six students sat on the deck.

"Tension is stored in the limbs of your bow when you draw the bowstring," Jace lectured the potential archers. "When you release the string, the tension gets transferred to the arrow. If, however, you release the bowstring without an arrow on the string, the tension goes back into the bow. And we get broken limbs and splintered risers."

"But the arrows are light compared to the limbs of a bow," a student pointed out. "How much difference can it make?"

Jace picked up a bow with a cracked riser.

"Let's see what difference an arrow makes. Stand up. I'll launch a shaft then you pull back and release the bowstring without an arrow."

Using a deep draw, Jace pulled the bowstring to his cheek and released the string. The arrow arched into the sky and the bow shook.

Before the arrow hit the water, Jace handed the student the damaged bow, "Your turn."

Hauling back on the bowstring, the Marine also pulled the string to his cheek. He grinned because the bow held under the tension.

"From the riser, down your arm, through your shoulders and back to your elbow should be a straight line," Jace coached while shoving the student into the proper position. "Always use the correct pose. But never release a bowstring without a notched arrow. Release."

Jace stepped away as the bowstring snapped forward. At first, the entire bow trembled in the student's hand. But less than a half a heartbeat after the release, the bow snapped. As if thrown, the limbs separated from the riser and spun over the shoulders of the Marine. The flying objects just missed the sides of his head and the men sitting behind him. During the dismemberment, the riser split, and a splinter gouged the Marine's hand. But he didn't notice the puncture wound. His worry concerned the slash under his eye from the whipping action of the bowstring.

"On Crete, we have several one-eyed archers," Jace explained. "All earned by students who questioned the weight of an arrow."

"I'll never pull and release a string without a notched arrow in place," the Marine promised while dabbing at the blood on his cheek.

"You mean we broke all these bows," another student remarked, "by releasing the bowstrings without arrows."

"Take parts and scrape off the excess glue and tendon," Jace told them. "I'll be around to look at the fit of the limbs to your risers."

Overhead, the sail snapped in the wind. With the memory of the shattering bow fresh in their minds, the student archers jerked. Their reaction let Jace know the lesson had been delivered and wouldn't be forgotten.

***

After five days of patrolling among the islands moving ever eastward, *Ra's Brightness* beached in a cove at Levitha. While sailors hiked to the freshwater spring, Jace guided his students up a side trail and away from the crew. Dressed in tunics and sandals, they resembled sailors from a transport. Except for Jace in his one aging garment, who resembled a beggar. Plus, each student carried a leather case and a bag of arrows.

"We won't string our bows until we've gently flexed and warmed the wood," Jace instructed. "And keep your arrows bound until you're ready to use them. Bundled together helps keep the shafts straight."

"Why are we leaving the ship?" a Marine inquired.

"Do you really want the oarsmen betting against you while you learn the bow?" Jace asked. "If so, let's go back."

"No, Archer Kasia, let's not go back," one advised. "We don't need an audience."

"That's what I thought."

The trail grew steeper before the land finely leveled. Jace halted the march, crossed the flat to the next rise. There he hung seven old, leaky wineskins against the hill. He'd just returned to the Marines when a voice called from the top of the hill.

"You can leave your coins and those bundles and return to your boat," a man recommended. "Or, merchants, you can stay, fight, and die."

Five spearmen appeared on the hill next to the speaker. From the slope beside the archery students, five more spearmen came into view. They had water skins hanging from their necks.

The six Egyptian Marines, given their spears and shields, were more than a match for the eleven pirates. But their heavy weapons were on the warship.

Noticing fear in the eyes of his students, Jace squatted and hovered over his bow case and the arrows.

"Three of you face the hill and block their view," Jace instructed. "You other three face the slope."

"Including their leader," a student warned, "I count eleven of them."

As he withdrew the war bow from the case, and began gently flexing the weapon, Jace talked to take their minds off the spears.

"You're standing on a famous island. Did you know that? In the distant past, King Minos ruled my Island of Crete. When Daedalus, the creator of the labyrinth, helped the King of Athens escape, Minos arrested the inventor and his son, Icarus. But Daedalus was a clever man. Using feathers, threads from blankets, and beeswax he constructed wings for him and his son. But he cautioned the boy not to fly too low, or the saltwater would foul the wings. And not to fly too high, or the sun would melt the beeswax. Icarus became over excited with flying and soared higher and higher. As

257

Daedalus feared, the sun melted his son's wings and the boy fell into the sea and died."

"I don't see anything except a committee meeting, merchants," the leader of the thieves announced. "I guess we'll just kill you and take what's ours."

He laughed and raised his arms to signal his men.

Zip-Thwack!

Both of the leaders' feet kicked out, together. Assisted by an arrow punching him in the forehead, he was thrown back. His feet came off the ground as his body stretched out. He hovered for a moment, before slamming into the ground.

Zip-Thwack!

The spearmen to the leader's right dropped his spear and grabbed the arrow shaft jutting from the meaty part of his thigh. He might have overcome the pain and recovered. But he never got the chance.

Zip-Thwack!

A shaft appeared in his other thigh. Spasms took his legs, and he collapsed while screaming in pain. The second and third spearmen paused to look at their wounded friend.

Zip-Thwack!

A shaft pierced the side of the second spearmen's mouth. Momentarily, teeth and gum tissue dangled from the arrowhead. But staggering steps shook the materials off, and they fell to the ground, along with the pirate.

Zip-Thwack!

The third spearmen thought about shouting an alarm. But the steel arrowhead on the end of the reed shaft drilled through his windpipe. Gagging, he dropped to his knees and clutched his throat.

Zip-Thwack!

The fourth spearman turned to the fifth to ask if they should retreat. Rather than voice the question, an arrow split his ribs, and the shaft passed through a lung before exploding his heart.

Zip-Thwack!

The fifth spearmen on the hill turned to run. The arrow separated his spine, and he dropped face first onto the crest of the hill.

"Go fetch their spears," Jace instructed. "Don't make me do all the work."

Five Marines raced uphill and returned with five spears. Seeing their victims armed, and being without a leader, the five remaining thieves ran.

"Do we go after them?" a Marine asked.

"Their boat must be on the other side of the island. We'll pay them a visit once you get your armor and shields," Jace replied. "Right now, I'm going to search the leader and get paid."

Jace started for the hill when one of his students inquired, "Archer Kasia. Why is the island of Levitha famous?"

"In their flight from Crete," Jace replied, "it's reported that Daedalus and Icarus flew over Levitha."

An Egyptian Marine scanned the sky before commenting, "that's not much fame, Archer Kasia."

"It's not much of an island," Jace observed. He hiked to the body of the leader and took a heavy coin purse and a long sica knife off the dead man.

Chapter 23 – Wallow with Pigs

Jace and two of the Egyptian Marines hunkered down behind an outcrop of rocks. On the beach below them, a liburna rested half in and half out of the water. Around the aft of the two-banker, thirty men argued. Although the sound of their voices drifted up, none of the words were intelligible. But their division into clusters and the exaggerated hand gestures revealed the nature of the discussion.

"Why haven't they rowed away?" a Marine asked.

"My first arrow removed the leader of the water detail. Looking at this, I'm convinced he was the Captain of the two-banker," Jace answered. "Without him, there's a power struggle in their ranks. I imagine the first officer of the liburna expected to become the Captain. But he's being challenged. Perhaps by a couple of section leaders."

"First Officer Midhat wouldn't like that," the other Marine offered. "If oarsmen challenged him, he'd have us throw the rebels overboard."

"That's the difference between a disciplined crew and a pirate crew," Jace told them. "In a period of crisis, you'll follow the second in command. In a rogue crew, the Captain doesn't allow his second in command to have too much authority. Remove the strong man, and the crew stands on the beach arguing instead of rowing to safety."

A scuffling on the rocks of the trail alerted them to a new arrival.

"First Officer Midhat wants to know the plan," a messenger informed Jace. He handed the Marines two short but stout Egyptian spears and passed a third one to Jace.

Jace hesitated for a moment. Somewhere during the days while he taught the Marines to repair the bows and lectured on proper archery techniques, the First Officer decided Jace Kasia was a qualified leader.

"Admiral Radames will want that ship," Jace told him. "Have the Marines come in from the sides. When we see the assault teams, we'll attack down the hill and secure the ship."

"Yes, sir," the messenger acknowledged.

While the man scrambled up the twisting trail, a Marine questioned Jace.

"We're going through the middle of them and taking the ship?" he inquired. "Just two Marines and an Archer?"

"The arguments tell us a lot about the crew," Jace commented. "Some will want to fight. Others want to escape. The fighters will stand their ground, especially when they see a small group of infantrymen on their side of the beach. And for the ones who notice three unarmored men coming down the hill, it won't panic them."

"That's what I meant," the Marine insisted. "Three men without shields against thirty."

"Our mission is to get to the ship and defend it," Jace told him. "Getting there is the least of your worries."

"What do you mean, Archer?"

"Once we're on the ship," Jace informed them, "they will all suddenly have a burning desire to escape."

"Then why are we going to the ship? We can't fight them all."

"If they get ten men on oars, they can row away," Jace advised. "We're going to prevent that."

A shout, then another, notified them the assault teams were approaching the crew.

"It's not as bad as it seems," Jace assured his two companions.

"It's not?" one asked.

"No," Jace told him, "sometimes it's worse."

Jace jumped to the top of the rocks then vaulted off the leading edge. Behind him, the Egyptian Marines mumbled, "sometimes it's worse?"

When faced with the raw truth, their logic fled, they shook their heads, and forgot their fears. Out of a sense of duty, they charged downhill, following Archer Kasia to a clash with thirty pirates.

***

Even with a little training, the clusters of men could easily repel, injure, or kill three men with spears. But only four pirates attempted to form a defensive line. And they held mismatched weapons of varying lengths. An iron spear, a curved sica knife, a war hatchet, and a heavy bronze sword completed the armaments.

Jace sprinted at the wall of iron, steel, and bronze. Being the tip of a three-man wedge, the blades came together to point at his chest. Four paces from the spear tip, the Archer glanced over his shoulder and waved.

Distracted by the movement of the running man's head and his over the shoulder hand motion, the pirate looked away. And for an instant, the pirate's spear pointed an unarmored Egyptian Marine.

When the long-handled weapon swung towards a new target, Jace Kasia shifted his spear and held it across his chest. Then he leaped forward. Using the shaft, he powered into the four defenders.

The spear shaft slammed into their ankles, and the four bandits tripped, and fell forward. Two reached their hands out for the attacker. But their fingers grasped only air. While they toppled to the ground, the man with the spear was gone.

***

"Don't wallow with pigs," Zarek Mikolas had taught. "On the ground, you have no speed, no leverage. If you find yourself down, get up fast."

To reinforce the lesson, Master Archer Micklas tripped and slapped Jace with a tree branch. For over a year, he instructed Jace to run in a circle. During the circuit, the branch came across and swatted him across the chest. Once taken off his feet, the branch beat him harder. And the longer Jace remained on the ground the harder the beating. From the front, the side, or from behind, the branch caught Jace and swept him off his feet. Then the pounding began in earnest until Jace regained his footing.

"If you wallow with pigs, you get dirty and the pigs like it," Mikolas explained between strikes with the branches. *"Being down puts you on the same level with untrained adversaries. All they need is to grab you and hold on while their partners pummel you to death."*

Running in circles, getting knocked down from every angle, caused Jace to cry and scream in frustration. But even knowing he would soon fall victim to the leafy branches again, he kept to the course. He did, until one day, the branch swished in from behind and Jace dropped to his chest. As soon as the branch passed harmlessly over his prone body, Jace jumped to his feet and began running the circle.

"What was that?" Zarek Mikolas demanded.

"I heard the wind through the branches," Jace replied. Then he challenged. "Shall we continue?"

Once he understood the lesson, Jace jumped over the branch or ducked under it. And the few times he went down, the Master Archer never touched him. Jace scrambled or tumbled away from the branch before coming quickly to his feet.

***

The Marines behind the Archer cringed when Kasia stretched out in a dive. Their objective was to gain the aft deck of the ship. If they got entangled in a melee to save the Archer, any hope of completing the mission would vanish during a losing fight. The four defenders toppled forward, and a pair of hands reached for Kasia.

"It always was a bad idea," one of the Marines called to his partner.

But the Archer didn't get caught or go down. Rather, he used his hands on the ground to summersault over the defenders.

Jace Kasia landed on both feet, balanced, and ready. And a good thing he was.

Two pirates noted the crew members down on their faces. Together, they rammed their spears at the Archer. Rolling a shoulder as he drew the sica knife, Jace dodged one iron tip. In a giant step, he got between the shafts. Using an elbow, he hooked one spear and shoved it out of his way. Then spinning, he reached out and nicked the neck of the second man. Still turning, he came face to face with the first spearman. While fighting off the spear the pirate used as a staff, Jace ran the curved blade into the man's belly.

Closer to the ship, a pair of pirates brandishing swords observed four crew members scrambling to get off the ground. Then spying two more who wouldn't be getting up, they advanced on the Archer.

Spreading his legs, Jace bobbed and weaved trying to confuse the swordsmen. But based on their coordination, the two had worked together before. Pressing their advantage, they boxed in the Archer.

Two long blades against a sica knife favored the bandits. Yet Jace Kasia wasn't without advantages of his own. While Egyptian Marines were less impressive with a bow than a new Herd at the Cretan agoge, the infantrymen were experts with their short spears. Planting their forward foot, they brought the spearheads from alongside their legs, and in a sweeping motion, they hooked Jace's attackers. Next, as if throwing slabs of beef, they flung the swordsmen away from the Archer.

Not having seen the Egyptian Marines in action, Jace was stunned by the brutal, yet accurate, stab and throw.

"Archer Kasia, remember the ship?" one suggested.

After snatching up a spear, Jace climbed to the aft deck of the liburna. The Marines scrambled up and flanked him. Being five feet above the beach, forced the pirates to stab upward against downward thrusts. Before the crew could organize any real threat to the three, the pirates turned away from the fight for the ship.

Coming in from the sides and protected by shields, armor, and helmets, the Egyptian Marines chewed through the remainder of the pirate crew. No Marine showed pity just as no pirate offered to surrender or requested mercy. The bandits died fighting down to the last man.

***

"Who were they?" Jace asked his Marines. "They certainly aren't Latians, Carthaginians, Egyptians, or Greeks. Yet they fought with the spirit of Spartans?"

One of his Marines scanned the bodies on the beach.

"That's why they argued," the Marine commented, "and didn't run."

"Why did they argue?" Jace inquired.

"Cilician pirates, Archer Kasia. They have a reputation for being nasty and staying with a fight until the end," the other Marine stated. "For a long time, men from rough Cilicia have taken to the sea as pirates. Most merchants, rather than fight, pay a ransom when approached by Cilician pirates. If you fight them, they will extract revenge."

"Not always," Jace remarked while pointing to the bodies.

He dropped the spear and went to the storage compartment under the steering platform. Bending down, Jace began rooting around and pulling out supplies. He needed gear. Soon he created a pile of new tunics, a pair of combat sandals, a war hatchet, and a set of leather chest armor.

When he lifted out a sword with silver wire wrapping the hilt, a Marine gushed, "That's a nice sword, Archer Kasia. You should keep it."

"Swords are too unwieldly. They snag on branches and can throw an Archer's aim off," Jace replied while setting the long blade to the side.

Then, Jace pulled out a wooden container and discovered an interesting document inside the chest.

***

The sun rested on the hills of Levitha as if the Gods had balanced an orange globe on the peak. From the mouth of the inlet to the south, Admiral Radames watched as a liburna sailed off the sea and into the bay. For long moments, he ignored the two-banker and maintained a vigil on the open water.

A warship in its natural habitat was formidable. And *Ra's Brightness* could handle the best of an enemy's ships-of-war while afloat. But on the beach, the oarsmen weren't infantry, and sailors made poor skirmishers. As a result of his missing Marines, the Admiral worried about being trapped on shore by a fleet of pirates.

Only when he recognized First Officer Midhat, and his Marines rowing the liburna, could he relax.

"Stand down the oarsmen and the beach team," Radames directed. "First Officer Midhat is back, and he seems to be bringing in a prize vessel."

"Yes, sir," the deck officer responded.

With no ram at the bow, the two-banker rowed right up to the shallows. Marines splashed into the water and shoved the hull onto the beach. Midhat jumped to the beach and Archer Kasia landed beside him. Together they marched to *Ra's Brightness*. Radames walked off the warship and met them at the bottom of the ramp.

"Mister Midhat, welcome back. May I inquire where you found the liburna?"

"Admiral Radames, I'd like to present a prize, an answer to a mystery, and a problem," the First Officer proposed.

"Obviously, the two-banker is the prize," Radames guessed. "But for the life of me, I can't recall a mystery and have no idea of what the problem could be."

"Kasia will explain the mystery," Midhat advised.

He handed Jace a scroll and waved the Archer forward.

"We couldn't understand why Lieutenant Diceärch deserted or where he took his garrison and the liburna," Jace reported. He unrolled the scroll and read. *"Let it be known that this warship sails under the protection of, and does the biding of, King Philip the Fifth. As such, the warship, its Captain, and crew must be granted every courtesy due to a loyal ally of Macedonia. Including ships and ports of Macedon, the Seleucid Empire, and the Aetolian League. By order of Phillip V."*

"Diceärch left the service of Rhodes, and the protection of the island's partners, to become a pirate for Philip the Fifth?" Radames questioned. "That's insanity."

"Sir. It seems that is exactly what happened," Jace assured the Admiral. "Your conclusion is correct. Both for the destination and the sanity in question. However, now that Diceärch has been freed from the restraint of a chain of command, I imagine he's going to be a problem."

"I know Kasia, if I ever go after him, I'll need your services," Radames recalled. "What is this about a problem?"

"Sir, the scroll and the two-banker belonged to Cilician pirates," Midhat answered. "Your prize can't go to Cilicia, or it'll be recognized."

"That would cause troubles with the locals," Radames stated. "It'll cut into the profits, but I'll have to hire a prize crew on Cyprus to sail it to Alexanderia. We just can't spare the sailors or oarsmen for the trip."

Jace shifted his feet uncomfortably in the sand.

"Sir, I have a request," he ventured.

"You want to be with the prize crew and go to Alexanderia," Radames said.

"Actually, three requests," Jace corrected. "Yes, I want to go to Alexanderia. But only after I train your Marines."

"What do you need, Archer?"

"For you to remain here for a few days so I can work with your archers," Jace answered. "And afterwards, for you to release me from our agreement."

Radames examined Jace's face for a moment.

"You took that serious?"

"Sir, we made a contract, and I took your money," Jace informed him. "I am a Cretan Archer and will work for you for as long as you pay me and hold me to the agreement."

"Tell you what Archer. You make my Marines proficient with bows and arrows and I'll release you from the contract and put you with the prize crew."

"Thank you, Admiral."

***

Four days later, the six Marine archers were able to put seven out of ten arrows in the old wineskins. Even their misses were close.

"The Admiral will be pleased," Midhat offered. "And I'm impressed. When you get to Alexandria, go to the city garrison, and ask for Captain Farouk Midhat."

"A relative?" Jace inquired.

"My older brother. Tell him I said, you are a man of your word."

Chapter 24 – A Lighthouse and A Village

A gentle wind pushed the captured liburna over the water. On the rear oar, the Captain of the prize crew guided the ship along the coast. An experienced skipper, Radames felt fortunate to find Arsi. And adding to the Admiral's luck, Captain Arsi had a partial crew at his disposal. After adding a few locals and Jace Kasia as rowers for the trip to Alexandria, they launched.

The afternoon slipped pleasantly by as the ship traced the shoreline. When the coast swerved to the right, Arsi nosed the two-banker to starboard.

"For those of you who've never been to Alexanderia," Arsi encouraged, "pay attention. It's a sight only sailors and a lucky few ever witness."

Then he eased the oar over, the wind snapped the sail, the ship cut left, and while the land retreated on the backside of the point, Arsi maintained the deep-water heading.

Jace Kasia climbed on his rower's bench and placed a foot on the rail. He leaned out over the side of the ship. Two and a half miles away, the land bloomed with greenery.

***

Trees, flowers, tall grasses, and leafy bushes existed in such abundance it appeared to be a mural and not a natural setting. The night before, they beached near the same type of display and spent the night listening to creatures click, chirp, and call in the dark.

"The Nile River delta," Captain Arsi explained. "Quite a difference, isn't it?"

His reference was a comparison between the delta and the five stops they made since leaving the Island of Cyprus. On those overnight periods, they camped beside the mouths of rivers. None were as green or as expansive as the Nile delta. Additionally, the farther south they sailed, the land became drier, and the rivers more shallow. Than as if a dream, the land went from arid to lush in half a day's travel.

"Can you see it over the bow?" the Captain shouted. "Look. Look carefully."

The eighteen men of the prize crew, like Jace, leaned outboard for a clearer view. Although they strained their eyes, most could only see a blue horizon. But a few gasped, Jace among them.

A sand-colored tower with a black cap jutted from the blue water.

"It's not much to look at," a farm boy remarked. "It's on a mountain island, right?"

Pushed forward by the steady breeze, the ship cut through the water. And as they drew closer, the tower became clear to all the crew members. Then in the blink of an eye, the tall tower with the black cap shrunk. Below the tower, a much broader structure, supporting the original tower, dominated the horizon.

Emerging from the sea and growing taller, the lower structure grew in height, pushing the tower higher into the sky.

"It is impressive," another of the crew remarked.

"Not yet," Arsi challenged. "Just you wait. Keep watching."

True to his word, a massive building appeared below the structure. Compared to the building and the structure on top, the tower compressed even more as it soared higher.

Transfixed by the emerging construction, Jace's nerves tingled. A Cretan Archer trained to know what was happening around him and not to be overcome by a single sight. He glanced across the ship at the farm boy and the empty blue sea beyond. Next, he looked to his left at the shoreline. While the ship sailed straight, the land pushed out into the water. From over a distance of two and a half miles when they rounded the point, it was now half that distance to dry land.

"Oh, oh," the crew members shouted with delight.

"It's magnificent, isn't it," Arsi exclaimed.

Although tempted to look, the Captain's over exuberant declaration warned Jace. He rotated to check behind him, and as he turned, the farm boy screamed, blood appeared on his back, and he fell overboard.

Throwing himself to the rower's bench, Jace dodged a knife blade. Another member of the crew cried out, followed by a splash. Kicking with his legs, the Cretan Archer caught an arm with the side of his foot. The knife flew out of the attacker's hand and Jace backflipped into the center walkway. A quick scan of the ship told the tale. Five men with knives out were running towards him.

"There are times to fight and times to run," Zarek Mikolas had coached. *"Just don't wait too long to decide which is appropriate."*

"Or time two swim," Jace added.

Grabbing his bow case, the quiver of reed arrows, and his bundle of gear, the Cretan Archer ran along the rower's bench, planted a foot on the rail, and leaped over the side.

***

The steady breeze on the sail may have saved Jace's life. When he surfaced, the liburna had traveled three ship lengths away. Captain Arsi and four of the crew stood on the steering platform looking back.

"Help," Jace screamed as he thrashed his arms about. In the splashing water, he appeared to be drowning. Then to add extra drama, he cried. "Help. I can't swim."

Between the rising and falling curtains of water, Jace noted the ship had not slowed or turned. In a final display of helplessness, he sank below the surface, never to be seen again.

Once underwater, the Archer pulled his water-resistant quiver and bow case to either side of his head. Resurfacing between the floating bags, he hid, breathed, and waited.

From the back of the two-banker, the luggage appeared to be drifting in the current. Satisfied with the eliminations, the Captain maintained the course to the harbor of Alexanderia. The foul deeds left and forgotten in the ship's wake.

Underwater, Jace Kasia began to gently kick his way to his partially submerged bundle of clothing and armor. Once collected, he aimed his small flotilla towards shore.

The Egyptian Marine had cautioned, "If you fight Cilician pirates, they will extract revenge."

With the Island of Cyprus only a day's sailing from Cilicia, Jace could only assume Cilician pirates had recognized the liburna. And while they couldn't attack an Egyptian warship, they could infiltrate a prize crew. After using the young farm boy and several others to make the voyage, Arsi and his crew extracted their revenge and disposed of anyone not a Cilician.

Chancing a look, Jace peered around the bow case. The tower, the structure, and a good portion of the lower building were visible on the horizon. After studying the three tiers of the lighthouse, Jace estimated it was too far to swim. He faced the coastline and returned to kicking his way to the nearest piece of dry land.

***

As a student archer, he had gone faster, and as a Legion recruit, he had longer swims. But never had he fought so strong a current. Coming not in waves but in steady pressure, the current threatened to push him out to sea. After a long period of struggle, he relaxed for an instant. And at that moment, all the progress he made was lost. Reaching deep in his gut, Jace Kasia smoothed out his kicks, inhaled and exhaled rhythmically, and kept his eyes on a narrow strip of brown visible in the distance.

Near dark, Jace felt the bottom and the current swirl around his legs rather than shoving him away from shore. In his exhaustion he tripped and fell face first into the water. Collecting a mouthful of sea water, he began to spit it out. But then he realized the water was only slightly salty. After swallowing the liquid, Jace wrestled his three bundles to shore, and collapsed next to them.

"Hello Egypt," he offered while patting the sand.

Then a star blazed to life. Not in the sky, but on the horizon. Hovering in the distance, the fire of the lighthouse glowed, announcing to all passing ships, the presence of the Capital of Egypt.

"I'm here," Jace reflected, "and Alexandria is there. How far? I have no idea. But every night for as long as it takes, I'll have the light to guide me. It's just a matter of putting one foot in front of the other."

***

At dawn, Jace built a long pack, strapped it on his back, and hiked off the beach. As his head came level with solid ground, and he saw the landscape, he laughed. Between his location and the walk to Alexandria was the widest river he'd ever seen.

Brown water extending into the blue showed where it flowed into the sea. And the location explained two things. The Cilicians choice of where to dump the bodies and why Jace had to swim against a steady current. But while the bodies had been swept out to sea, Jace Kasia won his battle against the mighty Nile River.

As far as walking to Alexander, that was out at the start. Having landed on the east bank of the Nile, first Jace had to cross the river.

***

Under the rising sun, the Archer strolled between areas of sea grass and tall wild grass that grew to chest height. Between the grasses crops of green bushes with yellow flowers sprang up. Under foot, the dark rich soil begged for a farmer's touch. The complete opposite of what Jace observed on the voyage along the coast where people struggled to grow crops, the Nile delta lay fertile and untouched. Pushing through a clump of stalks with feathery tops, his feet sank into mud, and he stopped.

Snapping off a stalk, he studied the broken end. Jace had seen reeds on Crete growing in wetlands. But the wet ground was merely damp, and the stalks had no more width than a blade of grass. Plus, they only grew knee high. Glancing down at the wet black soil that oozed around his sandals, Jace understood this land was different.

"They make arrows with these stalks," he muttered. Then Jace looked at the broken stalk in his hand. "How much water is necessary to grow a reed this size?"

He bent forward and divided the stalks with his arms. What appeared to be a shallow pond occupied an uneven circle in the center of the reeds. Although his throat was parched, drinking stagnant water, especially with no sign of animal activity to test for poisoning, ensured illness or even death. He retreated to an area of wild grass and firmer ground. Angling to his left, Jace went around the cluster of tall stalks with feathery tops.

***

Over a mile from the coast, it occurred to Jace that his quest for solid ground had guided him eastward of the Nile, and away from any crossing points. Still thirsty, he contemplated heading directly west to the river. A few strides after the thought, the wild grass ended, and he came upon a cultivated field. Part of it had been harvested. But the rest, a large area of wheat surrounded by green and ripening plants of beans, lentils, chickpeas, lettuce, onions, garlic, and tall green sesame bushes, remained to be picked. With his view cleared of wild grasses, he spotted a path.

"Not quite civilization," Jace considered, "but a trail in the middle of the delta has to lead somewhere."

Reinvigorated by the sight of the crops in the field and the well-defined path, Jace reached the trail and increased his pace.

***

The village was poor. Huts constructed with reed walls, and reed roofs, were unevenly placed around a well. On Crete, even the most impoverished hamlets protected their well by using mud as mortar between the rocks. Jace only knew it was the poor village's well by the rope and leather bucket resting on the loose and badly stacked stones. As he approached, he noticed frayed and unrepaired stalks in the reed walls of the huts. It was indeed a poor village.

But it had people, and people meant information, and that was all Jace wanted from the villagers.

"Where did you come from?" an older man inquired.

He squatted at a cookfire, tending a copper pot of bubbling broth suspended over the flames. The quality of the pot and the iron legs on the tripod took Jace by surprise. Then he noticed bronze farm tools with oak handles, and clean steel scythes on a rack. Expensive equipment in a rustic and barely livable environment caused him to hesitate.

"Are you addled?" the man questioned. "Is that it? Can you hear? Can you speak?"

Jace found his voice before his brain caught up to the extremes.

"My apologies," Jace offered in a fading voice. "It's that I, well I."

Three men appeared in the doorways of huts.

"What do you have there, Djau?" one inquired.

"Not sure," Djau replied. Then speaking slowly, he asked Jace. "Where did you come from? Do you remember?"

"That way," Jace choked out. While his arm indicated the direction, his voice completely failed.

Between the sea water he swallowed as he swam from the ship, the salty water when he reached shore, and not finding running water during his trek, Jace's throat had closed down.

"He is a little touched," a man proposed. "There's nothing out there beyond the fields other than wasteland, the beach, and the sea. He could have been wandering for days. Poor guy."

Frustrated at not being able to ask his questions, Jace pointed at a bucket of water beside Djau.

Mistaking the gesture, Djau grabbed a clay dish. He ladled in a scoop of thick stew and offered it to Jace.

"Go ahead, son," he advised. "There's nothing wrong with being hungry and lost."

There were times to fight and times to run, and then there were times to drop your long pack and accept charity. Once the load was off his back, Jace took the food with one hand and mimicked drinking with the other.

Moments later, Jace sat on a pile of stones shoveling stew into his mouth between sips of honey water. When he finished, his head drooped, and his eyes closed.

"Come with me," Djau instructed. "You need to rest."

Jace carried his pack and allowed the man to guide him to one of the reed huts. Inside, he dropped onto a reed bed with soft wool bedding and a clean linen sheet.

***

Mornings felt different than evenings: a lingering coolness from the night; birds flying away, seeking food, rather than returning to their nests and cooing; and the muffled sounds of people waking, and stretching, rather than the hushed tones of people relaxing before going to bed. In Jace's partially awakened state, he recognized the coolness of morning, but that was all. Snapping awake, he sat up in bed.

Outside, a gruff voice demanded, "Where's the food?"

"There's plenty in the field," Djau replied. "Go pick all you want, be my guest."

"Don't get smart with me, Cyrus. I'll cut the throats of your fieldhands," the voice threatened. "Slowly, one at a time, I will kill them. Give me the food."

Jace untied his bow case, removed the weapon, and flexed the wood.

"There's no food here," Djau informed the voice. "We've already sent the first harvest to the farm."

"I'm not here to listen to excuses."

With the bow in hand, and the strap of the quiver over his shoulder, Jace moved to the back wall. Streams of light identified a weak spot and he gently kicked out a section of frayed reeds. After crawling out of the hut, the Archer notched an arrow and went to investigate.

***

Pressed to their knees with spears poking their backs, the three men from the village trembled. Fear contorting their faces contrasted with the hard, serious expressions of the three men holding the spears. And while Djau stood and talked defiantly, his anxieties were just as obvious on his face. Standing behind a man in an officer's armor were three more spearmen.

"The cause needs your donations," the officer shouted in his gruff voice. He drew a sword and held the tip near Djau's nose. "Who dies first?"

"Isn't that obvious?" Jace asked.

Zip-Thwack!

The arrowhead smashed into the blade three fingers in front of the hilt. Steel on steel shattered the arrow shaft while snatching the handle from the officer's hand. The sword flipped away, leaving the officer shaking.

"Who do you think?" he began.

Zip-Thwack!

Thickness was a relative term. For deer and pigs the term described extra meat. For the tip of a bow's limb, it meant the depth of the notch that held the end of a bowstring. But when considering the thickness of a combat sandal, one could equate thickness to the tip of a thumb.

The arrowhead pierced the leather toe, split the difference between the man's big toe and the next one, penetrated the thickness of the sole, and buried itself in the dirt halfway up the shaft.

Roaring, the officer shouted in pain while trying to issue an order. Both came out garbled.

Zip-Thwack!

Of the three spears at the villager's backs, the arrow knocked the first one into the second spear. They rotated to the side and away from the fieldhands.

Zip-Thwack!

Sprouting an arrow's shaft, the third spear jerked away from that prisoner's back.

"Four well placed arrows," Jace exclaimed. "Is there any doubt I can take an eye and your life with the next arrow?"

Eleven pairs of eyes turned to the Cretan Archer. The four expended arrows had been replaced by ones with broadheads.

"Can your really put one of those through a man's eye?" Djau inquired.

"It's a tight fit," Jace answered. "The steel blades will do a lot of damage on the way in. But it won't matter."

"Why won't it matter?" the officer inquired.

Blood oozed from his sandal, and while trying to appear brave for his spearmen, the officer quivered from pain.

"Because my target will be dead."

A scraping noise by the three men on their knees drew everyone's attention. Jace ignored the fieldhands, assuming they were putting distance between themselves and the still armed spearmen. He assumed wrong.

Rising up in sprinter's stances, the three fieldhands kicked backwards. Caught off guard, the spearmen absorbed feet in their guts. They might have recovered, given a moment. But Djau's men swung their legs around and swept the legs out from under the spearmen. In fluid movements, the fieldhands grabbed the spears and raced over to protect their boss.

"Archer, can I get your name," Djau inquired.

"Sir, it's Jace Kasia. And yours?"

"I am Djau Cyrus, great grandson of File Leader Cyrus of General Ptolemy's right flank phalanx."

"And this officer and his men?" Jace inquired.

"Rebels who believe they can dethrone Ptolemy IV," Djau replied. "I appreciate your help. If I can ask one more favor, Archer Kasia?"

"You want to see if the blades of the arrowhead can truly fit in a man's eye socket?" Jace asked.

"God Ra, no," Djau laughed. "We're going to disarm them, that's all. Then I'll turn them loose. You see, rebels are like roaches, you kill one and two more take their place."

Jace hadn't adjusted his aim, yet he said, "they won't move. Unless they want to enter the afterworld with one eye."

"The next time you come to visit me," Djau said as he shoved the rebel officer towards the trail, "come to my estate. It's where I keep my sword and shield. Then you and I can have a proper conversation."

The rebels slinked away with the officer supported between two spearmen. Jace eased the tension off his bow.

"Sir, this isn't your village?" he asked.

"Son, the Nile floods every year, leaving the soil rich and ripe for planting," Djau informed Jace. "Where we're standing will be underwater for over a third of the year. No one in their right mind builds permanent structures in a floodplain. This is a planting and harvesting camp for the season. Are you hungry?"

"Yes, sir."

"Good. Join us," Djau proposed. "We were about to have breakfast before we were interrupted. Afterwards, we're off to harvest the ripe vegetables. Say, would you be interested in helping with the harvest and earning a few coins?"

Jace smiled and thought of his mentor and the code of the Cretan Archers.

"Sir, it would please me greatly to earn a profit today," he assured Djau.

(Intentionally left blank)

Act 9

Chapter 25 – Artichoke Flowers

Bundled reeds, bound together, then that bundle bound to others, and so on, created a long, shallow draft river boat. On the bottom of the vessel, a coating of pine tar kept the floorspace dry.

The fisherman swore the boat would hold two.

"I've crossed the Nile when it was low and when it ran deep," he bragged. "Never once have the reeds failed me."

"There's always a first time," Jace remarked. He set his bag of belongings, the bow case, and the quiver in the shallow depression at the front of the boat. "But you were recommended by Djau Cyrus, and I trust him, and by extension you."

The fisherman tied the luggage down and indicated the forward part of the passenger area.

"Sit on the hump, but watch your balance," he directed. Rivermen shoved the reed boat off the shoreline and the fisherman jumped in. He began rowing with a two bladed paddle. "Djau is a good man, but I fear for him."

The light vessel rocked in the current, causing Jace to tighten his grip on the top section of reeds. He wasn't afraid of drowning. But having to swim with his belongings in another emergency dunking didn't appeal to him.

Once Jace established harmony with the rhythm of the boat, he commented, "Djau and his workers are well trained. And they're not afraid of a fight."

"That's the problem, isn't it? He's set on resisting the rebels. But one landowner alone can't fight all of Horwennefer's men," the fisherman explained. "From the delta to Thebes at Luxor, the rebels are building in strength. And with that comes the power to compel farmers to donate to the cause."

"Djau refused to give the rebels food," Jace related. "They weren't happy about it."

"His great grandfather fought with General Ptolemy when he came to this land and declared himself Pharaoh," the fisherman stated. "Djau is fiercely loyal to the throne. But the throne has too much land to cover, and the rebels are strongest on the east side of the Nile."

Jace looked at the distant shore, felt the boat rock, and regretted getting on the flimsy boat.

"The Pharaoh has an army, doesn't he?" Jace questioned.

"Horwennefer is a man of the people," the fisherman offered. "As soon as the army marches through a town or a region, the rebels fade into the population. When the Pharaoh's army leaves, the rebels come out of the darkness. Until Ptolemy IV can bring the rebels to battle, farmers like Djau are in danger."

"For a fisherman, you seem well-informed," Jace noticed.

"I wasn't always a fisherman. When I was younger, I was led astray by my own self-importance."

"A philosopher named Plato, and his student, Aristotle created the concept of the earth being the center of the universe. And that all heavenly bodies revolve around earth," Jace lectured. "Are you referring to you or the world?"

"An excellent reference," the fisherman acknowledged. "I should inform you and confess that as a young scholar I took a position at the library of Alexandria. After years of studying scrolls, I became out of touch with my fellow man and with nature. So, I gave it up to become one with the Nile."

"A fisherman, you mean?" Jace inquired.

"Well, I couldn't actually become a fish. Now, could I?"

Jace sat silently as the boat pitched from side to side for the rest of the trip across the great river.

***

Only in a few fertile valleys had Jace seen such abundance. For as far as he could see, the land bloomed with crops. He walked through the fields never seeing a manmade structure, which troubled him. In his imagination, at any moment, a wave of water would come down the Nile and create a lake over the path he was on. It seemed impossible. Yet, as with Djau's harvesting village, nothing substantial existed in the vast expanse of farmland.

Per the fisherman's direction, Jace hiked westward. The former scholar estimated it would take three days to reach the sun gate at Alexandria. For others maybe, but not for a Cretan Archer. In a day and a night of jogging, the walls of the city came into view at mid-morning.

***

Three city guards walked the line of carts and herds of livestock waiting to enter Alexandria. The farmers and

287

herders answered questions and were released. They jerked the reins on their draft animals or poked the lead animal with a staff to get the herds moving forward.

A guard approached and eyed the war hatchet and the sica knife at Jace's waist.

"You have weapons," he mentioned.

"I do because I'm a Cretan Archer," Jace replied, "and weapons are the tools of my trade."

"About your trade," the guard inquired, "are you a thief or a robber?

"Neither, I'm a mercenary," Jace corrected.

"What's your purpose for entering the city?" the guard asked.

From the simple but direct questions, Jace figured out, the guards were nervous about the rebel threat. To ease the guard's suspicion, he used the name First Officer Midhat gave him.

"I'm here to see city guard Farouk Midhat," Jace explained.

"You'll find the Captain in the barracks across from the palace. Move along."

The abrupt release caused Jace to speculate about what position Midhat held in the city. Understandably, a Captain of the Guard demanded respect. But just the use of his name opened the gates for Jace. He didn't ask the guard for more information. He strolled through the sun gate, and immediately he squinted against the glare.

***

Brilliant white lime wash covered everything not the light brown of sandstone or pale granite. Every surface of every building reflected the morning sun. Adding to the white, quite a few people wore white linen robes that also reflected the light. Easier on the eyes were people in colored robes or workers in loin wraps and loose tops. Everyone wore something to shield them from the sun and to allow a breeze to cool their skin.

"Next time, I'll enter the sun gate in the afternoon," Jace complained to himself. "Now where did Djau say the lodgings were?"

He strolled down the crowded boulevard until locating a priest standing at the entrance to a narrow, but tall temple.

"What God is this shrine dedicated to?" Jace asked while craning his neck to see the roof line.

"This is the resting place of King Alexander the Great of Egypt," the priest answered.

At the agoge on Crete, old tales passed down through the decades from Archers who served with King Alexander told an interesting story. Every conquered territory embraced the Macedonian as a local hero. The secret of the transformation from enemy to liberator had to do with his fair treatment of the populace. And that after defeating a country's army, Alexander would marry his Generals and Captains to the daughters of men in high-ranking positions. Through those simple acts, shortly after conquering an enemy, Alexander would be hailed as one of their own. Based on the stories, Jace understood why the Egyptians considered Alexander, an Egyptian King.

"Alexander of Macedon," Jace wanted to say. But he held his tongue and gave the priest a coin.

Djau Cyrus insisted that Jace seek lodgings in a loyal household. To that end, Djau supplied the Archer with an address, or rather a description, of a house. A block from the Tomb of Alexander, Jace turned left and began looking for a blue door with a statue of Zeus on one side and a replica of the Egyptian God Apis on the other.

Near the end of the block on the right, he located the house. Acting as an awning, a balcony on the second floor hung over the street. Jace stepped into the shade and knocked on the blue door.

***

The sound of a locking bar being removed preceded the door opening. But it opened only a little. An eye peered between the frame and the door. It moved up and down, scanning Jace.

"No. Nope, goodbye," a girl's voice announced before the door closed.

Jace knocked a second time.

The door opened even less, and the girl stated, "No. The room isn't for a drifter, a sailor, a day laborer, or a soldier. Go away. Goodbye."

Again, the door closed. For the third time, Jace rapped on the blue door.

"This is a private residence," the girl informed Jace through a sliver of an opening. "If you don't leave, we will call the city guard."

"I'm not a drifter, a sailor, a day laborer, or a soldier," Jace rushed the words, trying to get them out before the door closed. "I wouldn't be at your threshold at all if Djau Cyrus hadn't recommended that I check here for a room."

From deeper in the house a woman called, "Nubia, dear, who is at the door?"

"Someone sent by Djau Cyrus," Nubia replied. "But I don't like the looks of him. He has weapons."

"Oh, child, when I was younger," the woman stated, her voice getting louder as she approached the door, "all our men carried weapons. Open the door and let's have a look."

When the door swung open, Jace saw an older Greek woman. Her blonde hair had started to turn gray while the young girl beside her had dark hair and the features of a native Egyptian.

"Ma'am, I am Jace Kasia, a farmer from Crete," Jace told her using a half-truth. "After helping Djau with a problem, he suggested I see you about a room."

"He smells and no farmer I know carries a sica and a war hatchet," Nubia complained. "I don't like him."

"Travelers rarely come off the trail freshly bathed," the lady offered. "And the road can be dangerous. But tell me young man, why would Djau point you in my direction?"

"Ma'am, he didn't say exactly," Jace admitted. "Only that I needed to stay at a home loyal to the Pharaoh."

"Did your help have anything to do with that sica and hatchet?"

"Technically no, ma'am," Jace replied.

"Then why," she stopped and thought over his choice of wording. "If not technically, what did you use?"

"My war bow and a couple of arrows," Jace told her.

"See, see," Nubia exclaimed. "Soldiers can't be trusted."

Jace adjusted the ropes on his long pack, nodded a farewell to the woman and the girl and apologized, "I'm sorry to have bothered you."

"Goodbye," Nubia asserted.

She began to close the door when the woman proposed, "I've known Djau since he was younger than Nubia. All his life, he's been confident to a fault and a man who plans for everything. I'm trying to figure out why he'd need with an archer."

A look of mischief crossed her face and she smiled.

"He's too smart for tigers, snakes, or Nile crocs," she listed. "Did your help have anything to do with two legged predators?"

"Yes, ma'am," Jace answered. "Seven of them to be precise."

"Come in Jace Kasia," the lady invited. "I'm Onella. You've met Nubia."

The sudden change sent a warning through Jace's mind. Onella had a problem and would probably pay with room and food. That meant, there was little profit for Jace behind the blue door. He started to walk away when Nubia's face paled, and she tried to slip into the space between the door and the wall.

Glancing over his shoulder, Jace saw the problem immediately. Across the street, Captain Arsi and two of his sailors came out of a house.

***

Typically revenge paid poorly. And because it was personal, an archer could make mistakes. Plus, there were always costs, further reducing any profit. For those reasons,

Jace had decided to ignore the Cilicians who attempted to murder him. The escape from the prize ship ended the affair as far as Jace was concerned. And it would have remained that way, until Nubia sniffled, and while trembling in fear, lifted a hand to wipe away a tear.

"Thank you, ma'am," Jace said as he crossed the threshold. Remembering he needed to earn a profit, he inquired. "Would you have a bite to eat for a hungry man."

"We've a bathhouse outback," Onella responded. "You head straight there, and we'll fix you a platter while you clean up."

"It's a deal," Jace said, substituting the word deal when he meant contract.

Onella and Nubia weren't aware of it, but they had just hired a Cretan Archer. And best of all, neither had Captain Arsi or his Cilician pirates.

***

Aromas from a platter of lamb, vegetables, and flatbread generously dusted with artichoke flowers, filled the room. Compared to the bowls of stew he'd been eating for the last month the platter represented a taste of hearth and home.

"That is beautiful," Jace gushed as he sat at the table. In his mind, any idea of deserting Onella and Nubia fled with the first mouthful. After swallowing, he encouraged. "Tell me what happened?"

Nubia trembled anew before Onella poked her shoulder and advised, "Tell him."

"It's really nothing," the young girl confessed. But she had to catch her breath before continuing. "Every three days, we go to the market to order fresh meats and vegetables.

293

Two days ago, Aunt Onella was feeling ill, so I went alone. On my way back, three men blocked the street."

She buried her face in her hands. Jace ate while the girl collected herself. When she spoke, Jace stopped eating.

"One pulled a knife, put the tip on my chest, right here, and said he was going to make me a wife," Nubia blurted out. Her finger rested on the top of her chest at her throat.

"She ran home in tears," Onella described. "The next day, feeling better, I walked over to talk to them. A middle-aged man answered the red door. When I told him about the harassment of my niece, he laughed. Sailors play rough and if your little girl doesn't like it, keep her off the street, he said."

She paused to hand Jace another piece of flatbread.

"Eat while I talk," Onella instructed. "Nubia feels trapped in the house. And to be honest, I don't feel safe going out either."

"Do you have any local garments?" Jace inquired.

"My deceased husband's linen robes," Onella replied. "You can have them if you like."

"Only enough to disguise me," Jace told her.

"Why do you need a disguise?" Nubia inquired. "Don't you want to show the men your weapons?"

"There are eleven of them," Jace informed her. The detail went by the girl without her questioning how Jace knew how many men lived in the house. "Flashing steel will accomplish nothing. Except, getting a few of them dead and me injured."

"If you don't want to fight," Nubia screamed. She jumped up from the table and remarked. "Then what good are you?"

294

The girl ran from the room and Onella leaned forward.

"How do you know," she demanded, "how many men live in that house?"

"A few days ago, I was on a boat with them," Jace informed her. "They killed everyone in the crew who wasn't a Cilician. I escaped and swam to shore. They think I'm dead and they've forgotten about me. But I'm not done with them."

"Is that why Djau sent you here?"

"No ma'am," Jace replied. "I think he just wanted to put me in a house loyal to the throne."

"It doesn't matter why. We're glad he sent you," Onella declared. "I'll get you the robes."

Jace returned to the feast. Eating hid his inability to form a workable plan to protect Onella and Nubia, and to punish eleven vicious Cilician killers.

Chapter 26 – Shadow of the Library

Early the next morning, the blue door opened, and Nubia stepped out of the house. Across the street, the red door opened, and two men appeared in the doorframe. They ogled the girl and took a step forward. But a tall figure in flowing white robes joined the girl, and the men stopped.

"Who is that?" one of the pirates asked.

"A barrier to our fun," the other Cilician answered, "and trouble we don't need right now."

Onella joined Jace and Nubia, and the three walked down the street. Behind them, the two pirates left the house and followed.

Unlike most cities and towns, Alexandria's designers built the city on a grid of straight boulevards with intersecting streets. At the end of the street, the trio turned left. On the next block, brick warehouses filled most of a lot.

"What's that on the other side of the storage facilities," Jace asked.

"The market," Nubia replied.

"I meant farther down on the other side of the road," Jace described. "The tall building with the massive doors."

"That is the library," Onella answered. "It's famous. They say the building contains more scrolls on more topics than any library in the world."

"It's certainly big enough," Jace admitted. "Will you two be all right if I go have a look at the building while you shop?"

"We know the venders and the farmers," Onella told him. "No one would dare cause trouble for us in the market."

"I'm going to have a look at the library," Jace told them. "Don't leave the market until I get back."

"We won't," Nubia assured him.

While Onella and Nubia entered the rows of vender stalls, Jace continued along the boulevard. As he got closer, the enormity of the library dawned on him. Looking up at the carvings high above, Jace veered off the boulevard. Still gazing upward, he crossed the street while admiring the craftsmanship of the stone carvers. He didn't see the legs of the man sitting on a bench.

When Jace walked into the legs, they both shouted. Jace out of surprise and the man from pain.

"When you visit Alexandria, you should watch were you're putting your big feet," the man scolded Jace. Rubbing his shin, he grumbled. "There is a need for a scroll on manners."

"How do you know I'm visiting?" Jace asked. Being proud of his disguise, he swung his arms. The light fabric flew around as if feathered wings and he was about to fly. Challenging the man, he said. "I might live here."

"In the desert, without shade, nomads wrap themselves from head to toe in those robes," the man replied. "In the city, we have shadows and shade on every corner. Thus, young nomad, you are a visitor to the city. Albeit, a clumsy, inattentive visitor. But still a visitor."

Jace felt as if he should take offense. But the man's language came out in the style of a caring teacher, and not in a rude abrasive manner.

"Allow me to apologize," Jace sighed, letting his temper cool. "My name is Kasia from Crete, and I am indeed a visitor to this city."

"It's impressive, isn't it?" the man proclaimed as if he didn't hear Jace. He indicated the building. "Within those walls is the knowledge of the world. Scholars spend their life on one topic but cannot get to all the scrolls and sheets of papyrus stored in that library."

"I met a scholar the other day," Jace said, because he couldn't think of anything else to say.

"You did. Here? Did you also bruise his leg?"

"Not in the city," Jace replied. "He's a fisherman on the Nile."

"Aw, I do miss him," the man murmured. "He left me five years ago to experience the real world."

"Left you?" Jace asked.

"I'm Eratosthenes of Cyrene, Chief Librarian of the Library of Alexandria," the man introduced himself.

"What do you study?" Jace inquired.

"A very astute question, young nomad. I study the field of Geography. Not that it'll mean anything to you, but if you look at the horizon of the sea, you'll notice it bends. Now imagine the bend continuing in a giant curve until it makes a circle. That and the mathematics of it, if you can understand the concept, mean we live on a globe."

"It fits with philosophers Plato and Aristotle's idea of the earth being the center of the universe," Jace mentioned. "If the moon and sun are round, it makes sense the earth is as well."

"An excellent layman's explanation," Eratosthenes stated. "Listen, but don't share this with anyone. While the outside of the building is impressive, inside is where the treasures are kept. If you go around to the side of the library, you'll find a servant's door. It's unlocked and if you go in and look up, you'll see the stacks of shelves holding the scrolls."

"I'll do that," Jace told him. "It was nice meeting you, Chief Librarian."

"Except for the bruise," Eratosthenes acknowledged, "it was a pleasure to make your acquaintance, Kasia of Crete."

As Jace strolled around the corner of the building and entered a dead-end alleyway, the two Cilicians stepped away from the side of a warehouse. They crossed the street and followed the Archer into the shadow of the library.

**

Out of the direct sunlight, Jace could feel the coolness through the linen robes. It felt good which elevated his mood. For a moment, he stopped worrying about Onella and Nubia, and enjoyed the anticipation of viewing the inside of the library.

**

Years before, Jace limped to the work shed with his legs in pain from raps from a staff and his eyes half closed from exhaustion.

"Here's a candle and a blanket," Mikolas said as he lit the wick. "You've all afternoon and early evening to study. I'll come fetch you for dinner."

"But I'm sore and tired," Jace complained. "Can't I skip it today? I could go to the pond and bring back fish."

"A Cretan Archer needs a broad range of knowledge and experiences," Zarek Mikolas preached. "Every situation an Archer finds himself in doesn't require a bow or a blade. Often, being good company will earn more than your arrows. And reading will reveal more than beating on a suspect or bribing a source."

So Jace studied, and eventually, he found that the words of philosophers and Greek poets took his mind off the pain. And freed him, for a few moments, for the never-ending tests that challenged his mind and his body.

**

Near the servant's door, Jace spoke to the memory of his mentor, "Master Mikolas, I'm about to witness all the knowledge in the world in one place. Wouldn't you like to see it?"

Out of habit, Jace softened his breathing and recalled the voice of his mentor.

In that moment of reflection, Jace felt the urge to duck and step to the side. Acting on instinct before he recognized the sounds of running feet, Jace Kasia ducked and rolled to his right.

The Cilician lashed out with his knife, slicing a shallow wound on his victim's shoulder. But his momentum carried him several steps beyond his target.

His partner, three paces behind, saw the other man from the blue house pivot and the knife draw blood. And while the first pirate traveled, stumbling out of range for a second attempt, the second Cilician adjusted his path.

The man, who escorted the woman and the girl, finished his turn, and stopped. Obviously confused by the violence, he stood still as he faced the onslaught of the second pirate.

With his blade extended, the pirate sprinted towards the man. The sprint usually panicked anyone fighting a Cilician. Crossing blades, either short or long, was frightening enough. Add to the conflict an attacker charging like a crazed bear, and typically the victim panicked, giving the Cilician an advantage.

***

"A running attacker either has a death wish or he's trying to intimidate you," Jace heard Zarek Mikolas in his mind. "He'll only have one chance to do damage. Give him something, take it away, than grant his wish."

"I'm sorry," Jace said as he swept his left arm up as if offering it to the pirate.

"No need to apologize," the Cilician mocked, "I'll make this quick."

Still running, he sliced downward in a bone splitting hack. But the blade only parted white linen fabric.

Jace swung his hips around the blade and captured the knife hand for a moment. Next, the Archer yanked hard and released the attacker.

The pull, combined with the sprint, propelled the Cilician forward at a tremendous rate. He smashed, face first, into the wall of the neighboring building. Bouncing off, the assailant dropped and sprawled on the stone pavers. With his arms outstretched, the Cilician appeared relaxed and looked as if he would spring up after a moment to collect himself. He might have, except for the blood pumping from the severed artery in his right wrist.

The first pirate stutter stepped to a stop and turned to see his partner on the ground. Insolence curled his lips. He snapped his blade back and forth as if testing his slashes.

Jace threw the robe off his head and revealed his face.

"Come on Cilician," he challenged. "Six of you sheep couldn't kill me on the boat. Let's see if you can do the job, one-on-one."

A rutting ram had nothing on the pirate. He lowered his head, pushed his blade out front, and sprinted at Jace as if defending his ewe.

"Sometimes," Zarek Mikolas mentioned once or twice, "your enemy will be too stupid to live. Help them out of their ignorance."

Jace dodged to his left and held the pose for a heartbeat. The Cilician altered course. But when the Archer's chest

301

filled the pirate's vision, Jace jerked to the right, threw out a leg, and tripped the Cilician.

Before his body finished skipping across the stone pavers, the Archer jumped on his back. Jace grabbed a fistful of hair and lifted the pirate's head.

"You lose," he growled.

"Before, I heard you say I'm sorry," the Cilician mentioned. "What did you mean?"

"Because of your interference," Jace said as he rested the skinning knife on the side of the pirate's neck, "I won't get to see the inside of the library. I was apologizing to my teacher for missing the opportunity."

***

Bleeding while wearing white fabric, especially in public, proved difficult to conceal. Jace rested a hand over the wound and walked with confidence to the market. Spotting Nubia, he went to her.

"Buy me a brown scarf," he whispered to the girl. "Take the coins from my pouch."

"Buy your own scarf," she shot back.

"Please, Nubia. Don't make a scene, just buy the dark brown scarf," Jace insisted.

Crossing her arms, Nubia stated, "No. And you can't make me."

Cries went up and, a moment later, city guards rushed by on their way to the library. Jace wasn't sure what the penalty was for a double murder in Egypt, and he didn't want to find out.

"Nubia," he begged.

The girl didn't answer, but Onella appeared off his other shoulder.

"Are you two having a good time?" she inquired. "What were you discussing?"

"He wants me to buy him a scarf," Nubia sneered. "He has two hands, let him purchase his own scarf."

Onella noticed Jace holding his arm across his chest. She moved around the Archer to the other shoulder.

Laughing as if she had an amusing thought, Onella said to the scarf vender, "The dark brown scarf almost matches my nephew's eyes. Let me see it."

With the dark fabric in hand, she placed the scarf over Jace's wounded shoulder.

"Oh, that's delightful," she exclaimed as she paid for the scarf. "I don't know about you two, but I'm exhausted from shopping. Shall we go home?"

They left the market and strolled down the boulevard. Along the way, more guardsmen rush by.

"I wonder what's going on?" Nubia remarked.

The girl slowed and turned to look back at the library. Immediately, Onella hooked her arm and eased Nubia back into line.

"I'm sure it's nothing, dear," Onella assured her.

***

They had just started down the street when a group of men came out of the red door. It took Jace a heartbeat to analyze how many ways the next few moments could go before he acted. Using his good shoulder, Jace crowded Onella and Nubia to the side of the road.

"What's wrong with you?" Nubia demanded.

"Onella, lean in and loudly scold me for my drinking," Jace directed.

"But you haven't been drinking," Nubia challenged. "If you had, I would smell it on your breath."

"Onella, loudly, and now," Jace demanded.

"You come from the country, and like your father, you fall in with slavenly drunks," Onella shouted. "Why are the men in my family all taken with drink?"

Overhearing the woman scolding a man dressed in nomad robes, Captain Arsi laughed as did the Cilicians with him. But the man beside the Captain only chuckled. Favoring a foot, he groaned with every step. An arrow between the toes had that effect on rebel officers.

"I won't have it," Onella blasted Jace. "If you keep it up, I'm sending you back to the desert where there is less temptation."

The men reached the end of the street and glanced back one more time to admire the tongue lashing. Then they strolled onto the boulevard and were soon lost in the crowd.

Jace announced, "That settles it."

"You're going to the desert?" Nubia inquired.

"No, little one. After I clean up, I'm going to see the brother of a First Officer I know. Good work Onella. Now, if I could ask one more favor."

"Before or after I sew up that knife wound on your shoulder?" she asked.

Chapter 27 – Search for Farouk

The palace walls blocked the view of half the piers in the harbor. But Jace didn't mind, he wasn't after a ship, at least not yet. Across the street from the Pharaoh's fortress, Jace walked into a crowded room. On the far side, a Sergeant of the city guard sat reading a scroll between sessions of scanning the visitors.

The Archer pushed through the bodies and approached the desk. The guard NCO looked up from the scroll.

"Are you a witness to the murders at the library?" the Sergeant questioned in a bored voice.

"What murders?" Jace asked.

"The murders everyone here claims to have seen," the Sergeant answered. "Ever since the library offered a reward, witnesses have been coming from every corner of the city."

"Do you have a description of the murderer? Or a name?" Jace asked. In his mind, the Archer planned an escape route out of Alexanderia, if he made it out of the barracks building. There was one comfort, although Eratosthenes of Cyrene had his name, the chief librarian never had a clear view of his face.

"Certainly. He is a nomad from the deep desert, a sailor from up north or down south, a rebel come to the city to cause mayhem, a Cilician pirate, which is odd because the victims are Cilicians," the Sergeant listed. "Or, the nameless killer could resemble any of the other descriptions the witnesses claim to have seen. But if you aren't a witness, what can I do for you?"

Jace congratulated himself on selecting a tunic rather than the white linens for his trip to the barracks. And with the brown scarf over the injury, he hid the bandage on his shoulder. As for the Chief Librarian, he either was too important to be interviewed, or for his own reasons, Eratosthenes didn't divulge Jace's name.

With more confidence, Jace answered, "I'd like to see Captain Farouk Midhat."

"So would I," the Sergeant responded.

"Excuse me?" Jace questioned.

"They transferred the Captain this morning. And left me with a junior officer at the start of an investigation of a double murder. Thus, I too would like to see Captain Midhat."

"That's understandable," Jace sympathized. "Can you tell me where the Captain was assigned?"

"Go out the doorway, cross the street, and ask for him."

"Where?"

"It's big, with stone walls, guards in shiny armor with shields, you can't miss it."

"The Pharaoh's fortress?" Jace guessed.

"It's the only thing across the street," the Sergeant grumbled. He went back to reading the scroll, dismissing Jace by his inattention.

***

All citadels had two things in common. They fended off attackers and protected the residents. For their walls they might use stone, wooden timbers, earthen embankments, or clay bricks. Whichever material was native to the region and easiest to collect. Some were rustic structures, utilitarian in design. Others were more stately with towers soaring above the walls. But none of the fortresses Jace had seen, or heard about, matched the Pharaoh's Palace.

Huge blocks of white granite, shaped and set tightly together, created an almost smooth façade. Towering over the street, they resembled a cliff face more than a manmade structure. At the entrance and adding to the majesty, two guards dressed in polished bronze armor and helmets, held bronze shields and steel headed spears.

Between the reflection off the royal guards' equipment, and the white walls, Jace held a hand over his eyes to fend off the glare. In Egypt, he was learning, the one constant was the presence of Ra, the Sun God.

"I'm here to see Captain Farouk Midhat," Jace explained.

"Who?" one of the guards replied.

"I think he's the new Ring Officer," the other sentry answered the first. Then to Jace, he directed. "Go ask at the harbor entrance. They might know."

**

Making it a long walk to the corner, the front of the palace covered more than a city block. When Jace reached it, he realized the side wall extended out into the harbor. No attacking army could marshal enough forces on the thin strip of land to be a threat to the Pharaoh.

After a long hike, the Archer could see three harbors and multiple piers in each. Merchant ships of all types and sizes filled berths at the piers. The traffic spoke to the amount of trade that passed through the Egyptian capital.

Jace tried to locate the prize liburna, but the beach harbors of Alexandia proved too vast. During the walk to the palace entrance, he came to the realization that if he wanted to find the prize ship, he'd need to walk the individual beaches.

Near the royal harbor, he located an entrance.

"I'm here to see Captain Farouk Midhat," Jace announced to the two sentries.

"Down the hallway to the third door," one directed.

"Thank you," Jace acknowledged.

Thinking 'hallway' would equate to a house or a normal building, Jace strolled into the palace. Once through the portal, he looked up at a stone ceiling and down a long doorless hallway. Based on the defensible corridor, the Pharaoh's palace proved to be more than a beautiful structure. It was a formidable citadel.

Although widely spaced, Jace found doors one and two, before finally arriving at the third door. He pushed it open and walked into an armory.

Around the walls were pikes, spears, helmets, armor pieces, and shields. None, however, were the quality of the gear used by the royal guards. As he crossed the room, the Archer noted the battle equipment was older and not well kept.

A clerk saw the visitor and inquired, "Are you lost?"

"I'm looking for Captain Farouk Midhat," Jace explained as he approached the desk.

"Wait here," the clerk instructed.

He vanished through a rear doorway and reappeared almost immediately.

"The Captain will see you."

After the long search for Farouk, Jace felt relieved as he entered a large office.

"What do you have to report?" a man inquired. Except for being a few years older, he resembled the First Officer of *Ra's Brightness*.

"Report?" Jace asked. "I didn't know I was supposed to report."

"Aren't you a member of the Third Ring?"

"No sir. I'm an acquaintance of First Officer Midhat. He suggested when I arrived in Alexandria, I should see his brother. And to say to you, I am a man of my word."

"My brother is a good judge of character. Always has been," Farouk remarked. "If I had a free evening, I'd be delighted to hear about his situation. But since I've been assigned as the Ring Officer, I have no free days or evenings."

"If I might, Captain, what is a Ring Officer?" Jace asked.

"When the Pharaoh takes the field of battle, he is surrounded by his personal bodyguards. Around the bodyguards are the palace guards. Seeing as both groups are charged with the safety of a living god, there is a need for a defensive ring around them. That's my new job, I'm the Ring Officer."

"You described the formation when the Pharaoh goes to war," Jace pointed out. "What's your job in the palace?"

"Other than preparing for war," Captain Midhat told him, "I protect the palace by keeping rebels out of the city."

Jace stepped around a chair, and uninvited, he sat.

"I've a tale to tell you Captain. One that fits into your job like a mortise and tenon joint."

***

To shade himself from the sun and to hide his features, Jace kept the brown scarf over his head. When he arrived at the blue door, he knocked. Nubia answered it.

"I went out this afternoon and no one bothered me," she gushed when Jace entered.

"They're probably too busy to bother a girl," Jace offered as an excuse.

Nubia huffed and stomped away. Not understanding why his explanation raised so much ire, he went in search of Onella. He found her checking the deliveries from the market.

"It's been years since I've purchased so much," she commented.

"I'm sorry if I'm a burden," Jace apologized.

"You're not, I can assure you," Onella told him. "Oh, and after you left, the men across the street returned. They were in a rush and talking loudly."

"I imagine they were," Jace remarked.

He hadn't mentioned the fight in the alleyway to Captain Midhat. Nor had he told the Captain about the prize ship. The liburna would link him to the dead Cilicians and that association might make him a suspect in the murders.

"Why would you imagine that?" Onella asked.

She knew he had been in a fight, but he hadn't told her it resulted in the deaths of two men.

"I need you to keep Nubia back here with you for the afternoon," Jace instructed. "The city guard will be arriving in force, and you don't want to get in the middle of a street fight."

"They've broken the law?" Onella guessed. "I knew there was something evil about those men."

"You have no idea," Jace said after she went to collect Nubia.

***

Their shields weren't bronze nor was their armor. But what the city guardsmen lacked in glamor - they made up for with intensity. As they gathered at the head of the street, Captain Midhat joined them.

A moment later, Jace stepped out of the blue doorway and waved. At the signal, Farouk and the guardsmen marched down the street. Scrambling to the stairs, Jace ran to the second-floor window. From the ledge over the blue door, he studied the windows and roof of the house across the street.

"They will fight," Jace warned the Captain. "But I can assure you, they won't use missiles from the roof or a window on your men."

"How can you guarantee that?" Farouk inquired.

"I'm a Cretan Archer. My bow and arrow will protect your guardsmen from flying objects."

"My brother does know character."

***

Before Captain Midhat started, guardsmen gathered at the entrances to the house. Midhat spoke to a Lieutenant behind him then he kicked in the red door.

As if a hive of angry bees, the Cilicians charged through the doorway. But short blades and ferocity were no match for spears and shields. In moments, the pirates lay dead in the street.

Farouk looked up at Jace and waved him down. When the Archer reached the street, he asked, "Can you tell if that's all of them?"

Jace roamed the small battlefield counting. When done, he returned to the Captain.

"Eight of them is all I've ever seen," he explained. "I think that is the entire rebel band."

"Come see me tomorrow Jace Kasia," Midhat directed. "I have a job for you."

"With the Ring detachment?" Jace questioned.

"When we go to war, yes," Farouk said. "Before war however, I need a resourceful man on the streets and the docks of Alexandria, searching out rebels."

"Does it pay?" Jace inquired.

"In fact, it pays a bounty for every rebel brought in alive for questioning. Less so, if you bring them in dead."

***

A week later, long before daylight, a hush blanketed the harbor. And except for a few sailors and dockworkers sleeping on the cool stones of the pier, the dock was empty. In the dark, two men came from the city, one limping slightly, and the other strutting.

"I've hired a crew for us," Captain Arsi bragged. "We'll cast off at first light and make a run to Cilicia to buy weapons. You'll be back in a week with enough blades to arm a hundred fighters."

"It's what I'm paying you for," the rebel officer commented. "But, can we trust the men you hired?"

"The crew wasn't told the destination, and they won't arrive until just before we shove off," Arsi informed his employer. "And none will be making the return trip."

Water lapped against one side of the pier. Turning away from the harbor, they took steps down to a beach. A short stroll along the sand brought them to a waiting two-banker.

"There should be a watchman," Arsi complained. He rapped on the side of the liburna, but no one responded. Frustrated by the absent guard, the Cilician Captain invited the rebel officer on board.

"It'll be more comfortable than sitting on the sand," he advised before jumping up. His hands grabbed the rail, and a swing of his legs gave him purchase on the gunwale. From there, he climbed onto the ship. "I'll get the ladder for you."

Long moments later, the rebel officer grew impatient.

"Arsi, where's that ladder," he called up to the ship. "Arsi. Is everything alright?"

A scraping announced the ladder being lowered over the side.

"I was worried," the rebel officer admitted.

He scaled the rungs until the top of his head reached the rail. Then, a large object flew over his head. When it landed, a thud revealed its mass.

"What was that?" the rebel officer demanded.

"No one important," Jace Kasia replied before bashing in the rebel's head with a club. "Just tidying up some old business before dawn."

The end

A sample of the start for book #8 in *A Legion Archer* series

The General's Tribune

The twin winds of greed and lust for power blew out of the west, racing eastward across the Mediterranean.

With Carthaginian forces removed from Iberia, the reinforcements and supplies for Hannibal Barca dwindled to a trickle. Even so, Hannibal held onto the southwest quadrant of the Italian peninsula and remained a danger to the Republic. Although secure in his position and made rich from his conquests, the architect of the victory in Iberia retreated to Rome.

Too proud to serve under another General, but too young to be a Senator or a Consul/General, Cornelius Scipio acted the part of a civilian. But under the toga, he burned with the desire to face Hannibal in battle. While trading political favors, he grew, thanks to his wife, in popularity with the elites and the citizens of Rome. To what end, few knew, and even less would understand his impossible plan.

And still the twin winds blew ever eastward.

Philip V, the heir to the Macedonian throne, cast his greedy eyes on the Island of Rhodes. And while his vaulted phalanxes were formidable on land, to shuffle an island nation, he hired pirates to interfere with shipping. Some of the privateers raided for coins, others for pride, and one pirate, Diceärch, joined the war as a way to quench his hatred of priests and temples, and to satisfy his yearning for cruelty.

Continuing eastward, the twin winds threatened a ruler and fanned the flames of war.

After smoldering in the desert sands along the Nile, a cause flared up. And while Cretan Archer Jace Kasia worked on a contract in an urban setting, his days of sleeping with a roof over his head were numbered. War was coming, but first, the rebel leader needed to declare his intentions. And when the rebellion materialized, God/King Ptolemy IV will raise an army of the Pharaoh, and march south to meet his fate.

And somewhere in route, there's a letter traveling to Crete. When it reaches the Archer, the message will recall Jace Kasia - carrying him eastward against the winds to the Roman Legions, where he will take his place as the General's Tribune.

Welcome to 205 B.C.

A Note from J. Clifton Slater

Thank you for reading *From Dawn to Death* (or To Victory), which would be the complete title of book #7. *A Legion Archer* series has taken us from the first battle of the 2nd Punic War to Cornelius' victories in Iberia, and Jace's early involvement in the Cretan War. By the number of readers this series of books has generated, I can now brag that I have a bestselling series on my hands. Thank you for that. Now, let's separate fiction from history.

We'll start with Cornelius Scipio in Iberia.

Before the Battle of Ilipa

After 12 years of war, Cornelius Scipio had become a formidable commander. During the march to Ilipa, Mago Barca sent a detachment to ambush the Legions. But Cornelius anticipated the attack and stationed cavalry in the hills. When the assault began, the Legion cavalry rode into the battle and destroyed the Carthaginian's detachment. It was the beginning of Scipio's lore as one of Rome's greatest Generals.

The Battle of Ilipa

Prior to the battle if Ilipa, Cornelius ordered his Legions to show the standard formation with light infantrymen on the flanks of his heavy infantry. But on the morning if the battle, he woke his Legions before daybreak and had them eat a meal. While it was still dark, he marched his Legions to the Carthaginian camp, and he made a change in the formation. Cornelius placed his light infantry in the center with his heavy infantry on the flanks.

Carthaginian Generals Mago Barca and Hasdrubal Gisco fell for the ruse. As I described in *From Dawn to Death*, when the Legions heavy infantry closed in from the sides and began butchering the Carthaginian army, a blinding rainstorm forced Cornelius to pull his men back from the fighting. Historians estimate that without the rain and the retreat, the death toll for the Carthaginians would have equaled the Roman's losses at the Battle of Cannae.

Fortified towns of Iliturgi and Castulo

Historian Livy wrote about the cities of Iliturgi and Castulo and how they treated escaping Legionaries. Located 16 miles from each other along the Guadalquivir River (the Romans called the river Baetis) the walled towns were regional centers of commerce. When the Legions of Publius Scipio, and later Gnaeus Scipio, were destroyed in 211 B.C., surviving Legionaries fled north towards Tarraco along the banks of the Guadalquivir River. Groups of infantrymen from the defeated Legions went to the fortified cities of Iliturgi and Castulo seeking shelter and supplies.

Iliturgi invited the Legionaries in, then attacked and murdered a number of them, before the rest escaped. At Castulo, the citizens closed and barred their gates on the desperate Legionaries and shouted insults from the walls.

Once the Carthaginians were pushed out of Iberia, Cornelius decided revenge was in order. He took a Legion to Iliturgi to punish the city and sent another Legion under the command of Lucius Marcius to dish out revenge on the city of Castulo.

Livy wrote that before the first probe of Iliturgi, Cornelius gave a long speech. Here's the part I paraphrased in the book. *"The time has come for you to avenge the atrocious massacre of your fellow-soldiers and the treachery meditated against yourselves had you been carried there in your flight. You will make it clear, for all time, by this awful example that no one must ever consider a Roman citizen or a Roman soldier a fit subject for ill-treatment, whatever his condition may be."*

On the second day of the siege, when the Legionaries hesitated, Cornelius Scipio ran to a ladder and exposed himself to enemy missiles. His actions shamed the Legion into attacking the walls.

Livy also mentioned African deserters being in Cornelius' Legion. I changed them to the African Corps for the story. But historically, the Africans climbed a cliff to attack the city from the rear. Per Livy's descriptions, *the Africans located narrow footpaths along the cliff face, and where none were found, they pounded in spikes to provide footing. Then they climbed to a low, lightly defended back wall of Iliturgi.*

In *From Dawn to Death*, I moved the timing of the attacks on Iliturgi and Castulo to a period before Cornelius went to visit King Syphax of western Numidia. But the sieges happened after his audience with the King.

In the chant '*As Sure as Hadad Wars with Reshef*', the African Corps reflected on the conflict between Hadad, the Carthaginian God of storms and rain, and Reshef, the God of fire and lightning. As with most songs in my books, for good or evil, I wrote the chant. As far as Cornelius being the last man to see the town square of Iliturgi, he probably was. After its destruction, the tribe relocated the city 12 miles from modern day city of Mengíbar to near the present-day city of Andújar, Spain.

King Syphax

Cornelius Scipio traveled to Western Numidia when Gaius Laelius failed to reach an agreement with King Syphax. As his two warships approached the harbor, seven Carthaginian ships-of-war noticed the Romans and prepared to row out.

According to Livy, the Roman quinqueremes had a stiff breeze from the sea which propelled them to the beach before the Carthaginians could intercept Cornelius' ships. History didn't give us action which forced me to invent a quick sea battle.

Safe in Syphax's harbor, Cornelius marched to the King's compound with a minimum escort. At the compound, Cornelius Scipio discovered Hasdrubal Gisco. The Carthaginian General had gone to Western Numidia after his defeat in Iberia.

Taking advantage of the presence of two powerful generals, King Syphax attempted to have them make a peace settlement between Rome and Carthage. To facilitate togetherness, at the evenings banquet, Syphax placed Scipio and Grisco on the same couch. While Grisco was not happy, Cornelius handled the arrangement with class.

Cornelius Scipio, however, got his digs in as Livy wrote, *"And so, he (Cornelius) said, it was not so essential for the Carthaginians to inquire how their Spanish (Iberia) provinces had been lost as to consider how they were still to hold Africa."* And, *"...that Scipio was not waging war in Africa, as Hannibal was in Italy."*

After leaving west Numidia, Cornelius sailed to eastern Numidia and visited King Masinissa. We have no details about the reason, but Livy mentioned the Kings nephew being discovered in New Carthage when the Legions took the city. I assumed, based on future events, the visit was to make peaceful overtures which included the return of King Masinissa's relative.

Sirocco

During the spring, the hot, dry winds from the Sahara Desert, blowing northeast, caused the gale force winds that made Sirocco famous. But year-around, the hot winds extend to the Mediterranean. The result of the Sirocco mixing with a large body of water regularly causes fog on the coast of northern Africa.

Cornelius Scipio in Iberia

As Prorogatio of Iberia, Cornelius Scipio created and trained Legions in Iberia for two purposes. He needed to stop the flow of supplies to Hannibal in Italy. For that, Cornelius had to clear Carthaginians from Iberia.

Once that was accomplished, he set his heart on the second purpose. Attacking Carthage and drawing Hannibal away from the Republic. After his achievements in Iberia, he began the preparation to invade Carthage. Like other successful Roman Generals, Cornelius thought he deserved a day of triumph, a parade where the General marched his Legions, displayed spoils, and captured enemy troops to the people of Rome. When Cornelius requested the parade, the idea was summarily dismissed, and he was reminded by the Senate of Rome that a Prorogatio was limited to a specific region.

City of Italica

Before leaving Iberia, Cornelius designated an area as a settlement for his veterans. Italica became the first Latin settlement outside Italy and the first Roman city in Spain. To demonstrate the success of the city, Roman Emperors Trajan, born 53 A.D., and Hadrian, born 76 A.D., were both from Italica.

And now, we'll take a look at the history around Jace Kasia's adventure.

The Cretan War

In 206 B.C., King Philip V of Macedonia set out to conquer the Isle of Rhodes. To accomplish the task, he planned to cripple the island by disrupting their shipping and ruining the economy by cutting them off from trading partners.

As allies, Philip selected the Greek cities in the Aetolian League, Spartan pirates, and the Seleucid Empire. Upon the death of 'Alexander the Great' in 323 B.C., General Seleucus I Nicator seized rule of Mesopotamian, and another of Alexander's generals, Ptolemy I Soter took Egypt. The two families, Seleucus and Ptolemy, had been enemies ever since. Egypt joined Rhodes, along with Athens and Pergamum, to oppose Philip's expansion.

On the island of Crete, the cities of Ierapetra and Olous joined the Macedonian cause. Being major centers of commerce on a poor island, Ierapetra and Olous forced the rest of Crete to join Philip's cause. Most did, except for the city of Knossos. Once the most prosperous city on Crete, Knossos had fallen far below its pinnacle.

Yet, Knossos had been a trading partner of the Island of Rhodes for decades. As such, the Cretan city sided with Rhodes. In doing so, Knossos became an enemy of Philips V of Macedonia and most of Crete. According to Greek Historian Polybius, having two or more cities on Crete involved in bloody conflicts, wasn't unusual for the island.

Diceärch, the Pirate

What we know about Diceärch is limited. An Aetolian officer who King Phillip V of Macedonia hired as a pirate, constitutes his background. What makes Diceärch an interesting historical figure was his habit of constructing two altars wherever he landed. One altar to *Asebeia*, meaning impiety or blasphemy, and another altar to *Paranomia*, meaning lawlessness or self-delusion. We don't know why he hated religion and priests.

Incomplete history, however, is where historical fiction writers work best. I created a backstory for Diceärch that explains his unique altars and his attitude towards priests.

As part of the story, Diceärch told Jace a brief overview of the conflict between Agamemnon and Achilles during the Trojan war. If you know Homer's the Iliad, you'll recognize that Diceärch slanted the story to fit his narrative.

And finally on the pirate, you might wonder why Jace didn't go after Diceärch in this book. Before he was captured, the pirate maintained a reign of terror for over a year. Keeping with the historical timeline, during that period, Jace Kasia had contracts to fulfill elsewhere.

Ancient Pergamon

The ancient Empire of Pergamon covered the northern end of modern-day Turkey. From south of the city of Bergama, east to Uşak, and north to the sea of Marmara, the empire provided a stabilizing force in the region and a foil to Macedonian expansion.

Pergamon had been mentioned in an earlier *A Legion Archer* book. The original The Dying Gaul stature, in bronze, was lost but the image lives on in a marble copy in Rome. Commissioned at around 225 B.C. by Attalus I of Pergamon to celebrate his victory over the Galatians, a Celtic people who lived in Anatolia, modern day Turkey.

Mortise and Tenon Joints

Readers have written that they find modern terms off putting in historical fiction novels. I can't argue the effect. But in my defense, just as with the use of port and starboard, for the left side and right side of a boat, no ancient historian left us alternative verbiage. The Egyptians invented the system of joining wood by inserting a shaved end of a board into a cavity carved into another. It soon became common practice throughout the Mediterranean region. And to me, mortise and tenon is the easiest way to describe an insertion that creates a strong 90-degree angle when connecting two boards.

The Lighthouse of Alexandria

Constructed on the Island of Pharos in the harbor of Alexanderia, the lighthouse towered 100 meters, or 330 feet above the water. Built of limestone and granite blocks in three tapering sections, the lighthouse had a lower square section at the bottom; an octagonal section in the middle; and, a circular section at the top to hold the furnace.

The Nile River

Before dams were built on the Nile, the river flooded every year. Once the water subsided, a layer of rich soil was deposited, allowing the floodplain to grow a variety of crops. The flooding made Egypt the breadbasket of the ancient world. For hundreds of years, whenever they had shortages, Rome and other countries purchased grain from Egypt.

Ptolemy IV

Pharaoh Ptolemy IV of Egypt faced a rebellion in 206 B.C. The rebel activity stretched from Thebes at Luxor north to the Nile River delta. While Captain Midhat is a fictional character, the Egyptian government was consumed with fending off the elusive rebels. There would certainly have been military men using sources like Jace Kasia to find people disloyal to the Ptolemy dynasty.

The Library of Alexandria

Many ancient cities had libraries. But Alexandria by all reports had the biggest building and the largest collection of scrolls and papyrus papers of any of the depositories.

Eratosthenes of Cyrene

Eratosthenes, a renowned philosopher of geography, created the first globe of the world. In 206 B.C., he was the head librarian at the Library of Alexandria. His conversation with Jace Kasia is purely fictional and any faulty conclusions are mine and not those of Eratosthenes.

Ring Officer

I created the position of Ring Officer to give Jace a boss and a reason to stay in Alexanderia. He isn't finished in Egypt. Although I've never seen a reference to a Ring Officer, as Farouk described in the story, the protection of a Pharaoh had to be layered – personal bodyguards, palace guards, and a ring of handpicked fighters to protect the soldiers defending the Pharoah. If you know of a different arrangement to guard a God/King in battle, please let me know.

206 B.C.

Most of *From Dawn to Death* occurred in 206 B.C. Here's hoping you enjoyed the story and the notes.

***

I appreciate emails and reading your comments. If you enjoyed *From Dawn to Death*, consider leaving a written review on Amazon or Goodreads. Every review helps other readers find the stories.

If you have comments e-mail me.

E-mail: GalacticCouncilRealm@gmail.com

To get the latest information about my books, visit my website. There you can sign up for my monthly author report (newsletter) and read blogs about ancient history.

Website: www.JCliftonSlater.com

Facebook: Tales from Ancient Rome

I am J. Clifton Slater and I write historical military adventure.

***

Other books by J. Clifton Slater:

Historical Adventure of the 2nd Punic War

A Legion Archer series

#1 Journey from Exile

#2 Pity the Rebellious

#3 Heritage of Threat

#4 A Legion Archer

#5 Authority of Rome

#6 Unlawful Kingdom

#7 From Dawn to Death

#8 The General's Tribune

Historical Adventure of the 1st Punic War

Clay Warrior Stories series